Heavenly Pleasures

Books by Kerry Greenwood

The Corinna Chapman series
Earthly Delights
Heavenly Pleasures
Devil's Food
Trick or Treat
Forbidden Fruit
Cooking the Books

The Phryne Fisher series
Cocaine Blues
Flying Too High
Murder on the Ballarat Train
Death at Victoria Dock
The Green Mill Murder
Blood and Circuses
Ruddy Gore
Urn Burial
Raisins and Almonds
Death Before Wicket
Away With the Fairies
Murder in Montparnasse
The Castlemaine Murders
Queen of the Flowers
Death by Water
Murder in the Dark
Murder on a Midsummer Night
Dead Man's Chest

Short Story Anthology
A Question of Death:
An Illustrated Phryne Fisher Anthology

Heavenly Pleasures

A Corinna Chapman Mystery

Kerry Greenwood

Poisoned Pen Press

Copyright © 2005, 2012 by Kerry Greenwood

First U.S. Trade Paperback Edition 2009

10 9 8 7 6 5 4 3 2 1

Library of Congress Catalog Card Number: 2007942868

ISBN: 978-1-4642-0009-0   Trade Paperback

Poisoned Pen Press
6962 E. First Ave., Ste. 103
Scottsdale, AZ 85251
www.poisonedpenpress.com
info@poisonedpenpress.com

Printed in the United States of America

This book is dedicated to a very dear Sister-in-Crime, Carmel Shute. A woman of remarkable determination, charisma and kindness.

With many thanks to Jean Greenwood, the remarkable Annette Barlow and all at A and U, the Gen-X Support Group, Sarah-Jane Reeh for Lucifer, David and Dennis and all.

Oppress not the cubs of the stranger,
But hail them as Sister and Brother,
For though they be little and fubsy,
It may be the Bear is their mother.
                                  —Rudyard Kipling
                                        'The Law of the Jungle'

Chapter One

Have I told you how I feel about four in the morning? Anguish, misery, existential dread, stubbing toe on cat?

Oh, I have. Right. Take it as read, then, that I rose, stretched, yawned, washed, and stuffed my XXL body into size XXXL trackies which have seen better years, as indeed have I. I made toast for myself and coffee, without which no early person or shiftworker can face the universe and its cold, dark emptiness. Four in the morning makes you contemplate your sins and count your blessings. So I contemplated and counted.

My name is Corinna Chapman, and I am a baker. I run a little shop called Earthly Delights on the corner of Flinders Lane and Calico Alley in the city of Melbourne. You've probably eaten my bread if you work anywhere near Flinders Street Station. I once was an accountant in a power suit, working grotesque hours doing accountant things: trying to get the balances to balance, arguing with the data entry persons about the implacability of the RIRO principle, wearing out my knees begging the Tax Office for more time, worrying about the state of the dollar. I don't worry about that now. I worry about yeast, which, unlike the dollar, is predictable and appreciates loving care.

So, one day I found I didn't care about accounts, and I did care about bread, and here I am. The ovens come on with a whoosh at four, which always wakes me. I lost my ex, James, along with the accountancy. As losses go, he wasn't one. I moved into this eccentric building, Insula, a Roman apartment house in the city, built by an architect whose mother, Professor Monk insists, was frightened by a copy of Suetonius. We have mosaics. We have Roman names for all of the apartments, though the shops on the street have Greek names. The Prof thinks this has to do with Roman jokes about Greek business methods. However it was, I am a baker and live in Hebe, Waitress of the Gods, the Lone Gunmen of Nerds Inc. live in Hephaestus, Smith of the Gods, the excellent cooks of the Pandamus family live in Hestia, Goddess of the Hearth, and my best friend Meroe, the witch, lives in Leucothea, the White Goddess, otherwise known as Hecate, Queen of Witches. We're the ones who have shops on the street, in the Roman manner, and the luxury of living upstairs from the job is magnificent, though it does tend to mean that until the shop is open I am not a sight to be seen by the fashion conscious.

Lately Insula has been busier than usual. In the space of a week in which I didn't get time to do much more than gasp with surprise, I acquired a gorgeous, ex-Israeli soldier called Daniel, a returned daughter Cherie for poor Andy Holliday in 4A, discovered that it was horrible old Mr Pemberthy who had been scaring the life out of all the women in the building, and walked out of a Goth club in full dominatrix gear with a murderer. A vampire murderer. It was a week I do not want to forget but have no mind to repeat and just now a little tedium would be nice. Just baking and selling and maybe a nice gin and tonic on the roof garden while all the other workers are hard at it…ah, schadenfreude, a reliable pleasure. Since there is nothing to be got from the newspapers but despair and misery and Iraq, and there are only a certain number of times one can say 'I told you so, you idiots!', I need a little schadenfreude sometimes.

A gentle paw on my knee reminded me that my partner, Horatio, had finished his ration of kitty dins and would now find a bowl of milk acceptable. Horatio is a tabby and white gentleman with impeccable manners and grooming. If cats have religions, he belongs to the one which venerates milk. I poured him a suitable amount and he folded down, paw by paw, disposed his tail prayerfully, and began his devotions.

Downstairs to the bakery, once Horatio had decided to take a little after-breakfast nap to prepare him for his afternoon sleep. I clattered on the stone stairs in my Birkenstocks. Every baker who wants to make it to thirty-eight uncrippled needs good shoes. I reminded myself that I ought to get Jason to buy himself another pair of proper shoes. You really need two pairs, worn alternately, but he still clings affectionately to sneakers. If you see what I mean.

As I hit the last step the Mouse Police collided with my ankles in a furry scrum, eager to demonstrate that they had been hard at work all night and deserved extra kitty dins. Heckle and Jekyll, two black and white cats, named after the cartoon crows. I noticed that Heckle, who is a retired street fighter, had a torn ear which Jekyll, a retired female, has been licking. I applied some disinfectant the vet gave me—rat bites are very dirty—and he didn't even seem to notice. Old campaigner, this Heckle. His ears have more holes punched in them than a punk nipple. He bounced up and down, directing my attention to a pile of dead rodents. Now that Horatio is no longer pinching them to feed a stray female cat on the roof—and that was a strange story in itself—the corpses have begun to mount up like an American election campaign.

I disposed of the six rats and four mice, washed my hands, fed the Mouse Police, and opened the back door into Calico Alley. Morning. Cool and fresh, before the car exhaust. Just the faintest scent of ozone from the trams.

The Mouse Police ran out and down the alley, convinced by previous experience that Kiko or Ian, the proprietors of the Japanese restaurant, will have fish scraps for a hard-working feline. Even Heckle, normally a cat you would not like to meet down a dark alley if you were between him and his predestined rat, can achieve fluffy for tuna.

Jason, my fifteen-year-old apprentice, was waiting on the step. I gave him my early morning glare, which checked his pupils for dilation and his fingernails for cleanliness. The eyes were bright and the hands cleaner than mine.

'Ginger muffins today,' he said bracingly as we poured the first flour and yeast mixture into the tub. 'I feel like something spicy.'

'As long as you make them, muffin man,' I growled. Jason makes much better muffins than I do, even though we use the same recipe, the same flour and the same oven. And him a recovering heroin addict. There is no justice. 'I've got rye bread, then seed bread, then pasta douro for the Greek restaurant and Cafe Delicious.'

'Then we can have breakfast,' he said hungrily. My need to feed people may have met its match in Jason's appetite. Then again, he is still as thin as an election promise. Since he gave up heroin his hair has thickened and I can no longer count all of his ribs. But he would still clock in as a flyweight and needs more covering, especially now that winter is coming on.

'Haven't you eaten?' I asked, measuring out seeds for my seed bread, which is a speciality and superb stuff, especially with blue cheese.

'A baguette or two,' he admitted. 'Some of that cheese and the leftover ham, and the rest of the herb rolls and a couple bottles of Coke. Nothing really.'

I got on with the bread and Jason started cutting up crystallised ginger to top his muffins. The Mouse Police returned, licking fishy whiskers, engulfed their kitty dins with gobbling enthusiasm, and settled down for a nice day-long nap on their favoured mattress, a pile of empty flour sacks. I know that animals are strictly forbidden in any place where food is prepared. But I'm not having poisons and traps in my bakery. The Mouse Police are neat, efficient, and work for peanuts—or kitty dins. To hell with Health Regulations. We are as clean as we can possibly be.

The mixers were all mixing and the dough was growing—you can practically hear it rising—and Jason and I had another cup of coffee. I bought a coffee maker for the bakery, now I have a helper. He helped himself to whatever leftovers he could find in the rack.

'Daniel been in?' he asked, surveying the remains of yesterday's baking.

'Not yet.' I suppressed a pang. Daniel volunteers as the guard on the Soup Run, a bus which circumnavigates Melbourne every night, feeding the lost and strayed. I met him when a junkie OD'd on my grate. What does a soup van always need? Bread. Daniel had stayed to lie in my bed with me and tell me he loved me, and then vanished again. For the last three mornings, Jen the social worker had come for the bread, with Ma'ani as her carrier.

And there was Ma'ani again. New Zealand manufactures Maoris in two sizes, Large and Extra Large, and Ma'ani is Extra Extra Large. He really must be about seven feet tall and about three feet wide and the most charming, gentle person that ever scared the hell out of a baker by appearing very quietly while she was thinking about something else. I jumped and swore. He grinned at me, his teeth making a perfect half-moon in the dark alley.

'Must you loom?' I snarled at him. Early morning is not my cheerful time.

'Sorry,' he said, stepping back from the door. I hauled the sack of bread out and he lifted it easily to his shoulders. He could have just as gracefully hefted anything up to and including a small car. I was snarling at a nice person and I called myself to order. I knew why I was snappy. I didn't want to sound anxious, and I didn't know whether I ought to ask, I didn't want to seem to be hanging out after Daniel, but I wanted to know where he was, and why I hadn't seen him for three days, and I bit my lip. Jason looked up from his muffins and saved me.

'Hey, Ma'ani!'

'Hey, Jase.'

'Jason,' said Jason severely. When he was an addict, he had been Jase. Now he was a baker, he was Jason.

Ma'ani grinned. 'Jason.'

'Where's Daniel?' asked Jason artlessly. 'Haven't seen the dude for days.'

I could have kissed the little ginger-scented omnivore.

'Sister Mary sent him up country somewhere—Ballarat? —to rescue a missing girl,' said Ma'ani. 'Gave me this note for you on Monday,' he added, retrieving it from his pocket while holding the load of bread with one hand. 'Forgot it, sorry. See you tomorrow,' he said, and walked down Calico Alley with that soft tread which huge people sometimes have. I suppose it would have had a genetic advantage in the old warrior days. I probably wouldn't have been able to sneak up behind him and bean him with a baguette, which is what I felt like doing. It was now Thursday.

'That's Ma'ani,' said Jason. 'And that Sister Mary, you do as she says.'

'True,' I agreed. Sister Mary was a very short, plump, charming nun with a heart full of Christian charity and love who had enough strength of will to drive a feather through a marble tombstone. Or keep the soup run bus running despite a residents' protest, a hostile council and a series of unimpressed police officers. There was literally nothing that Sister Mary would not attempt to ameliorate the lot of the poor. And if she had told Daniel to go to Ballarat, then to Ballarat he would have gone.

I unfolded the note: 'Ketschele, I have to go to Ballarat to find a girl. I already miss you, and I shall miss you more. I will be back and in your arms as soon as possible. Your Daniel.'

Now that was more like it. Suddenly the day improved. I picked up Jekyll and hugged her. I would have hugged Jason but he would not have liked it. Jekyll didn't like it much either but it was in her job description and she bore it pretty well.

Then Jason and I got on with the baking. In the course of which he ate four leftover rolls and a slightly failed attempt at a frangipani cake (too moist), and drank three cups of coffee and the rest of the milk.

Kitten, that was what Daniel called me. Ketschele is Yiddish for kitten. No one had ever called me kitten before. Fat women don't attract diminutives. My ex, James, used to call me—I retch to admit it—butterball. And that was when he liked me.

Lately he has been calling me 'that fat bitch'. He has reasons. I messed up a deal he had with a Singaporean bank. He has the delicate sense of ethics that one expects of a merchant banker of his type—bold, risk-taking, testosterone-fuelled—and I waited eagerly for the day when I read his name under bankruptcies in the court list.

First loaves in the oven, next all mixed and waiting, and time was ticking on. I went into the shop to take down the shutters, wondering why either Kylie or Goss had not come down. A long hard night on the fluffy ducks, I assumed. No, perhaps I do them an injustice. A long hard night on the cosmopolitans and the Long Island teas.

Shutters down, early morning Flinders Lane light flooded in. It's a nice shop, just a little slice out of the bakery, with a counter, space for people to queue and a lot of racks which will shortly be filled with bread. Muffins, rolls, loaves, knots, French twists; Cornish seed bread, Italian almond bread, Welsh bara brith. Wonderful stuff, bread. The staff of life. Jason came in with the first load for the shop. Ginger muffins. I took one, sniffed, broke a piece off to check the crumb, then bit. A strong taste without being overwhelming.

'Gorgeous,' I told him in answer to his anxious look. Jason isn't sure of himself yet. 'The girls aren't in,' I commented. 'Did they say anything to you about being late?'

'Nah,' he said over his shoulder. 'But they don't talk to me much. They're pretty pissed that their soap got delayed.'

I agreed with him. Kylie and Gossamer share an apartment and work in my shop until they can break into a TV soap. They thought they had made it with parts in an anorexic epic called 'Catwalk', but it had been delayed due to lack of funding. I hoped that this meant that they might dare to put on a few pounds before they died of malnutrition.

I dead-heated with Kylie as she rushed not into the shop but the bakery, holding a scrap of what looked like fun fur and sobbing.

'He fell into the sink!' she shrieked, thrusting the wet thing at me. 'Is he dead?'

It wasn't a scrap of fun fur, it was in fact Kylie's kitten Lucifer. The other two kittens, Soot and Tori, and the mother, Calico, were gentle sober creatures who posed prettily, ate daintily, and slept on the most expensive available surface in a photogenic group. Lucifer was an orange and white tom kitten with a splotch of ginger on his little head which would be flaming red later on, if he ever got to grow up, which at the moment seemed doubtful. This resemblance to a match had caused Meroe to call him Lucifer. His high-risk lifestyle bore out her theory that there had been some kind of diabolic intervention in his conception. He had begun his daredevil career by scaling the curtains and then staying there, crying pitifully, until Daniel climbed up and rescued him and had been scratched thoroughly for his kindness. Lucifer had been so glad to put paw to ground that he had dived into a kitchen cupboard and a lot of pots had fallen on him. He had then vanished until Goss found him packed neatly into her underwear drawer, bedded on pre-holed lycra and thoughtfully shredding pantyhose.

I had suggested buying him a cat cage but Kylie and Goss couldn't bear the idea. Now it looked like he had used up the last of his nine lives. He was soaking wet and so small in my hands. Poor little creature. I held him up by his hind legs and some water ran out of his mouth. Then I put him to my lips and puffed a tiny breath of air into the miniature lungs.

Nothing happened. I rubbed him in the handtowel to try to get some of the wet out of his valiantly orange fur. The little body rolled unresponsively between my hands. 'I'm sorry, Kylie,' I said. She burst into explosive tears.

'Too bad,' said Jason.

We were all standing looking at the kitten when the most amazing thing happened. Jekyll rose from the flour sacks and made an odd noise, almost a grunt. It was a demand. If it had been in words it would have been 'mine'. I put the towel down on the floor and said, 'Sorry, Jekyll, I don't think...'

Jekyll gave me an irritated look. She grabbed Lucifer by the back of the neck and shook him violently, then began to wash his face very roughly, pinning him down under her hard paw. Heckle had not stirred. Nurturing instinct was something that happened to other cats, he clearly felt. I was thinking how very sad it was that Jekyll should be trying so devotedly to resuscitate a dead kitten when the little orange scrap of fur sneezed, squirmed out from under the loving paw, sneezed again and wobbled to his feet. Wet but unbowed.

'That was fun,' he seemed to be saying. 'What else shall we do?'

Kylie grabbed him up and stroked him, heedless of the water on her stretch top. Wet cats hold more water than a sponge. Jekyll walked back to the sacks and resumed her nap. She seemed to have no further interest in him. Cats are very mysterious creatures. Thinking about them too much can give you a migraine.

'You wicked little thing!' cooed Kylie, kissing the top of his wet head so that Lucifer should know that he was in disgrace. He coughed up some more water and gratefully sank all his claws into her unformed bosom. You can always identify those with young kittens by the tattooing of little claws on all available skin surfaces.

'Ooh, the shop! I'm, like, sorry, Corinna! I was just doing the washing-up and I didn't see him on the shelf and then he took this extreme leap into the sink and the tap was running and…'

'Never mind,' I said. 'If this kitten lives to grow up, it will be a miracle. Is Goss coming today?'

'She's got an ad, left at five for make-up,' said Kylie. 'I'll just take him back and…'

We both thought about the possibilities inherent in leaving Lucifer in an unattended flat.

'Put him in the cat carrier,' I said. 'Just for the moment. At least he'll be safe in there.'

Jason got the cat cage down from the closet. It is a commodious one, with a wire mesh door. We put Lucifer, the handtowel, and a selection of kitty treats in it and locked the front carefully. I put the cage down near Jekyll and she didn't spare it a glance.

Meanwhile, there was bread to get out of the oven before it scorched and a shop to open. Kylie fled upstairs to change out of her kittened clothes and Jason opened the front door.

People were waiting. Poor overworked peons, required to get to the office before the boss and to stay until after he left, one of the most pernicious doctrines ever to waste the lives of its proponents. How much extra work really gets done by people who are exhausted, underslept, and longing to be home? Precious little, I bet. The Prof told me that when the spitfire factories worked round the clock with volunteers, they didn't actually produce more planes despite their dedication and their hard work. People who are tired get slow and clumsy. They make mistakes. They get injured. Even in a war, the government found that they got more planes built by sending their employees home after an eight hour shift than by working them to death. If it didn't work for a spitfire factory, it wasn't going to work for a modern office. Let the people go home and have a drink and meet their families and watch Reality TV or the Naked News according to taste. What the world needs, I am convinced, after more peace and charity and love and fresh water and food and literate women, is more time off to waste as the worker chooses. Everyone, at the moment, works too hard.

Including, I suppose, me. The scent of fresh baked bread— was dragging the famished hordes out of the cold street, where a nasty little Melbourne wind had whipped up, throwing dust into tired eyes. Like cigarettes or alcohol, but much better for the consumer, my bread is a special treat, an indulgence, a little warm mouthful just for that person alone. Although some of them buy enough for the whole office, bless them. Ginger muffins bounced off the shelves, everything sold well, and Jason was bringing in fresh supplies as the racks emptied.

Nine o'clock and there was always a lull until about ten, when morning tea became a priority. Jason was counting loaves into the racks for the carrier. I sell most of my bread to restaurants.

I don't actually need a shop. But I like having one. I like to see people's eyes light up, I like to hear that sniff as they inhale the delicious scent. Horatio had descended and was occupying his usual place on the counter, between the glass case and the cash register. This central throne means that everyone has to pay him homage. Most of my customers know him and he greets the favoured few with a polite nudge of the nose, and the importunate are dismissed with a lifted eyebrow. Horatio would have made a wonderful diplomat.

I was just stowing some fifty dollar notes—don't people have any change?—under the tray in the till when I heard a soft thud from the bakery. Jason said, 'Shit!'

When I went to the back, I saw that a whole ten kilogram bag of superfine baker's flour had somehow fallen over, breaking open and spilling all over the floor. And as I was grabbing the paper sack to stand it up and save some of the flour, a strange white object leaped out and headed for the door. I grabbed but missed and fell on my knees amongst the mess.

When I scrambled up, covered in flour and confusion, there was a tall, dark, leather-clad angel with trout-pool eyes holding a flour-coated creature at arm's length.

'Is this ours?' he asked dubiously.

'Yes,' I said, as a yowl announced that Lucifer had found that he couldn't get away from that firm grip on his scruff. 'Yes, Daniel, it's ours.'

Chapter Two

'I'd embrace you,' I said. 'But with this much flour we might be glued together for eternity.'

He smiled his heart-stopping smile. My heart stopped, and then raced.

'No complaints here, ketschele, but it might be inconvenient. What shall I do with this young gentleman? Can this be Lucifer?'

'Of course it is,' said Jason. 'Stick the little deadshit back in the cage.'

'He already got out of it once,' I said.

Jason's next suggestion—under a big overturned pot—was not acceptable either. Finally I opened the cage again, Daniel shoved the squalling Lucifer inside, and I tied up the door with a piece of twine. After a moment we both saw a tiny, flour-covered ginger paw emerge through the mesh and grope hopefully for the latch.

'Foiled you, my fine floury friend,' said Jason unexpectedly. 'You want to go and get changed, Corinna? Kyl and me'll mind the shop. Only I got to sweep all this flour up for starters. Hey, Daniel.'

'Hey, Jason,' said Daniel. 'How's life?'

'Going good,' said Jason. 'You gonna take Luce with you?'

'If he's lucky,' I said. 'He's going to need a wash. How I look forward to the multiple injuries I shall sustain giving it to him. Then we are definitely getting a cat cage. He's already run through his own nine lives and is overdrawn on his next three incarnations.'

'Blessed be, Corinna,' said a deep voice from the alley door. Meroe, a Wiccan witch with a carefully hidden talent for curses, had paused in her walk down to her shop from Kiko's, for whom she supplies various Japanese mushrooms. You know, the ones which look oddly like dried human ears. She was carrying an empty basket.

'Good morning, Meroe,' I said, dusting uselessly at my tracksuit pants. 'Might I interest you in today's special, pre-floured kitten?'

'Lucifer?' she asked in her dark brown, Hungarian accent. I love her voice. Listen to a voice like that telling you about your chakras and you feel better already.

'The very same. First he took a dive into the washing-up and nearly drowned, and then he tried suffocating himself in best quality flour.'

'Give him to me. I shall wash him, and then I shall make him a collar which may restrain some of his wilder impulses.'

'And the very best of luck,' I said gratefully, handing over the cage. 'By the way, he can lift the latch. Keep the cage tied up. And what is Belladonna going to think?'

'She is minding the shop. May I have a loaf of the seed bread, please?'

I supplied Meroe with bread and her kitten, and wondered what she meant about Belladonna minding the shop. I mean, Belladonna is a cat. A sleek, shiny, beautiful, exceptionally black cat. But a cat.

As he held the door for me, Daniel was clearly thinking the same thing. 'You never know with witches,' he commented.

I had to agree.

Daniel went upstairs and fetched my dressing gown and I shed the floury clothes. I took them into the alley and shook them in that cold wind before stuffing them in the washer and hoping that the filter would cope. Then, attired in dressing gown and shoes, I led the way into my private apartments and shut the bakery door.

Daniel took off his coat and slumped onto the sofa. It's a good sofa, with a grip of feathery iron. Once slumped, you tend to stay slumped. He looked very tired. There were dark marks under his eyes. Being a private investigator in this kind of town takes it out of you, all right.

'I'll put on some coffee and have a shower, you just close your eyes,' I said, dismissing certain fantasies about flour-covered grapplings on the floor. I'm too old to make love on the floor, anyway. Those carpet burns really sting. I started the coffee maker, took off the rest of my garments and washed the flour out of my hair. With difficulty. The stuff clung like glue. I wondered how on earth Meroe was going to restore Lucifer to pristine kittenhood so that he could go out and find another amusing way of committing felicide.

By the time I came back, Daniel had had one of his lightning naps and was drinking coffee, eating yesterday's apple muffins and smiling. The man can sleep anywhere. I suppose it is a function of having been a soldier. He looked better. I said so.

'So do you,' he commented. 'Less gluey, for a start, and all rosy from the steam.'

'I always seem to meet you when I'm muddy or floury or otherwise lacking in glamour,' I said ruefully.

'To me you will never lack glamour,' he said, taking my hand and kissing it. 'You are always beautiful. A beautiful thing does not become ugly just because it is temporarily covered in, as it might be, flour. Oh, by the way, ketschele, I met Juliette in the alley. She gave me these for you. She's trying out a new filling.'

'Speaking of glamour,' I agreed. Juliette Lefebvre is our chocolate maker. Her tiny shop, Heavenly Pleasures, is just down Flinders Lane from Earthly Delights and she, too, has a Hieronymus Bosch painting on the wall. She is tall, slim and radiantly blonde but I forgive her her beauty because she really cares about chocolate in the same way that I care about bread. I looked at the small, dark blue box. The last new filling had been violet; subtle, delicate, fragrant and (of course) delicious. I don't eat a lot of chocolate so Juliette uses me as a taster. I was, of course, eager to volunteer. If I was a chocolate fiend, I might end up broke purchasing Heavenly Pleasures' wares. People have been known to weep at the taste, it is so perfect. They have also been known to weep at the prices. Still, you don't expect to get an Easter egg made by hand in a nineteenth century Dutch chocolate mould with expert extra squiggles for the same as a Coles' one.

I wasn't in the right mood for chocolate so early in the day. I drank some coffee. Daniel ate another muffin. His fingernails were dirty. His t-shirt had something tarry spilled across it. He looked like he had been travelling hard class in Molvania, than which there is no harder class.

'Bad journey?' I asked. He drew a shaky breath.

'Journey was all right, but a bad trawl through the nastier parts of Ballarat and environs. I eventually found the girl, Belinda, in a squat on an old farm—a lot of farms have more than one house on them—and it was foul. I never saw such squalor.'

'Did she come with you?'

'Like a lamb. Thin as a skeleton, all bruises and lice, and the baby had pneumonia.'

'And you skinned your knuckles waving bye-bye?' I asked.

'I had to persuade this rustic polygamist that he didn't have any right to keep the girl against her will. Or such of her will as she had left, which wasn't much. Like most of these messiahs, he didn't have a lot of courage against a man. And I fear that his charisma didn't enchant me,' said Daniel, lips twisting in disgust. 'I left Belinda in the hospital with the baby and several loving relatives, and by now the local police will have captured the messiah. They were counting out warrants when I left. There was quite a pile.'

'Bath,' I said, and went to run one, pouring in pine salts.

'But Sister Mary…' he protested weakly as I dragged off his boots and horrible socks.

'Always says that good news improves with waiting,' I said firmly. 'I've got to go back to the shop. Soak all those bruises and then my bed is, as always, at your service. I'll wake you at three,' I said, and went down the stairs again.

Not that I wanted to, of course, but commerce is commerce. Everything appeared to be working in the shop. Kylie's navel ring was sparkling brightly under a short pink top. Jason was taking the last load of bread out of the oven. The floor was clear of flour.

'How's Daniel?' he asked.

'Tired,' I replied. 'Did you know this Belinda he was searching for?'

'Rich bitch,' said Jason. 'They always fall harder, the princesses. Not as much fun as they thought on the street. Went off with Darren the God Boy. Extreme nutcase. Daniel get her back?'

'Of course,' I said. I was about to ask for more details on Darren the God Boy, in view of Daniel's description of him as a messiah, but there was a rush of business and I forgot about it.

Most of the inhabitants of Insula come in during the morning for their bread. Excepting Mrs Pemberthy, of course, who is on a gluten-free diet since almost dying of pesticide poisoning. The Prof came in, looking elegant in a blue blazer and flannels, off to lunch at the University Club. His is the only apartment which has Roman furniture and decoration and reminds me that civilisation has been around for a while —though you'd never know it from the way the nations are behaving. Professor Dionysus Monk smiled at me and caressed Horatio's whiskers with a practised hand.

'Seed bread, if you please, Corinna. And perhaps a muffin or two. I note that Daniel has returned.'

'How do you know?' I asked, wrapping up the bread.

'You have your Daniel-is-here smile,' he said kindly.

He must have been a terror for students who were fibbing about why they hadn't done their essay on Juvenal.

After him came Trudi, our gardener and caretaker, descending from Ceres, her apartment, for some rolls and a loaf of stale bread for the birds. It's not that she likes pigeons. She hopes that if there is a good supply of food, a kestrel might decide to build in her garden. So far the kestrels have preferred nice bare ledges on higher buildings. Kestrels have no taste.

Then the day got busy. I did not forget about Daniel asleep upstairs, because one cannot forget things like that, but he receded into the background. He makes a very nice background. I sent off the bread with the carrier. I had sacked the old one, who was amazingly inefficient, and got a bright, sparky nineteen year old called Megan, starting her own business. She had a motorised arrangement like a rickshaw and so far the bread had always arrived at (1) the right place and (2) in good condition. Kylie told me tales of Lucifer and we wondered what was to become of him. Any kitten who at seven weeks was capable of picking the lock on a cat carrier was bound for a life of crime. I wondered if we should have called him Macavity and Kylie surprised me by knowing the reference.

'You've read Old Possum's Book of Practical Cats?' I asked.

'Saw the show,' she said. 'And the film. Tried out for a kitten when I was thirteen but I was too tall.'

I should have guessed. The only thing Kylie reads are scripts and *Girlfriend* magazine. Lately she has extended her repertoire to Wiccan magazines which she buys from Meroe and carries around ostentatiously. Who would have thought, early in the twenty-first century, that it would be cool to be a witch?

I still miss Buffy. Since Daniel was also a fan I was scheduling a couple of hours of season one—we were starting again—for the evening. Unless something better came up. So to speak.

We sold bread from the morning tea rush to the lunchtime rush and then, quite suddenly, it was two pm and there was no one there. Jason was doing the scrubbing, Kylie had cashed up and loaded the Soup Run's sack and the half-price racks, and I wasn't needed. It was a nice feeling.

'Have you found a home for the other kittens, Kylie?' I asked, lingering at the stairs.

'We're keeping Tori,' said Kylie. Tori was perfect for Kylie and Goss. She was a fluffy blonde kitten who adored being petted and who tolerated having a ribbon around her neck. They had already named her after their favourite singer. 'Cherie's taking

Calico. But no one seems to want Soot and who'd want Lucifer? I don't know what we're going to do.'

'He certainly needs more scope than an apartment,' I said. 'We'll see. Daniel might know someone.'

'Dude knows everyone,' agreed Jason. 'You want to move, Corinna? Only I haven't mopped that bit of floor.'

I knew when I was in the way. I left. Daniel was asleep in my big bed. Horatio was curled in the circle of his naked, muscular arm. They made such a pretty picture that I couldn't bear to wake them, and went pottering into the parlour to contemplate Daniel's clothes. Unlike all other men I had ever heard of, he did not strew his garments over the floor for someone else to pick up. By the time I left James, I calculated that I had spent close on a month of my valuable time just picking up things and putting them in their right place. I should have added that to the divorce settlement. At accountant rates of $100 an hour.

Daniel's boots were standing side by side on a sheet of newspaper. His filthy clothes were piled on top. His coat was hanging behind the door. His bag was next to the boots. He had come to me direct from the train. I was touched.

At a loose end, I glanced at the business pages of the paper. As I read, I noticed that there was a sly, almost invisible thread running through the editorial. It had been there for weeks. Something indefinable was wrong with an unnamed company in Trusts and Superannuation. A crash was to be expected. That was always an easy prediction to make, like Trouble in the Balkans or TV Evangelist in Shock Sex Scandal. I don't know why it's always a shock. I'm not shocked. Saddened, perhaps.

When I was in the business I would have known what that editorial insinuation meant. I would have said, aha! it's XY Pty Ltd, quick, get our money out of there and tell our clients to break the land speed record to the broker's. But I didn't know who they were talking about and it niggled me. Of course, I could find out by ringing my ex, James, but hell would freeze over before I did that. Did I still know anyone in the accountancy trade? Of course, and I hadn't seen her for years. Janet

Warren, a very good CPA who had been amazed when I kicked off my kitten heels for the last time and declared that bread was my destiny. I was just looking up Janet's phone number when I realised that she would have moved by now: She had been in the process of buying a house when I left. And I could not, for the moment, recall who she worked for. It didn't matter.

So I pottered into the kitchen and made soup. This is always a soothing occupation. Jason had been suggesting in his usual subtle manner—every ten minutes—that we should sell soup and a roll when the weather turned cold, if it ever did, and I was trying out various soup recipes. I had made chicken stock the day before, and now I shredded chicken and celery and spring onions into it, turning on the gas to 'smidgen' and slicing bread as it warmed and began to smell delightful. What would call a good Jewish boy out of his slumber better than chicken soup? I had a bag of vegetables to chop for my attempt at Scotch broth tomorrow and chopping is soothing, too. Now I didn't have to scrub the bakery every day I had excess energy. So far Jase's transformation into Jason was holding. It might not last. He was only fifteen, after all, and off heroin barely a month. His courage humbled me.

I had done all the veggies and was putting them into the big pot with my shanks when I heard Daniel stir. Then he sniffed. Then I heard him laugh.

Presently a man attired lightly in my Chinese silk gown came padding out to the kitchen and said, 'Chicken soup, ketschele? I'm sure I can smell chicken soup.'

'Have some,' I invited. He sat and sipped. He smiled. Daniel's smile is a smouldering thing in dark light which is probably powered by some sort of biological laser.

'As good as my mother's,' he told me. 'Chicken soup cures everything but a broken heart, she used to say. I never tried it on the broken heart but it's very good for bruises. I do not deserve you. But I'm very glad I have you.'

'Want some aspirin?' I asked breathlessly.

'A couple. But you should have seen the other guy,' he told me. The gown fell open to reveal a red splotch on his chest where someone had aimed for his heart. And missed.

'What did he attack you with?'

'A hockey stick. Makes a good weapon, a hockey stick. I had to take it away from him. Someone might have got hurt.'

Daniel drank soup and took his aspirins. He was aching. I could tell by the way he moved. Usually Daniel moves with an easy grace. Now he was being careful.

'In view of the weather, let us omit travelling to the roof garden today and instead sit on the balcony with our gin and tonic,' I said. 'Admiring the sort of tall leafy green things which Trudi has planted in those big pots.'

Botany is not my strong point. Trudi had given me the plants, swearing that unless I actually watered them with weedkiller or sprayed them with napalm, they would survive on rain and complete neglect. Which was what they were going to get. I am on record as the only person who killed a plastic hoya and who regularly ruins silk orchids. Of course, Horatio helps me in this. I think he likes the smooth feel of real silk in his claws. He had inspected the new plants, tried one delicately with a canine tooth, spat, sniffed the pot and approved of the fine, dark blue Chinese glaze, and ignored the plants thereafter. Trudi must have chosen green leafy things which cats did not find palatable.

Horatio accompanied Daniel and me onto the balcony, perched himself on the iron Pompeii table, and watched the street below. There is a fascination about being the only idle person amongst a crowd of workers. It was three in the afternoon and the street was crowded; women with shopping bags, messengers, couriers, shoppers, men in suits with important briefcases. Calico Alley is a short cut into two arcades which open onto main streets and is rarely empty, except at four in the morning. And no one ever looks up so the pleasures of idleness are augmented by the pleasures of voyeurism. My gin and tonic tasted more tonic than usual and my company could not have been better. I stretched happily.

Now, however, a truck was pulling up at the front door of our apartment house. This required a lot of backing and filling and obscenity as shoppers dived between fender and walls in the manner of chickens into whose yard a fox has nonchalantly wandered.

'Someone moving in?' asked Daniel.

'I've got the residents' group newsletter here—yes, a Mrs Sylvia Dawson. She's moving into 4B, Minerva. Next to Cherie and Andy in Daphne. That's been empty since old Mrs Prince died. Nice furniture,' I commented, looking at the sheen of the table being hauled inside. 'That's mahogany. Lots of book-shelves.'

'Lots of books,' said Daniel, equally fascinated, as box after box was carried inside. I read the legend on the truck.

'They're the expensive movers,' I noticed. 'You don't have to do a thing. They come to your house, pack everything, take it to the new place, unpack everything, put it all away, make your bed, put the kettle on, and remove all the boxes. They'll be a while. Madame will probably only put in an appearance when it's all done.'

An apartment in Insula is expensive. The shops are cheaper but even so it had taken all I had from my settlement to buy Earthly Delights and I had been a bit squeezed for the first couple of years until the shop began to pay. I was now in the delightful position of being debt free and making a profit. For the moment. Until, for instance, a cheap hot bread shop opened up in my near vicinity. But that hadn't happened yet. I didn't know why I was being so snippy. Mrs Dawson was a woman of some wealth and refinement, and why should she unpack boxes if she didn't feel like it?

Still, it struck me as extravagant. Leftover from Grandma's Presbyterian work ethic, I expect. I drank some more gin and tonic to suppress it and kept watching. That's how I saw my favourite police officer, Letty White (known to me as Lepidoptera) following a man with a suitcase into the building. From the ground, it would not have been obvious that she was following him. But I noticed how she looked around to see if she had been noticed. I didn't know the man. From above he was ordinary, with brown hair and a dark grey coat and a big navy blue suitcase with wheels. He went inside. So, after a moment, did she. Daniel had been looking at the unloading and didn't see either of them. But I'm sure it was Lepidoptera. I knew her steady, back-on-the-heels way of walking and her neat cap of hair. What was going on? The residents' newsletter didn't mention anyone else moving in today.

It took an hour for all of Mrs Dawson's things to be carried inside. They were taken up in the freight elevator, a temperamental beast which has to be treated with respect. We heard it groaning up past us. Only Trudi really understands that elevator and only she would dare to use it. I hoped Executive Luxury Removals were treating both of them with respect or they'd be contemplating their lack of manners between floors for eternity. Still, they'd have plenty to read.

Horatio leapt off the table. Daniel yawned. I finished my drink and put us all to bed for the rest of the afternoon. No one had hit him in the face so it was safe to kiss him, and I did, and then we all went byes, and it was so warm and cosy and lovely that I really didn't want to get up when the sun crossed my face at six.

So we didn't. We had some more soup and bread and opened Heavenly Pleasures' test chocolates for a treat. Daniel took one and allowed it to melt in his mouth. An expression of rapture settled on his face.

'Raspberry,' he said. 'Essence of raspberry.'

I bit into mine and then spat it out in sudden, jolting shock. Daniel stared at me. 'Sorry!' I jumped up, washed out my mouth under the kitchen tap, and then did it again, spitting vulgarly into the sink. 'There's something really wrong with that one. I just got a mouthful of chili sauce. Ooh, yuk,' I added, swilling and spitting again.

Daniel retrieved the spat-out chocolate and put it on a saucer to examine it.

'It's been filled with raspberry cream,' he said, lifting the saucer to catch the scent. 'Then—yes, ketschele, chili sauce it is. How funny,' he said grimly.

'I wonder if Juliette Lefebvre is laughing,' I answered.

At that, my bell began pealing, as though someone was leaning on the buzzer. I pressed the intercom.

'It's Juliette!' said a frantic voice. 'Corinna, let me in!'

Chapter Three

I released the door and waited. I did not hear the lift. Juliette must have run up the stairs, which is more than I could do, even under the impetus of panic. She knocked at my door seconds later and fell inside, gasping.

'Don't open those chocolates!' she said very quickly. 'I'm, I'm going to change the recipe.'

Then she noticed the open box on the table and the bitten chocolate on the saucer and stopped dead with her hands to her mouth.

'So that it doesn't include chili sauce?' I asked, still shocked. It's like missing a step. Expecting a delicious taste and getting another, like that salt in coffee trick which the humour-impaired used to perform to Amuse Their Friends while they had them. Daniel had taken the other chocolates out of the box and was examining the undersides with my magnifying glass (I use it for splinters and fine mending).

'Sit down, Juliette, let me make you some coffee, tell us all about it,' I said.

'No, I…' She was poised for flight. Her face was the colour of vanilla cream.

'Have they demanded money yet?' asked Daniel in that voice which suggested infinite understanding and compassion. It worked on homeless heroin addicts and it worked on Juliette. It worked on me, too, incidentally.

All at once, whatever had been sustaining her gave out. Juliette sagged down into a chair and put her decorative blonde head in her perfectly manicured hands.

'No,' she said. 'I don't know what they want.' She raised her head. 'I don't know who they are. And I don't know what to do,' she added.

'Not so much coffee,' said Daniel to me, 'as coffee and brandy, and probably something to eat.'

I supplied the last of the chicken soup, a large cup of coffee and a small glass of brandy and slices of bread with cheese. Daniel put the spoon into Juliette's hand and sat there willing her to drink her soup. She did. Then she ate some bread and cheese and drank the brandy. By the time she was onto coffee and apple muffins her cheeks had warmed to rose cream, if not strawberry. She drew a deep breath. I had never seen her with a hair out of place, and now she was distraught she still didn't have a hair out of place. Some people are like that and it is not an endearing trait. But her eyes were haggard, even if her face wasn't.

'That was very nice,' she told me. 'Thank you. I feel much better. I must have forgotten to have lunch. And maybe breakfast.'

'You've been worrying,' I said.

'I've been panicking,' she returned. 'Daniel, can I employ you?'

'To find out who is poisoning your chocolates?'

'That's the thing, they aren't poisoned, just ruined with chili sauce or soy sauce,' she said, lacing all her fingers together and pulling on them. 'No one would get sick eating them, just disgusted and shocked and deciding that they are never going to buy another Heavenly Pleasures chocolate again. The cops would say, no one's been killed, malicious mischief, tut tut, and I would get all the bad publicity and they wouldn't really be putting my shop high on the priority list, not with all these burglaries round here lately.'

'True,' said Daniel. 'When did it start?'

'That's just it, I don't know,' she wailed. 'The first one I found out about was when a customer brought back a box last Tuesday and told me that one of them had tasted foul, and I gave her some more, and I thought it was just an oversensitive person. You get that sometimes, Corinna, you know?'

I nodded. I knew. Not only did I have to make sure there were no peanut traces in any products that I used, because people with a peanut allergy are prone to die if they eat the stuff, but I had sometimes had customers complaining that their bread tasted of, for example, walnuts, when the only trace of walnut in the bakery had been in a mixing tub which had been thoroughly scrubbed. Two days before. I always apologised and handed over a replacement. Some people have very sensitive tastebuds. And some, of course, are insane. In all cases it is better just to give them a new loaf and not worry about it.

I couldn't help noticing that Juliette had grabbed Daniel's hand as she talked. I was struck with a pang of rampant, green-fanged jealousy. It hit me like an electric shock. I was amazed. I had never been jealous in my life. Then Daniel stretched out his other hand and took mine and gave me a look compounded of such amused understanding that jealousy lowered its head and retired abashed from the scene like a cat which has been out-cooled by Horatio. I had seen the poor things, slinking, utterly crestfallen, off the roof and retiring into private life, making feline resolutions never to cross that gentleman's path again. Jealousy went off just like that and I hoped it wasn't going to come back. I was shocked at myself.

Horatio leapt neatly onto the table and curled up under Juliette's other hand and she started to stroke him. I could practically feel her blood pressure going down. Unless they are diving into the washing-up or bouncing on your chest at three am, cats are very soothing companions.

'Nice cat,' she murmured. 'Then another customer returned a box, and when I offered to replace it she just wanted her money back, said she'd never be able to eat my chocolates with confidence again. I went through the boxes and found that three of them had been contaminated. Then I remembered that I had given one to you and…oh, what am I to do?'

'First, tell me about your shop. Tomorrow I will bring some gear and we will set up some electronic surveillance. Have a look at this,' he said, offering her the saucer and the magnifier. Juliette peered at the bitten chocolate.

'See, someone has punctured the bottom with a syringe, drawn off some of the cream, and put in some chili sauce. You can see how far it has penetrated. Then they have plugged the little hole by melting the chocolate.'

'Yes,' she said, 'the crosshatch pattern is smeared. And the chocolate is dull,' she went on. 'I use best quality couverture for these. Unless it is heated properly and cooled and heated again—tempered—it won't dry glossy. All right. That is how it was done. But why? And who?'

'And how?' I added to the questions.

'That, too,' said Daniel. 'Who works in your shop?'

'You can't be thinking…' Juliette began hotly, then subsided. 'Of course you can,' she said sadly. 'I own the shop with my sister Vivienne. It was our inheritance from our father, who was also a famous chocolatier. Viv does most of the manufacture. I do most of the selling. Then there's Selima who helps in the shop and Viv's apprentice, George. He's Greek. That's all. I can't imagine why any of them would want to do this. We all depend on the shop for a living.'

'How do you get on with your sister?' asked Daniel.

'Fine,' said Juliette. 'We get on fine!'

There was an element of defiance in that exclamation.

'Good,' said Daniel. 'You go along home, now, have a night's sleep. I'll be along tomorrow with the gear. That may be enough to stop this person's tricks. Nothing like knowing that you are being watched to regulate behaviour.'

We saw her to the door. She ran down the stairs, seeming happier than when she had run up them, which is the most you can hope for from most human interaction.

'We never seem to get any time, do we?' he asked sadly.

'I'll just pull up the drawbridge,' I said, 'arm the crocodile swamps and take the phone off the hook. You release the moat monsters and feed the cat.'

'Moat monsters released, check,' he said, more cheerfully, and went into the kitchen to feed Horatio.

We spent the rest of the evening watching Buffy meet Giles, and then slept the night away in perfect peace, until the four am alarm shattered the silence. I got up to find Daniel had already made coffee and was down in the bakery, washing his filthy clothes. I don't deserve him, either. I toasted extra rye bread for him, loaded a tray, fed Horatio his morning milk and left him to his devotions.

Jason was already starting the mixers on their first load of my mainstay, pasta douro. This means 'hard crust' and needs to be sprayed with water while baking but it really is delicious and most hot bread shops can't make it. Partly because it is labour intensive to make and partly because they didn't start out with my graduation present, old Papa Pagliacci's mother of pasta douro, a venerable yeast which had come—he said—with his great grandfather into Australia, nurtured in his great grandmother's bosom to keep it warm. A strain of yeast can indeed go on forever if properly cared for, so it might be true.

I looked at the orders and ate rye bread toast and cherry jam and drank coffee. Daniel sat in the baker's chair by the washer, nibbling rye toast with cheese. I noticed that Jason had brought his washing also. It was very domestic and pleasant. No one was talking, the radio was not on. Bliss. It was a household interior worthy of Vermeer, very quiet and soothing, throbbing slightly with rising dough.

When I opened the door at six for the Mouse Police it was one of those perfect autumn mornings, chill and clear, the sky above the alley as blue as blue could be. And along the alley came a lady wearing sensible walking shoes, a tweed jacket, a flame orange silk shirt and dark brown Fletcher Jones trousers. She was carrying a newspaper and a shoulder-slung brown leather handbag. She was an unusual sight for Calico Alley at that hour.

She moved with perfect self-possession, as if there were no such things as muggers in the world. The Mouse Police skidded to a halt at her feet and she bent to pat each furry head.

'Good morning, cats,' she said in well-modulated tones. 'A beautiful morning, isn't it?'

'Hello,' I said from the doorway. 'That's Heckle and that's Jekyll.'

'And you must be Ms Chapman,' said the lady. 'Sylvia Dawson.' We shook gloves. Mine were thin plastic and hers were bitter chocolate Italian glacé kid. 'I moved in to Minerva yesterday afternoon. A charming building. I'm sure I can be very comfortable here. Are you always up this early?'

'I'm a baker,' I said. 'Bakers start at four. But surely you didn't need to be?'

'I find early morning refreshing,' she said decisively. 'I went for a bracing walk through the Flagstaff Gardens. The leaves are turning. Well, I mustn't keep you from your work. Your bakery smells delightful. Would there be a loaf, perhaps? Or am I too early?'

'I can do you pasta douro,' I said. 'Fresh out of the oven.'

'Splendid,' she said. She paid me in exact coins, accepted the wrapped bread, and walked away. Her back view was as neat as her front view. Perhaps seventy, coiffed and trim and determined. I wondered about her. A widow, perhaps?

'Nice lady,' thus Jason. 'Can I do sour cherry muffins today? Only I ate the rest of your toast and that cherry jam is real nice.'

I should have known better than to leave anything edible near Jason. Daniel, whose clothes had graduated to the dryer, asked, 'Shall I go and make some more?'

'No,' I said.

'Yes,' said Jason.

'As soon as it clocks onto seven, you can go and buy breakfast at Cafe Delicious,' I told him. 'You know, that trucker's special which takes two strong men to eat? You won't starve to death before then. Have you got enough filling for your muffins?'

'No,' said Jason from the storeroom. 'Damn. I'll put cherry jam on the shopping list and today…tah dah!…we shall have blueberry. Bo-oring.'

'But sells well,' I reminded him. 'Get on with it, eh?'

I do not like too much talking in the morning. Ma'ani turned up for the bread. The day went on. I wondered how Meroe was progressing with the taming of Lucifer. She would need industrial strength spells to curb his enthusiasm for extreme sports. I was distracted by a picture of a bungee-jumping kitten when Daniel, re-dressed in clean clothes, put his arms around me from behind and kissed the top of my head.

'Got to go and get the electronic stuff for the chocolate shop from my stash at The Open Eye,' he said. 'Should be finished by this afternoon. Can I come back then?'

'Please,' I said fervently. He was walking with more freedom; a night's rest had loosened all those bruises. Bungee-jumping kittens faded and were replaced by much warmer speculations. Daniel left, Jason made muffins, I made bread. Outside it got almost warm. I made more bread and Jason went to eat his breakfast, the preceding meals having been more in the nature of little snacks.

There is always good money to be made at Cafe Delicious by betting how long it is going to take my thin scrap of a Jason to eat his way through three eggs (fried), three sausages, three rashers of bacon, two grilled tomatoes, a stack of toast and two hash browns or potato pancakes, depending on whether Grandma Pandamus or the Hungarian relief cook Kristina is dishing out the food. His record is three minutes, which I would have thought was barely enough time to physically shovel all that food into the mouth, without fiddling refinements like cutlery. Or chewing.

Still, it is well known that a boy of fifteen has the digestion of an ostrich. I took his very good blueberry muffins out of the oven. While I encouraged his experimental streak, there was still nothing like a good hot blueberry muffin with sifted icing sugar. Jason came back. Five minutes, but he had also had a free piece of baklava, a present from the patriarch Del Pandamus (who had probably won his wager). Jason learned to make French plaits. Bread made, I went into the shop to admit Goss.

Because of their frequent changes of hair colour, eye colour and even stature, the only way I can tell my assistants apart is by their navel rings. Goss's is gold and her navel has a little lip on the upper edge. She had what I would have called day-glo green hair this morning and a top to match.

'Good morning, Gossamer,' I said. 'How was your ad?'

'It was, like, gross!' she replied candidly. 'It was a new chocolate bar and I had to eat, like, hundreds of them! Well, bite them. Lots of times.'

'I thought you liked chocolate,' I said. I should have known better.

'But, duh, Corinna, my diet?' she said. 'There must have been a thousand calories in every bite. I had to keep spitting it out. And I won't be able to eat anything till tomorrow.'

'Goss, if you spat them all out, you haven't eaten anything,' I said patiently. 'And you can't fast and work in the shop. You'll faint. Let me send Jason for a skinny milk latte and have a muffin. Or some of that nice nourishing Cafe Delicious salad.'

They really worry me, Kylie and Goss. Their adherence to the 'famine' diet, which allows them to eat no fat or starch, one steamed chicken leg a day and a few grapes, must be ruining their constitutions. I live for the day I can see them eat a square meal. The trouble with starving like they do is that now and again they just break out and eat a whole tub of ice cream and fifteen doughnuts and then they are ashamed and have to starve again. Since they are both naturally slender, it seems like a modern form of martyrdom of the flesh to me. And even the extreme Catholics have got over that. Goss nodded and I yelled into the bakery for some breakfast for my assistant. Then we opened the door and the hordes came in.

'We've got a new person,' said Goss, after she had eaten a salad roll without margarine and drunk a cup of decaf latte with artificial sweetener.

'I met her,' I said. 'Mrs Sylvia Dawson. Nice lady.'

'No,' said Goss. 'It's a man. He's moved into 7B. Pluto. He came in yesterday. With just a suitcase. Who used to live in Pluto? It's been empty as long as Kyl and me have been here.'

'It belongs to a trust,' I said. 'Part of a big family trust. Squattocracy. Western District, I believe. They own Heracles, too, 7A. Sometimes they sublet it, sometimes the grandchildren or their friends live there. Both of the apartments are furnished. The grandfather bought them as a pied-à-terre for his children so they wouldn't have to stay in hotels when they came to Melbourne for the races or the Show. He had some sort of quarrel with a hotel manager who wouldn't let him keep his sheepdogs in the hotel, and went straight around and bought those two apartments, just after Insula was completed. What does this man look like?'

'A man,' shrugged Goss. 'Oldish. Older than you,' she clarified. 'Not as old as the Prof. Looked boring. Sort of creepy. Had a suit.'

And that was about as much as I was going to get out of Goss. I'd know more when I next saw Meroe. She was in charge of orienting new inhabitants.

The day went on as Fridays usually did. I liked Fridays because tomorrow and Sunday I would not open. Nothing much happens in my end of the city on the weekend, when the action moves across the river to Southbank. Tomorrow morning I would get to sleep in and with any luck I would have company. And I didn't mean Horatio.

When I shut at three I gave Goss and Jason their wages, left them to clean up and, escorted by an elegant cat, climbed my stairs for a bath.

There is nothing like a deep, hot, well-scented bath at the close of a long day. I was in the mood for lush violet foam, and sloshed around in it for some time. Just when I was thinking of getting out, a vision of male beauty, perfectly naked, slid into the tub beside me and kissed me on the mouth.

He was something out of a fever dream, my Daniel. Long limbs, a smooth torso only marred by the shrapnel scar, sweet mouth, strong arms and the most beautiful buttocks in captivity. I was flooded with heat and scent and grabbed, which you shouldn't do in water. We rolled out of the bath onto the floor and coupled like seals.

When I became aware of my surroundings again I found that I was lying partly on Daniel and partly on a tiled floor and I was beginning to get cold. I disentangled some limbs and Daniel said, 'Well,' and sat up.

'Well' is equivocal. An expression of approval or disapproval? I wiped some wet hair out of my eyes and said 'Hello,' and Daniel began to laugh.

'I love you,' he said, dragging me to my feet. 'I never ever met anyone like you,' he said, and kissed me very gently and caressingly. I was melting again and my knees were becoming unreliable. I grabbed his shoulder. I had never ever met anyone like Daniel, either. For one thing, he was strong enough to hold me up.

'Bed,' I suggested.

'Get dry first?' he asked.

I found a towel. The bathroom floor is self-draining, which is lucky, because most of my bathwater was on it. Wrapped in towels, we sloshed into the parlour and dried ourselves. Horatio, from his resting place on Daniel's clothes, eyed us benevolently. Cats, he seemed to be suggesting, did this sort of thing better.

'Let's not be greedy,' I said, regaining my breath. 'We've got tonight. And tomorrow night.' Greedy indeed. I watched the towel slide across the admirable slopes of Daniel's chest and along his thighs and had to look away. My whole body was tuned to him, as though we vibrated on one string.

Now I could see that his bruises had bloomed nicely into velvety dark patches, marring his olive skin. He caught me looking at them.

'It's all right, ketschele, they hurt most before they turn black. Shall we go up to the roof, then?'

'Just let me put some clothes on,' I said. He dropped to one knee and planted a soft kiss on my navel. Then I found a gown, put together the esky which contains the afternoon potation, and Daniel re-dressed.

We rose to the roof garden via the lift. I had the esky, Daniel had Horatio. We sat down in the roofed temple of Ceres in case of light rain and smiled at each other with perfect satisfaction. Horatio pottered off into the undergrowth on business of his own. I poured a gin and tonic for us both.

The roof garden had survived the mad demolitions of the sixties, when everyone in Melbourne was a property developer and most buildings like Insula were torn down in favour of a million square metres of office space which would never be sold. Some benefactor had chained the door and the vandals hadn't noticed it. It ran wild, watered only by rainfall, for years before Trudi applied a taming hand (or machete) and brought it back into cultivation. It has Roman garden furniture, a rose bower and a small temple of Ceres with a statue of the earth mother, arms full of grain.

It is overlooked by a lot of tall buildings, and part of the compensation for getting up at four is sitting in the garden at three thirty in the afternoon, watching tongues hang out in all of the windows. And now I was sitting in the garden with an incredibly beautiful lover who also loved me, which is something I thought would never happen, basking in an afterglow that was still warming my face and breast. Bliss.

The sky was blue and cool. Trudi's linden tree was losing its leaves. Soon the garden would be snuggled down for the winter. The roses would be cut back to prickly stumps, the bulbs which Trudi had persuaded us to buy would be poking little green noses through the ground, and the flowers would be gone. The bower would be a bare ruin'd choir where once the wisteria hung in scented garlands. Horatio and I would spend our garden time in this temple, which was weatherproof and a perfect place to watch storms, because it had a 360 degree view through the glass walls between the columns.

Horatio and I liked storms. I thought I'd ask our new friend. 'Daniel? Do you like storms?'

He thought about it, sipping his drink.

'Being in one, weighed down with a pack and no prospect of refuge, no. In a ship on the sea—no. In this place, with glass all around—it would be wonderful. Why is it warm in here?'

'The architect circulated the waste heat from the building into pipes which run under the garden and keep the soil from freezing. That's why Trudi has to put some of her bulbs in the fridge. Or so she says. And this temple was designed as a winter shelter. Professor Monk says it is a very Roman idea.'

'Those Romans were smart,' he said. 'Perhaps we should forgive them for burning down the Temple of Jerusalem. You haven't replied,' he said, turning his brown eyes on me.

'To what?'

'Do you love me?"

'I love you,' I said. It was true. Had I a song, I would have sung it. As it was, I snuggled into Daniel's side and watched the cool wind picking up the leaves and swirling them in little circles until it got tired and dropped them again.

Meroe arrived just as I ran out of gin, but that was all right, because unless events get atrociously bad, she doesn't drink alcohol, which dulls the chakras. She was carrying a thermos of herbal tea and what appeared to be a furry orange yoyo. She sank down onto the bench next to us.

As it happened, it was not a furry yoyo but a kitten enmeshed in a blue harness and leash. He was wrapped up like a parcel and trying to chew his way out. 'Lucifer is not yet used to his harness,' she explained, unravelling the kitten and setting him down on his paws. He immediately dived onto Daniel, ascended him, and began chewing a shirt button with an expression of innocent enquiry. 'He needs to explore,' said Meroe, pouring herself a cup of what smelt like raspberries. 'This way he can investigate the world without getting himself into too much trouble.'

'You got all the flour off him, I see,' I said. Lucifer was not only clean but shining. 'How? It turned to instant glue on me.'

'I had to wash him very thoroughly,' said Meroe, a shade martyred. 'And I found that he can swim, which is useful to know. He seems to like water. He joined me in my bath.'

Instantly, I blushed red. Meroe looked at me as benevolently as Horatio had. 'Never know what you'll find in your bath these days, eh, Corinna?' she murmured. Daniel laughed and hugged me closer.

'What did you make of Mrs Dawson?' I asked, changing the subject with a wrench.

'Just as you said, a nice lady. Her apartment is furnished with new furniture in perfect taste, a few antiques which must be family treasures and photographs of her children and her late husband. She wanted to know all about the city. For instance, she is off today to join the Athaeneum library, have a light lunch, go to a movie and dine out in Chinatown. She is determined to enjoy herself and I am sure that she will. Any woman who drinks the best gin, chooses linen sheets and wears Arpège is sure to appreciate the finer things in life. I liked her. I explained about the garden. I also asked her if she would like a kitten, but she refused.'

'Good try,' said Daniel. Lucifer abandoned his hope that the button would either (1) detach so that he could choke on it or (2) produce milk, ascended further and poked his nose down the collar of Daniel's shirt.

'But our other new tenant, that is another thing,' said Meroe, dropping her voice.

'Goss thinks he is creepy,' I said.

'I would not go that far, but he is strange,' said Meroe, sipping her tea. 'He was only interested in services which meant that he did not have to go out. Grocery delivery, for instance, takeaway menus, video hire. Pluto is already furnished, of course, mostly in the original art moderne stuff. All he seems to have brought are clothes, a few books, a laptop and a couple of awful sculptures. You know, those objets trouvés things which people build to exhibit their lack of any artistic talent? One has a bronze skeleton of a fish on it.'

'Perhaps he has a broken heart,' said Daniel. 'And he is hiding until he feels ready to face the world again.'

'Perhaps he is an artist,' I said. 'Preparing for a show.'

'Perhaps,' said Meroe in her best oracle's voice. 'But he is a man of secrets. There are shutters behind his eyes.'

'What's his name?' I asked.

'White,' said Meroe. 'Ben White.'

'I wonder if he's a relation of Lepidoptera's?' I suddenly remembered seeing her track him into the building.

'The man is doing no harm,' said Daniel. 'Why not ask Letty when you see her again? If he's her relative she'll be visiting him. Now, can one of you kind ladies relieve me of this kitten? He seems to be trying to dig his way to my spine through my abdomen.'

We removed Lucifer from Daniel's shirt and set him on the ground again. He sprang into Meroe's lap and curled up, folding his tiny paws across his ginger nose.

'So he does sleep sometimes,' I marvelled.

'Very lightly,' warned Meroe, and, joined by Horatio, we tiptoed out.

Chapter Four

We decided to cook dinner. Usually more than one cook in a kitchen leads to snarls, arguments, collisions, spills, and occasionally homicide by saucepan, but Daniel and I moved around each other and Horatio as though we had been working together for years. This so touched me that I was almost in tears by the time we had assembled chicken breasts with herb and garlic stuffing, a warm potato salad and a vivid tomato concasse. Then I cheered up, because I was hungry and dinner smelt fine.

'The only thing I miss about summer is the tomatoes,' said Daniel.

I sat down to eat astounded. He had just read my mind. I opened a bottle of red wine and we had a very civilised meal. When I am on my own I tend to take my plate to the TV, in which lazy habit I am encouraged by Horatio, who has a better chance at the food that way. Now I was sitting up and having to remember how to converse.

Of course, we talked about our neighbours. What else are neighbours for?

'Mrs Dawson will be happy here,' I said. 'But what do you make of Mr White?'

'Not enough data,' said Daniel. 'I've never seen the man. We need to know more about him before we can make any judgments. On another topic, I'll slip down presently and get the tape from the chocolate shop. On fast forward it won't take too long to scan. Not the viewing you had in mind, Corinna, but I do need to check. Or would you rather I did so in my own house?'

'No, of course not, bring it here. I've never seen a surveillance tape.'

'They are amazingly boring,' he told me gravely. 'Like watching an episode of *Big Brother*, but worse. This is the real Reality TV. Mind-bogglingly dull, just like the imitation. Then we can watch some more *Buffy*.'

'Good.' The chicken was very tasty. I ate some more.

'Juliette seems subdued today. Often happens when you decide to call in a private investigator. You worry about what else he might find. But I did pick up some gossip. Jon is coming back, and they say he has a boyfriend.'

'But I thought that Kylie…or was it Goss?…seduced him.'

'If they did, it hasn't taken,' said Daniel. 'Word is that he is a remarkably beautiful Asian man whom Jon met on his travels. Due in tomorrow, says Juliette. One thing about this place, ketschele, there's always something happening. Oh, and I met Mistress Dread this morning. She wants to know when we are going back to the club.'

'I hadn't thought about it,' I lied. I had. Mistress Dread, the leather queen who runs a costume shop in the lane, had lent me the most beautiful dress I had ever worn. I would love to wear it again. Daniel was not deceived for a moment.

'We could go on Saturday night,' he said. 'The crypt is closed now that Lestat is in jail, but the dungeon is still open and I am sure that Mistress Dread runs a very well conducted dungeon.'

'I'll think about it,' I replied, mopping up the last of the concasse with rye bread. I was sleepy with food and wine and sated lust. 'Why don't you go and get the tape and I'll clear away? Are you on the Soup Run tonight?'

'Yes,' said Daniel. 'But not tomorrow night. Very well. Back soon.'

He went. I washed dishes. Then I sat down on the sofa and just closed my eyes for a moment.

When I woke, the TV was on and Daniel was watching a grainy black and white film of a shop. A time clock ran along the bottom of the picture. There was no sound. It was an odd experience.

'It'll never replace Buster Keaton,' I commented.

'I agree,' said Daniel absently. 'There was that trick he did with a falling house which no one will ever surpass.'

'I remember. The house just comes down and he is left standing in what would have been an open window. Must have had nerves of steel. What are we watching?'

'A day's trading in Heavenly Pleasures,' said Daniel.

I curled up next to him. He radiated warmth. I could smell the cinnamon scent which was his signature.

'What can we see?' I asked.

'That's Selima,' he said, pointing out a pretty girl in the chocolate shop's elegant smock. 'Behind the counter. Juliette is just out of the frame at the edge of the screen. Here she is.'

Juliette came into view, carrying a large stainless steel tray. With a pair of tongs she placed chocolates very gently into the display cabinet. I knew that the sweets were all ranked according to filling. These were all of one sort. 'Orange creams,' said Daniel. 'I marked the placements on my chart.' He scribbled the time on a list which already had several entries. I noticed that Selima, with another pair of tongs, was making up the little boxes of eight chocolates which had refreshed many an afternoon, farewelled many a personal assistant and made up many a quarrel. She ranged all over the displays, seemingly at random, filling the little boxes and then sealing each one with a sticky gold label before tying the ribbon.

'She's made ten boxes,' said Daniel.

The boxes were piled artlessly on the end of the display case, for customers who were in too much of a hurry to select their own. Blue and gold packaging. Very dramatic. I remember someone saying that you couldn't package food in blue or green because people wouldn't like it, but this did not apply to Heavenly Pleasures choccies. I would personally buy them in brown paper and string. Or bright orange plastic. Or even bare in the palm of my hand.

People came in. Every person was greeted politely by Selima or Juliette, and every person bought something. Considering the prices of their wares, the sisters must be coining money hand over fist. Most customers gave themselves the pleasure of considering which fillings they would like and ranged up and down the glass case, pointing and, in two cases, slavering.

Each person was given a nickname and entered into Daniel's log. The customers were varied. Men, women, children; well-dressed, ill-dressed, trackpants to Italian handmade suits and some tradesmen in overalls. The men were either hoping to heal a quarrel or intending to behave in such a way as to start one when they finally got home. Or they had forgotten someone's birthday. They all looked rather apologetic and embarrassed at being in this dainty blue and gold palace of sweetness. Women, however, settled in for a good long conversation. Chocolate is a female birthright.

One elderly lady was definitely Mrs Sylvia Dawson. I pointed her out to Daniel. She must have been buying a box of eight chocolates for her own consumption and was indulged with several tastes by Juliette before she closed her eyes in ecstasy and purchased a whole box of one type, and another for good measure.

'Caramel Delight,' diagnosed Daniel, checking his list. 'In milk chocolate. She likes hard centres. And the other box she bought was chocolate covered hazelnuts.'

'A decided character,' I said. 'Oh dear,' I added.

'What?'

'It's Kylie,' I said. 'Or Goss.'

'And they can't eat chocolates?' asked Daniel.

'They're on a famine diet,' I explained. 'It's too much for flesh and blood to stand, all that chicken and grapes. They'll eat all the choccies and then they'll starve for two days to stay thin.'

'Amongst your many virtues,' said Daniel, noting down Kylie or Goss's purchase of two boxes of soft centred chocolates, 'is your total refusal to diet. I do admire it. What do you do when people say "just follow this diet and you'll be thin"?'

'If they said it,' I said, snuggling, 'I'd spit in their eye. But they don't.' I had heard from other fat women that perfect strangers came up to them in the street and offered them diet plans or magic herbs. No one had ever done that to me. Which is fortunate, of course, because I would not have been pleased and might have been armed. I assumed that people who left me alone had some elementary sense of self-protection.

Perhaps I didn't give off the right air of being sorry for existing. Even when I was imprisoned in a tough girls school and forced to play hockey and ridiculed because I couldn't, I have never been sorry that I existed. I have, of course, been sorry that a lot of other people existed, beginning with certain politicians (they know who they are; George, are you listening?) and my ex, James, but not, as it happens, me. Daniel spoke suddenly and I snapped myself out of my reverie.

'Here's Vivienne,' he said.

Vivienne was a carbon copy of her sister except she wasn't pretty. It was hard to say why. Especially in a black and white fast forward. But I made Daniel freeze the picture so that I could get a good look at her. She was tall; in Juliette tall was willowy, in Vivienne it was gawky. She was blonde, but her hair seemed paler than Juliette's and was dragged back into an unbecoming ponytail. She was pale, but with Vivienne it looked pasty while Juliette was milk and roses.

The two of them were standing behind the counter as Selima took what must have been her lunch break. Vivienne was placing chocolates tenderly into their ranks. Juliette was trying to talk to her but each time she approached, Vivienne turned a bony shoulder and looked away. I could not see if she was speaking. Finally Juliette gave up and retreated to the far end of the cabinet and stared out of the window, biting her lip.

'I get on fine with my sister,' I quoted.

'Doesn't look like it, does it?' asked Daniel.

'No, but we don't know the source of the quarrel. Could be she's just grumpy because the chocolate isn't setting. Cooks tend to be highly strung,' I said.

'Don't I know it!' said Daniel. 'I worked in a hotel kitchen in Paris once and the chef used to throw pots. And that's when he was in a good mood.'

'And when he was in a bad mood?'

'Knives, mostly,' said Daniel. 'Or choppers. All that army experience was useful. I ducked and took cover really well.'

I had to ask. 'What were you doing in Paris?'

'I got out of the army when my wife died,' he said quietly. 'I didn't know what I wanted to do or where I wanted to go. So I went to Paris,' he said, as though this was self-evident.

'Ipso facto, as the Prof would say. Come to think of it, that's how I ended up there, too.'

'Paris is very good if you don't know where you want to be,' he told me. 'I worked in a cafe which only made onion soup. I'll make you French onion soup, ketschele. I'm really good at it. It was a nice job. I only quit when people started to move away from me on the metro. The onions had soaked into my skin, I swear. Ah. Vivienne has gone back to the kitchen and here we have—George.'

'The apprentice?'

'Just so,' said Daniel. We stared. George was young, tall, dark, handsome, and really, really aware of it. He had an armload of boxes which he put down behind the counter. Juliette laughed at something he said and he gave her a fleeting pat on the cheek. Then we saw George jump at some summons from behind him, and he fled back into the kitchen.

'Aha,' said Daniel.

'I second your "Aha!",' I said. 'What a very decorative young man.'

'Knows it, too,' said Daniel.

'Not my type,' I said. 'I have always found that that sort of young man is more interested in his mirror than any living female. They hang about in gyms, I believe,' I said, never having entered one. If I want to be tortured, I'll join the wrong political party in some benighted African republic. Actually, mostly just being female will do it in places like that.

'More customers,' said Daniel.

Several girls, giggling, bought wicked chocolates. An elderly gentleman with a stick came in and Juliette talked to him for ten minutes, going away to serve other people and coming back to him. He was given tastes of four different chocolates, more than anyone else, before he bought a box of the miscellaneous ones from the pile on the end of the counter. He was a magnificent talker, flourishing with his elegant hands rather than just waving them. I wondered if he was an actor.

'Someone she knows,' Daniel guessed.

'A relative,' I said.

'Why do you say that?'

'He didn't pay for his chocolates,' I said. 'Relatives never pay. Neither do old friends. I had an uncle who went broke because his cafe was too successful.'

'And that happened because…?'

'All his old schoolfriends and relatives came in practically every day and he had to feed them all,' I told Daniel. 'There wasn't room for paying clients. Mind you, he had a wonderful time while it lasted. The same could not be said for his wife, who was doing the cooking,' I concluded.

'You really are amazing,' said Daniel.

'It's a gift,' I said modestly. He laughed.

The elderly man left. Several customers bought sweets. Then a woman came in with an opened box of chocolates and slapped them on the counter.

'Aha,' said Daniel.

'A complaint,' I said.

'A dissatisfied customer who has bitten into a mouthful of chili sauce,' said Daniel.

Juliette did her best to placate the woman. The woman waved her arms. She was expressing just how ruined her evening had been. She clutched at her throat to demonstrate how shocking had been the taste which had insulted her innocent mouth. Juliette pleaded. She grovelled. She offered a new box. The woman gradually allowed herself to be pacified. She accepted two boxes, specially chosen, as compensation, and stalked out, still upset.

'Oh dear,' said Daniel. Selima had come back into the shop and Juliette had fled in tears.

'I suspect she isn't going to get a lot of sympathy from her sister,' I commented.

'Probably not,' he agreed. 'But maybe she isn't expecting any from her sister.'

'George?' I asked.

'They would be nice arms to throw yourself into, ketschele.'

'George wouldn't like it,' I said nastily. 'Tears might stain his shirt and emotion might disarrange his hair.'

'You really haven't taken to him, have you? All right, we are getting to the end. Shop is closed. Juliette and Selima do something to the cash register…'

'Count the money apart from the float, write it all out on the bank voucher and put it into the bag for the night safe,' I said, repeating what had to be done every day the bakery was open. Then someone will go to the bank…it appears to be Selima,' I said, as the young woman doffed her smock, picked up her handbag and the bank bag and went out. 'Now we clean the shop and then everyone gets to go home.'

This is, in fact, what happened. George condescended to sweep the floor, the chocolates were carefully covered with a cloth and the display cabinet glass and the window were cleaned. George left, followed by Juliette. Vivienne remained in the shop. She turned away into the back room and shut the door behind her.

'Fin,' said Daniel. 'Applause.'

'You know, watching too many of these could make you feel very sorry for the human race,' I said, leaning on him.

'It does,' he responded. 'It also makes me want to go to bed with you,' he added.

That sounded like a good idea. We did that. And Horatio, who is a perceptive animal, stayed where he was on the couch.

Chapter Five

Horatio was there, purring, when I woke, however, promptly and automatically at four. I stroked him, momentarily regretted the lack of Daniel, and did my favourite Saturday morning thing: I turned over and went firmly back to sleep. Extra sleep is such a luxury. One reason why I had never had children is that I might have been woken up once too often and then had to donate them to the Salvation Army to get some sleep, and that isn't socially responsible behaviour.

Another reason is that James would have been their father and I would not wish that on any child. Poor creatures, isn't a world with George Bush in it bad enough, without adding James to the mix? Out of the question. Whatever Jason might say, I am not a cruel woman.

I snuggled down into my pillow and only had time for one groan of pure pleasure before I was waking up again and it was ten in the morning and high time to get some breakfast. As this was also Horatio's opinion we went into the parlour, picked up our current novel, and settled down with pasta douro toast, marmalade and coffee—and kitty dins for him—to spend a quiet morning. I took my breakfast out onto the balcony where Trudi's green leafy things were (remarkably) still alive and idly watched the alley. Always something to watch in Calico Alley.

The day had clouded over. We might actually get some rain. Horatio, who is a very good forecaster (he hates getting wet and is convinced that rain is caused by some negligent human omitting to keep the sky in good repair), had moved under the canopy and was washing his ears. Rain coming, all right. I didn't have to go out. I had yielded to laziness and emailed my grocery order to the supermarket. I was tired of hauling all those heavy tins of cat food up to the apartment. Did the cats thank me for it? They did not. Let someone who is paid to haul things haul them. My excuse was that bakers put a lot of strain on their backs already, heaving sacks of flour around, and I should preserve my spinal health. It was a good excuse and I was sticking to it.

And here came the grocery van, on schedule. Brisk persons in dustcoats got out those ingenious trolley things and began wheeling boxes into the building. I opened my door for a young man who wheeled the trolley in, unloaded the boxes, smiled, and was gone in an instant. But not before I noticed that the other boxes were marked for Pluto, and that Mr White had laid in really quite a lot of booze and what looked like the whole range of frozen cuisine.

I put away the groceries. Since someone else was carrying it I had bought a new sack of kitty litter, enough tinned cat food to feed a group of full grown tigers, and a lot of heavy things like new bottles of brandy and gin, a fresh chateau collapseau, a lot of potatoes, ingredients for a number of meals and soups: lentils, dried beans, chicken stock, vegetables and both ham hocks and lamb shanks. I stuffed all the perishables into my commodious fridge and went back to the balcony.

I had a new Jade Forrester. And another cup of coffee. And although slightly sore in several places which hadn't felt any friction since I left James, I was very happy.

Mrs Dawson came past just as it began to rain, and opened one of the most beautiful umbrellas I had ever seen. It was patterned with Van Gogh sunflowers. It cheered the whole alley until she disappeared inside, furling it as she went. Her silk shirt was mushroom pink today, softening her severe grey serge trouser suit. We at Insula were lucky to have a woman of such impeccable taste living amongst us. I made a mental note to be watching when she went to church tomorrow. I was quite sure that Mrs Dawson would go to the cathedral for matins.

I could see down the lane a little. Heavenly Pleasures was open and doing good business, to judge by the number of people who passed with little blue and gold boxes in their hands or tucking them into pockets. I reflected on the strange position which chocolate held in my society. How had a paste made of crushed cocoa-beans become so important? How had a bitter bean come to mean comfort, reconciliation and kindness? These were deep matters.

I finished my coffee and pottered off to do Saturday things. The washing. Feeding the Mouse Police and cleaning out two litter trays. Reading all the bits of the paper which did not concern politics, due to politics at present not being good for my digestion or my temper. Meroe came to the door at noon with her furry yoyo and a basket of her special salad leaves, which (despite what she says) I know are flown in by express broomstick from Fairyland every morning. Nothing earthly tastes that good.

Set down, Lucifer immediately dived on Horatio, who, woken from rightful slumber, hissed and swiped before he realised that he was slapping a kitten. Then he ascended the sofa and sat with his back to us, mortified.

'How is Belladonna taking this invasion of kitten?' I asked, laying out cheese and bread and various fruits of the earth.

'With complete lack of poise,' sighed Meroe. 'She refuses to leave the shop if Lucifer is in my apartment and is presently not speaking to me at all. And he's such a dear little thing,' she added, watching fondly as Lucifer sprang onto the table, investigated the cheese and butter, and was gently dissuaded from curling up for a brief rest in the salad bowl. Exhausting the possibilities of the table, he dived down again and devoted some time and energy to finding out whether a silk tassel from the curtain would unravel. It held out gamely, even when bounced on and then pinned down under paw and chewed.

I was getting tired just watching him.

'I've an idea about Lucifer,' I told Meroe. 'I think he needs broader pastures and new challenges,' I went on.

'That,' sighed Meroe, 'is true.'

'Therefore I suggest that we pay Trudi to take him around with her, safely secured in his harness, on all her worldly occasions,' I said. 'She's on the move all day, gardening and so on. Get him out into the fresh air. Get his paws dirty.'

'But Trudi doesn't like cats,' objected Meroe, taking a large helping of salad.

'I bet she'll fall for Lucifer after a week or two,' I said. 'Anyway, it ought to give him something to do. He might even learn sense,' I added, though not with any real confidence.

'I'll go halves,' she said, as the tassel finally gave way and enveloped the kitten in about a hundred metres of yellow thread. In which he rolled, entangling himself like a fly in a web. Then he lay there, waving his one free paw and waiting for someone to get him out. I was all for leaving him there until we finished lunch but Meroe insisted and eventually we had to cut him out. Then he bounced up onto the couch to try for Horatio's tail.

Horatio glanced around, glared, and returned to his station. His back conveyed his immovable resolve not to come down until this small detestable beast was gone, and probably not for some time thereafter. Lovers are bad enough, he seemed to be trying to convey. But kittens are the end.

By mutual consent, Meroe and I put off our cup of coffee (me), camomile tea (her) and took Lucifer up to Ceres. Trudi was home, looking through a bulb catalogue. We explained our problem. Lucifer sat on the table, paws together, looking as though he was plotting something dreadful.

Trudi is Dutch, sixty-ish, with short white hair and strong hands. She is responsible for fixing recalcitrant machinery, replacing light bulbs, understanding the cargo lift, maintaining the garden, harassing tradesmen and letting people in when they have forgotten their keys or their passcodes or, like Andy Holliday, who they are and where they live. Since he got his daughter Cherie back, he has been going easier on the bottle, but he memorably once woke the whole building with his feeling rendition of 'Heartbreak Hotel'. Trudi had hauled him up to his apartment single-handedly. She is formidable.

And she didn't look very happy about being landed with Lucifer. But she needs the money and after Meroe had explained that Lucifer needed scope for his adventurous nature, agreed to take him for a week.

Before she could change her mind, we provided her with a litter tray and a bag of litter, kitten food and dishes, and instructed her on how to remove and replace his harness. The kitten dived on Trudi and, as we were leaving, was trying the edge of her bulb catalogue for edibility.

Meroe and I retreated to my apartment for our beverage of choice.

'I hope he'll be all right with her,' said Meroe guiltily, as though we had just sold the little ratbag to a furrier.

'Of course he will be,' I said bracingly. 'Now Belladonna may forgive you and Horatio may forgive me, and Lucifer will get to see the wide open spaces. Have a citrus muffin?'

'Few situations cannot be improved by a muffin,' she said, and bit. 'Lovely! One of Jason's inventions?'

'He's working on new ones all the time,' I said. 'This is made orangey by candied orange rind. He candied it himself. He has the instincts of a really good pastry chef. I'll have to let him go in a few years, to do a proper apprenticeship. But he's still a little shaky on reading and writing and of course he might go bung at any moment. He's always messed things up before, he says so himself.'

'Self-fulfilling prophecies,' said Meroe. 'He might not. Well, that was lovely. Thank you for lunch and the solution to the Lucifer problem.'

'Thank you for the salad,' I said, really meaning it.

Meroe left to go back to the Sibyl's Cave, her magic shop. It has a little doll in a bottle by the door, marked 'A Present from Cumae', which always makes Professor Monk laugh. I keep meaning to ask him about that. There the seeker after knowledge can purchase anything from sheep's shoulderblades for divination to herbs, runes, books of spells, occult jewellery, holy water from a variety of sources, little statues of any given deity, Egyptian oils, incense and tarot cards. They may also have a refreshing look at Belladonna, a cat so black that light almost falls through her, who lies in the tiny window and attracts custom by batting idly at the Celtic symbols and looking inscrutable, depending on mood. It is considered lucky, in the occult community, to stroke Belladonna upon entering the Sibyl's Cave. I had detected amongst the magicians a tendency to talk to Bella as though she was Meroe. I suppose, under some circumstances, she might be. You never know with witches, and you certainly never know with cats.

I cleared the table and sat down to read some more of my Jade Forrester. She has been diversifying into sci-fi lately. She's very good at it, if light on for detail of where the crew got this ship and how it works. But how she was going to get her Avon and Roj together—given their mutual loathing and total refusal to understand that they were made for each other—I could not imagine. I read on, through another cup of coffee. Horatio got down from the sofa, sniffed the areas which Lucifer had marked with his profane little paws, sneezed, then levitated to the table for a conciliatory scratch behind the ears.

'He's gone now,' I said soothingly. 'Trudi has him.'

Horatio sneezed again, implying that Trudi was welcome to him. Then he settled down next to my book rest in his usual loaf shape, paws folded under, and began to purr. What with the rain and the purring and the Jade Forrester, I was well occupied until about five, when Daniel came to my door. He rang, even though he had a key. When I let him in he was carrying a rucksack.

'I thought you mightn't mind if I left a few clothes and things here,' he said. 'In case I come in like I did before, in need of first aid and smelling like a drain. If you don't mind? I don't want you to think that I'm moving in on you, Corinna.'

'A good idea, there's an empty wardrobe in the spare bedroom,' I offered.

'I'll stash the stuff, then,' he said.

My spare bedroom is always ready for anyone who wants to sleep amongst the things which somehow I can't throw away and might still need, like old clothes, and the things which I will need but needn't keep on display, like my sewing machine and box of fabrics. I also keep my To Be Read pile of books there. The TBR is now taller than me, and never seems to get any shorter. The wardrobe, however, is empty, if hard to get to. Daniel had brought two changes of underwear, a pair of jeans, a pair of boots, two t-shirts and a jacket. He also had a plastic bag which contained shaving things and spare keys, judging by the clunk as he put it on the shelf. I delved for an emotion. When men start leaving clothes in your house, sooner or later they move in, that was the maxim. I did not feel threatened.

Besides, it was Daniel. I made him some coffee and we sat down. Horatio elevated his chin for Daniel's attentions. I explained about Lucifer and Daniel approved.

'Nice for him to get out into the fresh air,' he remarked. 'Trudi may not like cats but she will take care of him. A good solution, ketschele. By the way, I met your mystery man in the lift. Most odd.'

'How?' I asked.

'He wouldn't look at me,' said Daniel, puzzled, 'yet I'm sure that I have seen him somewhere before.'

'In person?'

'Possibly,' he said. 'I really can't remember. I might have just passed him in the street, of course. But I agree with Meroe. There are shutters behind his eyes.'

'What did he look like?' I asked.

'Tallish, dark hair turning to grey at the temples. Brown eyes, what I could see of them. Nice suit, but not handmade. Glasses. Well-kept hands. Looked like an accountant, something like that. Maybe forty years old. He had a shopping bag with him. I didn't try to talk to him.'

'Good move, why set out to be snubbed? What shall we do tonight?'

'Do you feel like going out? I'm in favour of an earlyish night, but I'd like some dinner.'

'Not to the club,' I said. Blood Lines needed preparation, like black nail polish and a full cosmetic makeover, which I did not feel like doing. 'Just for a bite of dinner?'

'Nice. Anywhere in the city?'

'Let's be bold,' I said, 'and go to my favourite cafe in the world. In Brunswick Street. And we shall travel by tram.'

We had negotiated our first date! I was elated. Daniel had said what he wanted to do, it happened to be what I wanted to do, and we were agreed. I leaned over and kissed him, just because I could. The kiss was deepening agreeably when we were interrupted by the doorbell.

I opened it grumpily, swearing that if it was Trudi trying to return her kitten I would be cross, and was confronted by three people. One was a tall, willowy Chinese man of surpassing beauty. Another was a short Chinese boy with a cheeky smile. The third, who explained the other two, was Jon, the international charity exec. He was tall, too. And had red hair. And was an absolute darling, now looking slightly wounded at being scowled at for no reason.

'Corinna? I'd like you to meet my friends. Have I come at a bad time?'

'No, not at all, do come in,' I said, slightly dazed. Gorgeous male persons were certainly parading my way today. First Heavenly Pleasures' George and now this vision of loveliness. Where had they all been when I was eighteen? All the boys I had seen then made James look good. Only by comparison, I hasten to add.

Jon brought his friends in and I offered chairs and drinks.

'This is Charles Li, known as Chas,' he said, introducing the boy, who had scanned the apartment in one fast, comprehensive glance, and was now considering Horatio. Who was also considering him. Boy and cat looked at each other, not in a hostile but in a very feline, measuring way. Then they broke their mutual gaze, satisfied that the other was not a threat.

'Hey,' said Chas, in pure Australian. 'Nice to meet you, Miss. You Daniel? I've heard about you.'

'And I've heard about you.' Daniel shook Chas's hand gravely. 'You sell stuff at the Queen Vic, don't you?'

'That's me!' said Chas, beaming. 'Pile it on a barrow, gone in ten minutes, no problems.'

'And this,' said Jon, pausing for effect as well he might, 'is Kepler Li.'

'Miss Chapman,' said Kepler in perfectly modulated English. 'Mr Cohen.'

'On these eight minutes…' said Daniel, obscurely.

'I will build a new theory of the universe,' concluded Kepler.

It must have been some sort of code that they both recognised. Was Daniel a member of a secret society? Nothing would have surprised me about Daniel. I looked at Jon. He shrugged. Chas giggled.

'We picked English names for ourselves,' he said. 'In the camp. I got mine off a book he was reading by Charles Dickens and found out he was also called Chas. He named himself after…'

'Johann Kepler,' said Daniel. 'A very good choice. Do sit down. A glass of wine?'

'Red for Kepler and me,' said Jon, knowing that I always had red wine in the house. For medicinal purposes, like the brandy. 'Chas will have mineral water if there is no Coke.'

'As there isn't,' I said apologetically. About every six months I get an urge to drink Coke and then I drink the whole bottle.

'We should have brought our own,' said Jon. 'You know, I never thought to ask you why your name was Kepler, Kep dear.'

'I chose him,' said Kepler, tossing his long, shiny, ebony hair out of his eyes, 'because when I read about all the great scientists, Kepler was the only one who was both right most of the time and nice. Everyone liked him. Nice scientists are very rare. He had a medieval mind but a true understanding and when he was asked to accept either the Ptolemaic system with all its circles and deferents was wrong or that Tycho Brahe's observations were wrong he chose to believe Tycho. He knew Tycho was a complete obsessive who would stay out in the freezing Danish night until his toes dropped off rather than fudge an observation.'

'And he was right,' said Daniel eagerly.

'Even though he did think that the planets were swept into place by God's celestial broom,' said Kepler apologetically.

'Well, he was right about the three laws,' said Daniel, displaying a knowledge of astronomy of which I had not suspected him. 'They were proved right by Newton. Especially R cubed over T squared. Newton proved that it had to be true because gravitational acceleration a equals GM over R squared which equals 4 pi squared R over T squared. Therefore R cubed over T squared equals GM over 4 pi squared, therefore Kepler was right.'

'As these are all constants for our solar system,' agreed Kepler, beaming at Daniel. He looked like a Chinese deity who had discovered especial acts of piety amongst his people. Except most Chinese deities didn't wear handmade Mandarin-collared suits in fine shadow-grey shantung, which perfectly matched the streaks of grey in his hair. A least, as far as I know. I've never actually met any Chinese deities. I'd have to ask Meroe.

'Perhaps it's a code,' I said to Jon.

'I have always thought so,' he agreed. 'Kepler has just arrived.'

'Where from?' I asked, as the words 'five regular solids' and 'harmonia mundi' were used in my parlour for the very first time.

'I met him on a trip when we were dealing with famine relief in Cambodia. It was a terrible situation and he was very kind to me. He comes from Hong Kong, but from China initially. Chas came here when he was only five,' he added, which explained Chas's accent. I never saw two brothers more unlike. Chas was like Jason: bright, interested and, if I knew my artful dodgers, a player. Kepler had a vague air, as though his mind was in the sky and his thoughts on the planets. He and Daniel were having such fun that I didn't like to interrupt.

'He's a computer genius,' said Jon fondly. 'Microsoft Games Division pay him a huge retainer in case he comes up with anything. The rest of the time he teaches tai kwon do.'

'And he's useless on the stall,' put in his brother with scorn. 'He gives stuff away to people because they look poor.'

'And you would never do that,' teased Jon. Chas scowled fondly at him. 'I've got a month's leave, that last Cambodian placement was a bit hairy. So I thought I'd show Kep around Melbourne.'

'A nice idea,' I agreed, sipping. 'What is he interested in?'

'Everything,' said Chas. 'I'm just here to help him carry his stuff. And see the apartment so I can tell Mum. Then I got to get back, I got a load of t-shirts coming in tonight.'

This counted as a delicate hint, and Jon obediently drank up and put down his glass. Kepler had hardly tasted his. Jon touched his shoulder.

'We had better get going, Kep,' he said. 'Nice to meet you, Daniel.'

'Perhaps you would like to visit us for a game of chess?' asked Kepler Li. He cast such a loving, confiding look at Jon that I was taken aback. 'When we are settled.'

'I'd really like that,' said Daniel, shaking the long, slim hand. Kepler smiled ravishingly at both of us and went out, ushered by Chas, who was clearly in a hurry to get back to his load of t-shirts. Jon took Kepler's hand as they went out. The door closed.

'Weren't they just so sweet together?' said Daniel. 'Come along, ketschele, if we are going out let's go, or I shall just have to propose other ways of passing the time.'

I kissed his soft, silky mouth, then pulled myself out of his arms. I liked the way they automatically closed around me.

'Clothes,' I said, and went into my bedroom to dress. I chose black trousers, comfortable shoes, a bright blue silk shirt and a black jacket. If it worked for Mrs Dawson, it might work for me. I took up the backpack without which I never travel, and we went out into the cooling darkness.

We caught the tram in Collins Street. I love trams. I like the new super-quiet air conditioned ones which whisper along the tracks. I also like the old clacky ones which bump and grind like a Las Vegas showgirl. There is something about sailing through the traffic in a machine which weighs nine tons and can hold its own against anything except a tank which engenders a feeling of superiority. I had a bunch of tickets, because attempting to co-ordinate the money, the movement of the tram and the slots in the machine is not to be attempted by any but the ballet trained.

It was, as it happened, a clacky old tram, and Daniel and I validated two tickets and sat down in the middle to watch the city flee past. We chugged up Collins Street past the bulk of the town hall and the sad statue of that pair of utter losers, Burke and Wills. I love Collins Street. The chestnuts were losing their leaves and flurries scraped across the road under the traffic. The white holiness of the Baptist Church flashed past, Greek and pure. The tram laboured up further, past Scots Church and rows of genteel buildings, to the awful cliff of the Australia Hotel, and then we paused as a flood of traffic shouldered past us along Spring Street.

Then, with a feline wriggle, we were sliding past Parliament, the home of lost clauses, the trees almost meeting over the roof of the tram.

'What was all that about Kepler?' I asked Daniel, his hand warm in mine, resting on my thigh and sending little wriggles of sensation along my spine.

'He was a remarkable man,' said Daniel. 'But the theory I love best was the harmonia mundi.'

'I haven't got time to nick back and ask the Prof what it means, so you will have to translate,' I said comfortably.

'The music of the spheres,' said Daniel. 'Each planet, he thought, must have its own note, and as the planets move, they generate music. The cosmos sounds continually with the grave, slow fugue of the planets, the music of the spheres.'

'What a beautiful idea,' I said, thinking about it as the tram wriggled through the mass of tracks and, having made up its mind, swooped down Brunswick Street at last. I tried to imagine what such music might be like; so slow and deep that we could not hear it.

'Like trees,' I said, as we clattered past the Housing Commission flats, going downhill and faster.

'Trees?'

'If we were listening to what trees had to say, their language would be too slow to hear,' I explained. Daniel thought about it.

'Nice,' he approved. We sat in silence for a while and then he said, 'Where are we going, Corinna?'

'We get off here,' I said, as the tram slammed to a halt at the corner of Johnston street. 'Up there,' I pointed, 'is the Night Cat, a good place if you are feeling like grunge and ex-garage floors. Along here,' I took his hand, 'is the best second-hand bookshop in the city. And we pass the fashionable cafe,' I said, passing it, 'because I do not go to a cafe to be seen where other people go to see celebrities. Poor things ought to be allowed to have their cafe latte in peace.'

'I do agree,' said Daniel as we fell into the Brunswick Street amble, a slow passegiata stroll which did not conflict with the people, dogs, skateboarders, small children and cafe tables which littered the pavement. The night was cool, not yet cold, and the street was thronged.

'You must have been here before,' I said to Daniel. He was walking directly behind me as we slid past a large board advertising shiatsu massage and aromatherapy.

'Certainly,' he said. 'On business. But never—as it happens—for fun. I'm trying not to look for homeless kids, drug deals or missing children. If you would come back and hug me it would materially assist this process,' he suggested.

I fitted exactly under Daniel's arm. Somehow we had not discovered this before. Not just easily—exactly. To embrace me he did not have to stoop or stretch. It was almost as easy to walk along entwined with him as it was to walk by myself, and that was another thing which had never happened to me before. I felt a little light headed and giggled. I do not usually giggle.

Past the gorgeous Grub Street Bookshop and a little further on and there were the second-hand iron tables outside my favourite cafe.

'Vertigo?' asked Daniel. 'Why here, more than any other?'

'It has no celeb watchers,' I told him. 'And the staff are genuinely glad to see us, and that doesn't happen very often. Hello,' I said, pushing open the door.

The young man in the long white apron smiled and ushered us toward the back of the cafe, where it was warmer.

I liked Vertigo. I liked their Parisian bar, with the ranked bottles behind it. I liked their style and I really liked their pasta. But it wasn't just the food. No one survived on Brunswick Street for long selling indifferent food. One got the feeling that Vertigo liked feeding people. I had been sneered at by head waiters in enough expensive restaurants when I had been married to James to be super sensitive to snubs from food handlers. If it was slung across the table with an unvoiced 'I hope it chokes you' then I suddenly wasn't hungry.

'Pasta,' said Daniel, reading the menu. 'Something simple, I think. Fettucine with tomato and basil sauce, that sounds good. What about you?'

'You've already made up your mind?' I was astonished. James had taken classes in advanced menu study. He always cross-examined the waiter as to all ingredients, too. It had driven me mad, actually, now I came to think of it. I knew what I wanted, already.

'Tagliatelli with smoked salmon and cream,' I said hungrily.

'And a nice bottle of...?' asked the waiter, who had seen me before.

'Red,' I said, naming a very good one. 'We're celebrating.'

'So I see,' said the waiter, grinning. 'Half your luck.'

I looked around, indulging in the sport of 'eavesdropping', which has always been one of my guilty pleasures. There was a big group at the back. There was the table of girls on a girls' night out, drinking house champagne and eating their own negligible weight in Cafe Vertigo cakes, which tend to be exceptionally rich in exceptionally large serves. With King Island cream. They were talking about a club they were going to later, where all the boys were cute.

'And other dreams,' said Daniel. I had met a fellow eaves-dropper! And I had thought I was the only one. No pervert who finally found someone who shared his own unique vice involving boiled eggs, leather straps and raspberry ice cream could possibly have been more gratified.

'But you have to admire The Herd,' said a young man at an adjoining table dressed in a red Midnight Oil t-shirt which had seen better years. 'They've introduced politics into hip-hop.'

'Political hip-hop,' sneered his friend. 'It was always political. Now if you want philosophy, you want McLusky. No one does it better than McLusky.'

'Crap! I don't know how you can say that,' said his friend, and I lost interest.

The big group were intent on solving something. Suggestions were being called out and shouted down. They were all eating cake and drinking coffee.

'Could it be in Austria?' asked a ravishing brunette with a short, shiny bob and a biro in her hand, which she twiddled as though it was a cigarette.

'Maybe Bavaria,' said a wizardly person with a beard and long white hair.

'No, Prussia,' said a deep-voiced man, raising his cake fork in a commanding gesture. 'We'll have to look it up in the atlas later. What's next?'

'Nine across,' said a plump woman with curly red hair and a green cheesecloth shirt. 'General who ate peaches and became a legend for steadfastness shares name with a famous bare-knuckle fighter.'

'Well, we know who that is,' said the deep-voiced man.

'An eighteenth century pugilist called Gentleman Jackson,' said the redhead.

'And Stonewall Jackson,' said the deep voice. They put in the clue and smiled at each other. And ordered more cake and coffee.

'A crossword,' said Daniel. 'That fiendish general knowledge one. Ah. Dinner,' he said, as plates of pasta were carried forth and we both realised that we were starving.

'Yum,' I agreed.

We ate sumptuously and drank the wine and listened to the cafe. The boys talked about Super Furry Animals and Idlewild. I knew about the Super Furries. They did a very funny parody of Santana dressed as golden retrievers—or possibly yetis, it was hard to tell. The girls talked about boys and *Big Brother*. The crossword collective howled with rage about the inaccuracy, idiocy and natural sadism of the crossword maker and threatened retribution in the form of flung dictionaries. Vertigo went on with its business. People ebbed and flowed past the windows and the street murmured its own private self-satisfaction. We paid and went out into the Brunswick night.

Hot chocolate in the Spanish manner at Bocadillo, or ice cream?' I asked.

'Ice cream,' said Daniel.

We crossed the road to Charmaine's Temple of Ice Cream and ordered a pink grapefruit gelati (me) and a tiramisu (Daniel) and strolled along the other side of the road, licking and looking around. The sorbet was sharp and not very sweet. The tiramisu was velvety and rich. The shops were as eclectic as ever. We had finished our dessert by the time we got to the tram stop.

'Home?' said Daniel, as the tram slid to a halt.

'Home,' I agreed.

We sat down in the tram and I leaned my head on Daniel's shoulder. The city flicked past in red and green and white lights, in sudden intimate glimpses into upstairs windows where people were doing things; pouring tea, lighting a smoke, turning a page. Then around the squiggle into the city and down the long slope of Collins Street, past the Reserve Bank which, with all its money, couldn't have been happier than Daniel and me. Down to Elizabeth Street, where we got off and ambled along, sleepy with wine and good company, towards our own home and bed.

Which we were not going to get to immediately, it appeared. Insula was buzzing with people in various stages of undress, and cops.

'Is it a fire?' I asked Meroe, who was clutching a wire carrier in which Belladonna was howling a protest.

'It's a bomb,' she said.

'Who'd want to bomb Insula?' asked Daniel.

Meroe set down the cat carrier so that she could throw up both her hands in a Hungarian Gypsy gesture of despair. She said a thing which very few professional witches like saying.

'I don't know!' she cried.

Chapter Six

I looked around. Everyone appeared to be here. Mrs Dawson in a dark brown cashmere dressing gown and soft, terracotta-coloured Russian leather boots. Professor Monk wearing a voluminous dark blue gown rather like a monk's robe, holding an armload of papers and books. I observed Mrs Dawson walking across to assist him with the pile, which was beginning to topple. I sighted Goss and Kylie, who were, of course, dressed for an evening at the clubs, in skimpy but expensive outfits which seemed to have been stapled together with gold wire. Kylie was hugging Goss.

Jon and Kepler were sitting on the top stair, looking bemused. I stepped over the Lone Gunmen, three young men who ran Nerds Inc. They were sprawled on the stairs. Taz, Gully and Rat appeared no worse for their fright but apprehensive, as they always were when forced out of their burrows and made to converse with humans face to face. They had a carton full of DVDs.

'Corinna, Trudi let your cats out,' said Taz as I tried not to stand on any part of him.

'But we don't know about Calico and Soot and Tori,' sobbed Kylie. 'I left them inside because I didn't know what all the noise was about and now they won't let us back into the building and now…'

She sobbed again and Cherie Holliday, who knew all about loss and fear, put an arm around her. Cherie had brought her teddy bear, Pumpkin, with her. Her father Andy, I noticed, had brought his briefcase and his bottle of scotch. Everyone, in fact, had brought their most precious things. Mrs Dawson had a suitcase which, I would bet, was full of photos and books. Professor Monk had his Aristophanes translation on which he had worked for years. I didn't actually have many precious things, and all of my papers and so on were on me. My mother was a hippie who didn't believe in material values and my grandmother brought me up. I had her bluebird pin. And some pictures I supposed I would miss.

Kylie and Goss had their make-up cases. Trudi had a box of bulbs and Lucifer, who was now riding on her shoulder. His little ears were laid back and he was having the time of his life. I noticed that Trudi had tucked a leather glove under the strap of her overall, for him to shred with his claws and save her shoulder. The Pandamus family were gathered together like chickens threatened by a hawk, with the children and Yai Yai in the middle. Mrs Pemberthy and her rotten little doggie Traddles were having hysterics in a police car. Mistress Dread, the leather queen, was talking to a police officer who seemed unfazed at being towered over by a six foot woman in fishnets and a red leather corset who punctuated her statements by slapping a riding whip on her muscular thigh.

Oh, my Horatio, where was he? The policeman who was standing by the door did not look sympathetic. While Horatio could protect himself from most ordinary threats, what could he do about a bomb? Daniel's arm tightened around my shoulders.

'Trudi let him out,' he said to me. 'By the usual feline rules, he ought to stroll down the stairs about now.'

And blow me down if he wasn't right. Horatio, Calico and the kitten Tori came bounding down the stairs and out into the crowd of people, followed by the Mouse Police. They were abashed and turned and slunk down the alley. They knew a lot of places of refuge. They would be all right on their own. Horatio sat down at my feet, folding his tail over his paws and radiating smug satisfaction. Calico rushed to Cherie, complaining loudly, and Kylie and Goss smothered Tori in kisses. She bore it pretty well, considering how hard it is to wash lip gloss out of fur.

'Well, my boy, you have done well,' I told Horatio. 'You wouldn't like to tell me what's happening, would you?'

'You have a possible bomb,' said a level voice which really couldn't have been Horatio's. I turned. Police Senior Constable Letty (aka Lepidoptera) White was standing next to me.

'Someone left it in the foyer, or whatever it's called,' she said soberly. 'It's a brown paper parcel. It's ticking. Then someone phoned what sounds like an identical threat to everyone in the building and also to us. So here we are, waiting for the bomb squad. A nice way to spend Saturday night,' she added.

Senior Constable White is a neat, stocky woman of about thirty-five. She has carefully tamed brown hair and brown eyes and I like her, in a careful sort of way. She does not approve of Daniel, but we all have our blind spots.

'Do you think it's a real bomb?' I asked. She shrugged.

'Could be. If so, I wonder why anyone would bother trying to blow up this building when there are such a lot of more important ones.'

'True. Not the place to make a political statement,' I agreed. 'Unless you really have it in for the Roman Empire.'

This was all feeling strangely unreal. Mrs Dawson and the Prof came down the steps and suggested adjourning to a nearby pub, where it had to be warmer. I beckoned to Jon and Kepler and we began to edge away, as a large truck arrived and practically jammed itself into the alley. Out of it came men in flak jackets or whatever that armour is called, and helmets, and it was all getting too military for my liking. We were going to cause a sensation in Young and Jacksons on a Saturday night, but I didn't see any point in hanging around. I asked Letty White if we could go to the pub.

'Take all of them, and I wish I was joining you,' she said in a heartfelt manner. Jon brought Kepler, Cherie brought Andy and Kylie and Goss, the nerds hauled themselves up off the street, Trudi hefted her box of bulbs and the Pandamus family picked up babies and helped Yai Yai to her feet. We were all moving when Meroe remembered something.

'Oh, Goddess,' she said quietly. 'The mystery man!'

'He's not here?'

'No!'

'You go on,' I said. 'Stuff Horatio into that carrier with Bella, would you? That'll give her something to scream about. I'll tell Lepidoptera and catch you up.'

Along Flinders Lane they went. Leading the way with quiet authority was Professor Monk and Mrs Dawson, both well and warmly, if unconventionally, clad. There followed Kylie, Goss, Cherie and Andy, Jon and Kepler, the Pandamus family in a huddle, Nerds Inc in a group, Meroe with the cat carrier (now strangely silent), Trudi and Lucifer and Mistress Dread bringing up the rear with her predator's stalk.

'There might be someone still left in the building,' I said to the senior constable.

'Who and where?' she asked.

'In 7B, his name is Ben White. You know him. And a black kitten called Soot,' I added.

'What makes you think I know him?' she asked sharply.

'I saw you coming behind him when he moved in,' I returned. I was not in the mood for sharp retorts. 'Of course, he might not be home,' I added. 'It's Saturday night.'

'Very well,' she said. 'We'll check. Now if you want to get along to the pub,' she added, 'you should drink one for me.'

'What's your favourite?' I asked, moving away as the armoured men ramped up the steps.

'Cosmopolitan,' she said.

I had no objection to cranberry juice, so I nodded and walked on. I was almost to Swanston Street when I saw that the Insula inhabitants had stopped and were gathered around something on the ground. It was groaning.

'Corinna? Go back and get Lepidoptera,' said Daniel from a kneeling position. 'Professor, take everyone on to the pub, I'll

stay with him. Tell her we need an ambulance,' he said to me.
'But that the building is clear. We've found Mr White.'

I didn't stop to look. I ran. Fortunately it was not far because
running is not my skill. I grabbed Letty White by the arm and
gabbled out my message. She tore her eyes away from a strange
robot thing which looked like a collection of old vacuum cleaner
parts clanking into the foyer, snapped out an order on her radio,
and followed me back up the lane. Actually, she preceded me,
because I was out of breath.

'How is he?' she snapped at Daniel.

'Beaten,' said Daniel. 'Might have a few broken ribs. Not
conscious but breathing well, good pulse, no major bleeding
unless it's internal.'

'One assailant?' asked Letty crisply.

'Got to be more than one,' said Daniel, getting to his feet.
'And by the way his pockets are torn, I'd say he's been robbed.'

'Ambulance is on the way,' said Letty. 'Thanks,' she said awk-
wardly. 'Why don't you go and get that drink? You've earned it.'

They looked one another in the eye for a while. Then Daniel
smiled at the senior constable and she smiled at him. I would
have put considerable money on that not happening. Ever.

'I will,' he said. 'Coming, Corinna?'

I fell in beside him. He held his hands away from his body.
They had blood on them and he was trying not to touch me,
which was nice of him.

'We do have strange evenings,' I said, tucking a hand into
the crook of his elbow.

'We certainly do,' he sighed.

The management of Young and Jacksons, faced with an influx
of refugees, had opened a back room and by the time we got
there the party was becoming hilarious. The young women were
drinking the cocktails for which the hotel is known, and I joined
in, ordering a Cosmopolitan for Letty's sake. It was delicious.
Mistress Dread drank, of course, a Bloody Mary. Daniel went
and washed his hands and emerged to buy a bottle of red wine.
He shared it with the Prof and Jon and Kepler. Mrs Dawson

had a gin and tonic and the Pandamus family were handing out beer and ouzo to all hands except the youngest, for whom the hotel had concocted Coke spiders, the taste sensation of my schooldays.

The nerds were drinking Arctic Death, a mixture of vodka and bitter lemon, to which they are famously addicted. If you want any computer magic done, all you need is a six-pack of Arctic Death. Meroe had forgotten about her chakras and was drinking Bombay gin with Trudi. And smoking a Gauloise. She smokes very rarely, and so do I, but I was going to have one of those smokes before the night was out. These qualified as special circumstances.

I was very impressed by Mrs Dawson and the Prof carrying off that parade down the street in their nightclothes. I said so, partly to take my mind off the bomb—where was I going to live if Insula blew up? Would my insurance cover it? Had I, in fact, actually paid my insurance?—and the assault on Mr White and partly because it was true. Mrs Dawson gave my arm a brisk pat.

'My dear, I have been in circumstances more dire than these and in garments less comfortable, as I am sure has the Professor. Haven't you, Dion?'

'Certainly,' he said, smiling his Juvenalian smile. 'I recall being blown out of a window by a flying bomb, stripped all the clothes off me. And I landed on shattered glass, which rather frayed my...er...confidence. I had to conceal my blushes in a watchman's coat until I could find some clothes. And it was freezing cold. And you?'

'Oh yes, dear me, I was caught in a bushfire. I was taking a bath in the river at the time and although I was safe enough my tent and all my garments were completely destroyed. And there were mosquitoes. And flying embers. Not comfortable at all. And I was young, then, and I did get embarrassed. But I found that as I got older, I lost fears. There didn't seem any point in them anymore. So if anyone wishes to be amused at my clothes, they are entirely welcome, but it doesn't bother me.'

'Or me,' said Professor Monk. 'Another gin and tonic, dear lady?'

'Thank you,' said Mrs Dawson.

I bought another bottle of wine. Jon said to Kepler, 'I didn't mean your first night in Insula to be this exciting,' and I heard Kepler reply, 'It doesn't matter. I'm with you.'

I went back to Daniel. Subconsciously, we were all listening for a bang. I poured a glass for myself. Sometimes, wine is the answer. And one of Meroe's Gauloises.

About an hour later, Letty White came into the crowd and said, 'It's all right. You can go home,' and we were having such fun that she had to raise her voice and yell.

'No bomb?' asked Del Pandamus.

'Just a device which ticked,' said Letty. 'A practical joke.'

'Oh, very funny,' growled Meroe. We gathered ourselves together, finished our drinks and went back into the street, taking our worldly goods with us. I detained Letty as we were going out.

'And Mr White? Is he all right?'

'Bit of a bump on the head, they're keeping him overnight,' she told me. 'Do you know what this might have been about?' she asked Daniel suddenly.

'Me?' he echoed.

'Yes, you. Anything you're investigating which might attract the wrong sort of attention?'

'No,' he said honestly. 'Unless it's Darren the God Boy. But he wouldn't have set up an attack here, would he? I don't live in Insula.'

'Tell me all about it,' said Letty, sitting down and taking out her notebook.

As Daniel began to explain about his commission from Sister Mary, I poured another glass of wine and lit another Gauloise. Meroe had left the packet behind. Possibly prompted by the Goddess.

By the time we got back to the apartment, everyone had gone inside, checked their own apartment for damage and either settled down or gone out for the evening. Horatio was in my apartment, ruffled and cross. He had been lifted and confined—confined!—in a cat carrier with another cat! He was threatening to call his union. And the Mouse Police had come back in through the bakery cat-door. They were waiting in a body in the kitchen.

'There's a delegation to see you,' said Daniel, as three pairs of accusing eyes lifted to his. Tails were being lashed. The feline part of this household were royally pissed off and were not bothering to hide it.

'Cat food can cure all ills,' I said. 'There's meat in the fridge for a special treat. This looks like a special occasion. A handful each, Daniel. I'll sit down. I'm more than a tad drunk,' I said.

'Me too. So let's just go to bed like good citizens,' he said. 'And sleep it off.'

So we did. I woke in the night, which is what happens if you drink too much, but I fell asleep again beside Daniel. So it wasn't until we had completed the ritual silences of breakfast that I remembered.

'Oh, shit,' I said.

'What?' Daniel put down his empty coffee cup.

'Soot is missing,' I said. 'Last night Calico and Tori came with Horatio, Trudi had Lucifer on her shoulder. But not Soot.'

'And she's a very small black kitten in a building which abounds in shadows, set in a dark alley?'

'Yes,' I sighed.

'We will check,' he said. 'Later. I need to look over my notes about the chocolate shop, and you need to sleep some more.'

'I do?' I asked, yawning for the fourth time.

'You do,' he said, leading me gently back to my bed, where Horatio was now sprawled. I lay down. I closed my eyes. Daniel was right. I drifted off into gentle slumber.

I woke gently, too. It was Daniel kissing me, not Horatio. The absence of whiskers gave it away. He whispered the word guaranteed to bring me out of any coma short of actual death.

'Coffee,' he said. I woke up and kissed him back.

'What time is it?' I stretched.

'It is noon on Sunday,' he said. 'I suggest that we have a little light lunch—I observe that you have made vichyssoise, a good soup for a rainy day—and then you decide if you want to come with me to talk to Sister Mary.'

'About?'

'Darren the messiah. Sister Mary told me where poor Belinda was, though she didn't tell me how she knew. If Darren is responsible for that little joke last night I will need to talk to him, and so will Lepidoptera White.'

'Indeed, that might have been a real bomb,' I said, shuddering slightly.

'Or it might be a real bomb next time,' said Daniel.

'I expect that Darren was rather cross with you,' I said. 'I mean, you stole his slave.'

'And I punched his nose,' agreed Daniel. 'Few messiahs can let that sort of thing pass. '

'So, are we going to Ballarat?' I asked.

'No, we are going to MAP—the Melbourne Assessment Prison,' he said. 'Just down the road in Spencer Street. Darren breached his probation and is in custody; I believe that he has quite a lot of time left to serve.'

'Why should he talk to you?' I asked. 'You're the reason he's back in jail.'

'Actually, if you think about it, he's the reason that he's back in jail,' said Daniel. 'If he'd done as he was asked, got a job and stayed out of trouble, he wouldn't be there. He is back in jail because he had to go out and seduce some more followers. And mistreat them.'

'Yes, I agree, but I don't put Darren down as one of history's clear thinkers,' I responded, getting up and finding some socks. Because my socks are always attempting to wriggle off to find a more sock-centred existence, I used to have trouble matching them. Now I just buy a lot of black socks, and it doesn't matter if the pairs stay true to each other. Undies and trousers and shoes, shirt and jacket. Right. Corinna was ready to face the world.

'Sister Mary will meet us there,' said Daniel. 'I rang her. Are you sure you want to come?'

'Yes,' I said, not sure.

Daniel carefully took his small Swiss army knife off his key ring and laid it on the table. 'Have you got a pocket knife? Leave it at home,' he advised.

I removed my pocket knife from my backpack. I use it for opening bottles. From the number of attachments I could also build a small house and remove stones from horses' hooves.

'And off we go,' he said.

Because it was Sunday and trams were few and far between, we walked down Flinders Street, past the Gothic bulk of the station, which went on far longer than one thought, past the Banana Vaults and the new walkways along the river, then across to the remade end of the city. It used to be agreeably broken down. Now even the wharfies' pubs have gone upmarket, sporting new paint and a small supermarket next to the tattoo parlour.

'I hardly know the city these days,' I sighed as we struggled up past Spencer Street station with its fleet of country buses, lost tourists, people hauling wheeled suitcases up over kerbs and drivers reading newspapers.

And there was the Melbourne Assessment Prison. It was made of red brick, still unfaded and raw, and tastefully surrounded by aluminium barrels on high fences looped with razor wire. Very hospitable.

But there, deep in conversation with a scruffy woman festooned with children, was Sister Mary, one of the world's Forces for Good. She saw us, said, 'God bless you,' to the woman with such deep conviction that even the brats were impressed, wiped one child's nose and turned to greet us.

'Corinna! Daniel! How nice to see you. Thank you for coming. Visiting the prisoners and captives is one of the corporeal works of mercy, and God is well aware of what you do. Come along,' she said, and we followed her small, plump, determined back into the prison.

I had never been into a prison before, though I had seen this one every time I had taken Spencer Street beyond the confines of the city. It was ugly without and I found that it was ugly within, though not in the deep-pit-with-scorpions—Chateau D'If—aha-Lord-Monte-Christo-you'll-never-escape way of, for instance, the Old Melbourne Jail. In that dank bluestone building I had had my very first and only attack of claustrophobia and had to demand to be let out before we got to the high point of the tour: the gallows on which Ned Kelly had personally expired.

This was a sort of bureaucratic ugliness, a bought-cheap by the contractor ugliness. To be imprisoned here would be like being stranded for life in the waiting room of a not very successful dentist. The walls were painted cream, there were security guards everywhere, all talking to one another, and the place smelt of—I tried to analyse it with a nose badly damaged by years of heated steam—yes, male urine, disinfectant, and despair. In about equal parts.

The disinfectant was pine scented. This did not make it better. I took Daniel's hand.

'You can smell it?' he asked. I nodded. 'It never gets better and you never get used to it,' he said consolingly. 'It's the same whatever sort of prison it is. Desert camp, new inner-city building, old dungeon. Misery soaks into the walls. Just come along,' he said, following Sister Mary, who had already persuaded the guards to let her through to the first gate.

'Daniel,' said the guard. 'You on business?'

'With the sister,' Daniel replied. 'So is the lady.'

I got the impression that the guard might have said something else if it wasn't for the growing impatience of Sister Mary, who was beginning to swing her rosary beads. I was patted down by a short female guard and sent through a metal detector a few times, and they took my backpack and most of the stuff in Daniel's pockets, but we weren't a lot of fun. A big sign said 'Sharps, knives, syringes or pointed objects prohibited' and I saw that Daniel had been wise to leave his Swiss army knife at home. The guards kept up their conversation about some TV show which had been on the previous night. 'They got it better than us in LA' observed the small woman in the big uniform. I wondered if they would have been so casual if I had been that scruffy woman with those screaming children.

The place was giving me the creeps, as Jason would say, big time. We got to the first sliding door and a guard with a radio signalled someone beyond us to open it.

This let us into a shiny empty corridor worthy of Kafka. We walked along it.

'Daniel?' I asked. He understood the implied question.

'We're on camera,' he said, pointing out the telltale black disks. 'When we get to the other end they will open another door.'

'If they don't?' I quavered. This was hi-tech terror I was feeling. Trapped inside the machine. And I have never liked machines.

'Then we ask Sister Mary to call down divine wrath. Everyone here knows she's in damn big with God,' he said easily. His hand felt comforting and warm in mine. Nevertheless, that walk is not going to make it into my memoirs as one of the great promenades.

We got to the end of the corridor, facing another featureless door. It hissed open promptly, to my unspeakable pleasure. There was a human on the other side. A cheerful human. He had a red face which spoke of whiskey, and scant reddish hair. And he was smiling. He came as such a relief that I could have hugged him.

'Sister, is it you indeed,' he said in a strong Irish accent. 'Which of our malefactors and bad boys are you interested in today?'

'Darren Smith, Mr Halloran,' she said.

'Darren the God Boy? You'll have your work cut out with that one,' he said dubiously. 'But come into this nice little room and I'll have him brought right to you. And you're the woman to deal with him, so you are,' he added, taking comfort.

We went into the room, which was not nice, though it was little. Plastic chairs creaked under our weight. There was a huge no smoking sign on the wall but no other decoration.

'Daniel, I doubt that Darren is going to be pleased with you,' said Sister Mary. 'Why don't you sit behind me?'

'Is that a slur on my masculinity, Sister?' asked Daniel, grinning.

'No, dear, but if he attacks you he'll be in even more trouble,' she said practically. Daniel sat behind Sister Mary and the guard brought Darren in. Darren was in chains and leg irons. Halloran sat the prisoner down in a chair then retreated to lean against the wall in the corridor, out of easy earshot but in constant eye contact. Darren shook his handcuffs at Daniel.

'You cunt!' he snarled.

This was my first look at Darren the God Boy and he did not impress at first sight. He was tall, yes, but running to fat around the waist. The prison jumpsuit did not emphasise any of his good points. It strained over his belly and draped his slack chest and thin arms. He had long brown hair, now in need of a good wash. The prison smell had been augmented by unwashed human, never my favourite scent. His face appeared extensively bruised.

'You shouldn't have beaten her,' said Daniel quietly. 'You had a good thing going; hot and cold running girls, never had to lift a hand. Why did you have to beat her?'

'She didn't know her place,' growled Darren, and turned the full force of his dark eyes on me. 'Women should know their place.'

Oh, my. They were compelling, those eyes. For a moment I could not look away from them. I was being sucked down into them, weakening as I went. I dragged my gaze away and re-read the no smoking sign. But I was thirty-eight and had considerable strength of will, or I could never get up at four every morning. What effect would those eyes have on an already traumatised girl?'

'No tricks,' said Daniel unpleasantly. 'Have you given your little friends any orders about me?'

'Hah!' Darren didn't so much laugh as choke. 'Been making your life difficult, have they?'

'Then it has to stop,' said Sister Mary firmly. 'You're in enough trouble, God knows. More will just mean that you stay here longer. You know that I'll speak on your behalf. But you must call off your friends, Darren, or they will also be in trouble.'

For a moment I thought she would prevail. For the flicker of an eyelash, Darren faltered, exerting his own evil will which bounced off against the stainless steel sanctity of Sister Mary.

But the moment passed. Darren coughed and spat on the floor close to Daniel's foot. Then he began to chant, but he was chanting nonsense. At least, it sounded like nonsense to me, but it meant something to Sister Mary. Darren's eyes rolled back in his head, leaving only a flickering glimpse of white. It was very disconcerting. He began to shake, one muscle at a time, beginning with his thighs and working both upwards to his head and downwards to his feet. I thought that he must be having an epileptic fit.

'Stop that at once,' said Sister Mary, springing to her feet.

'What do we do?' I asked.

Halloran came in, shouting into his mobile phone. An alarm started to ring.

'Lay him on the floor,' said Daniel. 'Put something between his teeth.'

'Don't you go anywhere near him, either of you,' said Sister Mary firmly. 'He might bite. This is not disease, this is hysteria. You need to call the psychiatrist, and put him on twenty-four hour suicide watch,' she told the guard. 'I fear for the state of his miserable body, but more for the state of his soul. Do you hear what he is saying now?' she asked me.

'Sounds like bzzz, bzzz,' I replied, astonished.

'He is calling on Beelzebub, Lord of the Flies,' said Sister Mary. 'Christ have mercy upon us! The last thing we need is a Satanic scandal. Take him away, Halloran, lock him up on bread and water, and don't listen to a word he says. He has no power. It is all fake, to get attention.'

'If you say so, Sister,' said Halloran, not seeming very convinced.

'He's not the messiah,' said Sister Mary unexpectedly, and I concluded the quote from the *Life of Brian*. I didn't know they let nuns watch movies. Except *The Sound of Music*, of course.

'He's just a very naughty boy.'

This got a reluctant laugh from Halloran. The inner door hissed opened and two men with a stretcher came in. They loaded Darren the God Boy onto it and went out. We could hear him screaming and calling on Satan all the way down the corridor, where Halloran let us out.

'You're sure, now?' he asked Sister Mary. 'The lad's got no contact with Him Below?'

'May God have mercy on you and give you more sense,' she said brusquely. 'He's a bad man and he was a bad boy and he's faking it all. You watch him, Halloran, and if you see one thing which you can't explain, you call me and I'll bring a priest. But there won't be anything,' she said, and sailed out. Daniel and I followed in her magnificent wake.

When we were out on the street and I was wishing that I hadn't stopped smoking, she gave Daniel a brisk pat on the arm.

'Don't you worry,' she said. 'I'll get to the bottom of this. Satan is only involved here in tempting a foolish boy to play games with his captors. I'll spread the word to his friends that Darren has no power over them. Now, God bless you,' she said, and walked off down Spencer Street.

We stood and watched her go. If there was some diabolic intervention in Darren's fit, I'd back Sister Mary to sever the line to Hell, even if she had to do it with her own scissors.

I said so to Daniel. He agreed.

'Of course, they'd have to be the good scissors,' he said.

'What do you mean?' I asked.

'Haven't you heard that call in every household: "Where's the good scissors?". That presupposes there must be evil scissors,' he said. 'Darren may have the evil scissors, but I bet Sister Mary has the good scissors.'

We were feeling so tired by our encounter with the supernatural that we took a taxi home and cooked an early dinner, for it was Sunday and I would have to get up on Monday morning to bake the world's bread. On Monday morning Daniel was going back to Heavenly Pleasures to talk to the staff.

We had excellent pies made by the Other Bakery, which specialises in pastry as Earthly Delights specialises in bread, and hot chocolate with rum. Horatio was placated with kitty dins. Everyone in the building seemed unaffected by the scare of the night before. I could feel the place settling down for a nice long autumn nap, and soon Daniel and I did the same.

Chapter Seven

I was woken by the alarm as usual. Daniel slept through it. That man could sleep through a major war. It must be a wonderful talent to have. I left him in the middle of my big bed and went down to start the rye bread, taking my cup of coffee with me. Jason came in. We fed the cats. We concocted the first rising of the day.

Jason now knows how I feel about mornings so, even though he was bursting with news, he kept it to himself until everything was proving and I had drunk my third coffee and eaten some toast and lemon butter. Jason had eaten three rolls with cheese and a leftover bag of stale baguettes which he reheated in the microwave and tore at with his teeth. Even the Mouse Police watched anxiously as he ripped chunks out of the fossilised crust. But he was a growing boy and it was two whole hours to breakfast time at Cafe Delicious. Finally he choked down the last of the baguette and I took pity on him, he was so obviously brimming with news.

'So, Jason, what is it?'

'You know that Selima chick who works in the choccie shop?' he asked.

'Yes,' I said cautiously. 'And you know I've warned you about what I'll do to you if you keep calling women "chicks".'

'Whatever,' he shrugged. 'She's gone,' he told me. 'Run away.'

'Does Daniel know?' I asked.

'Can't see how he could,' he said.

'How do you know?' I asked. Morning is not my best time.

'Heard the Juliette ch…woman talking to her sister,' he said. 'As I was going past. On the way here,' he added, to make it all clear.

'How did you hear them?' I pressed.

'They were yelling,' he said. 'I couldn't help it. Chick's been missing since Saturday. Can I tell Daniel?'

'If she's been missing since Saturday then there's no rush. Daniel always says the first twenty-four hours are crucial and they've already gone past. You can tell him, though. When he gets up. Which won't be for hours yet. We had to go to the prison to talk to Darren the God Boy yesterday and it rather took it out of us.'

'Crazy dude,' said Jason.

'No shit,' I agreed.

We made more bread. Horatio, who had been sleeping sprawled out along Daniel's agreeably warm back, stepped downstairs and suggested breakfast. I went back upstairs to feed him and found Daniel silently making coffee. I did not interrupt. Now that I have actually found a man who doesn't want to talk in the small hours I am not going to blow it by talking myself. I fed Horatio, found out that I had been flim-flammed, in that Daniel had already fed him, and went downstairs again. I would have to watch Horatio's talent for playing both sides. Anyone who says cats are stupid hasn't ever been defrauded by one.

First batch of bread in and out of the oven and Jason was making a new sort of muffin. I sat down, prepared to learn. Jason was quick and sure in his movements and a pleasure to watch. He had mixed the muffins in a few sharp strokes and then plopped a spoonful into the tin, followed it with a spoonful of cherry jam, and then the rest of the mixture. I waited until he slotted the muffin tins into the oven and closed the door, for muffins are acutely impatient of delays, and asked, 'Why put jam in the middle?'

'Well, if it works, it'll be like a jam doughnut,' he told me, wiping his floury hands on his apron. 'People love doughnuts but they're really fatty. This will be a low-fat doughnut. At least I hope. I never tried this before, it might go soggy. Any more coffee in the pot?'

'Plenty,' I said. 'Have you thought about chocolate muffins?'

'Yeah, but they never seem to have that real taste. Hey, perhaps I can ask the Juliette ch…woman about it. She knows her chocolate. There must be some trick to it. Like that French bread, the one called *pain*. Why do they call it *pain*? Not a nice name for a roll.'

'Pain,' I said, pronouncing it in French. 'Pain is French for bread. You mean *pain au chocolat*, don't you? My baking encyclopaedia might have an entry. Have a look while we time your muffins out.'

Jason dragged down the encyclopaedia and flicked idly through the pages.

'If you go to the back of the book there's an index. Look up *pain au chocolat* in the list under 'p', which is between 'o' and 'q', and it will give you a page number.'

He gave me a look compounded of respect and resentment. Jason had never heard of an index before. He found the page, though, and soon was stammering through an entry on the sort of brioche that had chocolate in the middle.

'Aha,' he said. 'There is a trick to it. See, if you cook chocolate for as long as you need to cook the bread, it goes dull.'

'No way around that,' I answered. 'And in any case, who cares if it's dull? It tastes just as good. Your muffins are ready.'

He levered one out of the tin, looked at it, sniffed it, then bit. He yelped with pain as a stream of hot jam trickled down his chin.

'Ouch,' he observed. 'But it tastes real good, Corinna. Just let it cool down a bit.'

Like most Jason muffins, the cherry ones were superb and I told him so. I ate one with another cup of coffee and then my remaining synapses kicked in.

'Oh, Lord, I forgot about Soot,' I groaned. 'I promised I'd help look for her and I forgot all about her. The poor little thing!'

'Nothing to be done until we finish the baking,' said Jason practically. 'Then I can go and ask if Kiko or Ian have seen her. Anyway, maybe someone's found her by daylight. She's a black cat. They're pretty hard to see in the dark.'

'You're right. Are you going to make some more of those muffins? I've got an order for Health Bread, see how much bicarb we have.'

'I still don't believe people eat that stuff,' said Jason, going into the storeroom for more cherry jam and finding the bicarb.

'I don't care if they eat it,' I said. 'I just care that they buy it.'

Time passed. We finished the bread and the muffins, sorted out the orders for Megan, stocked the shop, and Jason started the scrubbing while I opened the shutters. It was a bleak day outside. Mrs Dawson came in briskly, rubbing her gloves together. Today she wore a brown cashmere jumper of the finest knit, a heavy woollen coat and her usual tailored trousers and sensible shoes. She had thrown over the outfit a pashmina figured with golden pheasants and vines. She was a very decorative figure. Her cheeks were as red as apples and her blue eyes were very bright.

'Chilly morning,' she observed. 'Going to rain, I believe. The great advantage of an early morning walk is that one can spend the rest of the day in guiltless luxury. I, for instance, have a pile of books, a nice view of the weather, and a warm apartment. And, I hope, some of your bread and the excellent Jason's muffins.'

'These are cherry, and they're really good,' I said honestly. I sold her three muffins and a loaf of rye bread. 'Can you keep your eye out for a small black kitten?' I added. 'She might be lost inside the building.'

'And if I find her?'

'Call Kylie or Goss and they'll fetch her.'

Mrs Dawson nodded and took her leave. I heard Jason laughing with the carrier as he handed over the bread, and then his footsteps as he went down the alley to ask Kiko about Soot. Escorted, no doubt, by the Mouse Police in search of raw endangered species of the Antarctic Ocean. It was very quiet, one of those little oases of calm that cities sometimes have, which vanish a moment later as if they had never been.

Horatio sauntered into the shop, leapt up onto the counter, and took his accustomed place. Daniel followed him, and kissed me on the back of the neck.

'Good morning,' he said. 'I'm going to talk to Heavenly Pleasures.'

'First catch Jason, he has something to tell you,' I said. 'And Soot is still missing, so grab her if you see her. And I love you,' I added, overwhelmed with affection, burying my cold nose in his warm neck.

'I love you,' he said. 'I'm going,' and he went.

Kylie came in, all blonde today, pale hair and blue eyes. She took her place behind the counter, within easy stroking distance of Horatio. There was no news of Soot. I took a muffin and went to see Meroe.

The Sybil's Cave was a very small shop with a great many things in it. Meroe was sitting in her big chair with a spread of cards laid out before her. Belladonna was stretched along the high back, stropping her claws. The fact that the black cat had returned to her perennial occupation presumably meant that she had forgiven Meroe for Lucifer's intrusion into her well-regulated life.

I ducked under a lot of hanging dream-catchers, removed a bundle of Wiccan magazines from the other chair and sat down. It does not do to interrupt a witch, so I put the muffin down on one corner of the table and perused a magazine. Its leading article was 'Evil in the Modern World' and I grew steadily more depressed as I read it. I didn't think all this calling of the light and contemplations on peace were going to cut any ice with the likes of al-Qaida or the good old Military Industrial Complex. I sighed and Meroe said, reading my mind as she often did, 'But you never know what will turn a scale. We would be negligent not to continue trying.'

'I suppose you are right. I brought you a muffin.'

'And a problem,' she said, shaking back her long dark hair. I have no idea how old Meroe is. She could be a youthful sixty or a weathered forty. She always wears a long skirt and top, both black, and some sort of shawl or wrap. Today's was a length of brilliantly scarlet Chinese silk, a bright note in an already bright shop.

'Yes,' I said. 'I met a man who is undoubtedly what Jason would call an extreme nutcase. He thinks he is a messiah. But he looked at me and I had to drag myself away.'

'Do you believe in the devil?' asked Meroe.

'No,' I said.

'But you believe in evil,' she pressed. Belladonna shredded some more upholstery with an unsettling sound, like a knife being whetted.

'Well, yes, you can't read a newspaper and not believe in evil.'

'This man believes in himself with such power that he can convince other people to believe in him as well, isn't that true?'

'Yes,' I agreed. 'Until Daniel rescued one of his slaves and punched him in the nose, he had a group of fanatic followers. Indeed, he might still have. They might have set that bomb hoax.'

'Hmm,' said Meroe, turning over another card. I don't know the meaning of tarot cards, but this one looked benign. It was a naked woman dipping water up from a pond. The sky was dominated by a star. Meroe made a tutting noise.

'The Star,' she said. 'Not helpful. All things are strange, is the meaning.'

'There's a tarot card that says that the future is unpredictable?' I asked.

'Certainly. I know the man you are talking about. This spread is for him. I have been trying to work out if it was him, and what he is likely to do next. He is certainly evil. He is very angry with Daniel. He would always try to injure him by sidelong methods—he is too weak and scared to attack Daniel directly. Therefore he is likely to attack...'

'Through me,' I said. A cold shudder ran down my spine.

'So I will provide you with this,' said Meroe, looping a thin ribbon over my head. I examined the pendant. It was a small bag made of white silk. It had something crackly—paper?—inside it, and something hard. It smelt of oranges. I might not be magically protected—I really didn't believe in magic—but at least I would smell nice.

'Will it work even if I don't believe in it?' I asked.

'Oh, yes,' said Meroe, smiling her witch's smile. 'Does the light come on when you press the switch? You aren't required to make sacrifices or chant prayers to the god Electricity. Evil is bound by metaphysical laws, just as Good is. This will protect you and yours, and I will conduct a working to reflect any evil back onto its perpetrator.'

'Sister Mary said he was faking,' I protested, tucking the little bag into my shirt. 'He was chanting and calling on Beelzebub and had some sort of fit.'

'Oh, he was faking if Sister Mary said so,' agreed Meroe. 'But he is evil. Sister Mary knows about evil. She will take care of what remains of his soul, and we will take care of his nasty habits.'

'Is this a spell?' I asked suspiciously.

'Just a working,' said Meroe, which didn't answer my question. Meroe knows that she would be very good at Evil if she gave the left hand path a try. She stays away from outright curses. Mostly. Remembering those dark brown eyes and that feeling of horrible suction, I figured that Darren deserved all he got.

I left the muffin, bought a Wiccan magazine for Kylie, and went back to Earthly Delights, where everything was going beautifully. Goss was serving a queue of customers and Jason had joined her, supplying and wrapping as she took the money and gave change. They were working very smoothly together. Considering that only four weeks ago Jason had refused to come out of the kitchen at all, I thought this a significant improvement.

'Cherry muffins need twenty seconds in the microwave to be ace,' he told the customer. 'Hey, Corinna.'

'Hey, Jason,' I replied.

'Daniel wants you to go to the choccie shop,' he told me. 'Dude's real angry about not being woken up.'

'I'll go now,' I said. 'If you can manage?'

'Sure,' he said blithely. Goss nodded at me. I went.

Out into the lane and past Mistress Dread's leather shop and in through the gold-lettered door of Heavenly Pleasures, with its cherubs and clouds. Juliette came out of the kitchen when the bell rang and waved me inside.

'Corinna,' said Daniel. He drew me aside behind a large machine which was burbling to itself. He looked like a dark angel who is disappointed in humanity.

'The girl is missing,' he said to me, his voice deep with reproach. 'Jason says he told you at five. Why didn't you call me?'

'Because you were asleep,' I said.

'She's run away,' he told me. 'A lot can happen to a girl in a few hours. You know that.'

'Is it your problem?' I asked. He took his hand off my arm. I felt entirely disconcerted. As I usually did, I attacked. 'No, consider it. Is it your problem? Aren't the police looking for her?'

'No,' he said flatly. 'She is over eighteen. They are not looking for her. Juliette is my employee. Selima is her employee. It is now my problem.'

'All right,' I said tentatively. 'If your instruction is to call you when such a thing happens again, I will call you. Now are you going to stop glaring at me?'

'That will depend,' he said.

'On what?' Now I was getting angry as well.

'On whether the delay would have made a difference to her fate,' he said, and began to walk away.

'Daniel, that isn't fair,' I called after him, hating the quaver in my voice. He stopped for a moment and looked straight into my eyes, quite unsmiling.

'No, it isn't,' he said, and went.

I kicked the machine and swore. How dare he speak to me like that? Who did this Daniel think he was? And why did he think I cared?

I swore again and then became aware that Juliette was hovering just out of slapping distance.

'Corinna, I'm sorry, I didn't know…'

'That he'd react like that? Neither did I,' I said, getting control of myself. I had been through low spots and bad times before. Even if Daniel never came back, I would, I knew, recover. Eventually. Thirty-eight has few advantages over eighteen, but knowing how strong you are is one of them. And that grief, however deep, never lasts.

'Talk to us,' she said. 'He has a list of questions, here they are, but now he has to go and find Selima. I can't imagine where she's gone. She seemed like such a good girl. And imagine, she was trying to ruin the business!'

'And you don't know why,' I asked.

'No, I don't.'

'Well, even if it seems unnecessary, let's do the questions anyway, then I'll ask mine. I've always wanted to know more about chocolate.'

'I'll shut the shop,' said Juliette.

I was getting my breath back. The quarrel, if that's what it was, had erupted so suddenly that I felt like I once did in an Irish pub, where someone who had indulged in more Bushmills Black than was good for him had punched me in the solar plexus by mistake. He had been aiming for his friend, who had dodged at the last moment. I had the same feeling that the world had gone out of focus. And it was going to be very bleak without Daniel in it.

I drew in another breath as Juliette came back from putting up the 'closed' sign. There was a big shiny metal table, and we sat down at it on metal stools.

The kitchen also contained, reading from right to left, the Adonis-like apprentice George and the unbeautiful sister, Vivienne. They were both wearing white smocks.

I looked around. The manufactuary had several machines of unknown purpose, piles of moulds from little tiny cupcakes to large Easter eggs, several vats of creamy fillings, a huge refrigerator and a strange scent composed of far too many sweet smells from bitter lemon to hazelnut to rosewater.

'What do you want to ask? Only we've got chocolates to make,' said George.

'I need to talk to you one at a time,' I said. 'Who wants to go first?'

'Me,' said George. Both sisters looked at him, Juliette dotingly, Vivienne with some dislike. The women got up and left the room.

'Name?' I asked. I had a notebook and took a pen from Juliette's phone table.

'George Pandamus.'

'Any relation to—'

'Uncle,' he said. Smart boy, eh? He was so beautiful that it was hard to retain a suitable detachment while looking at the curve of that lovely throat, the arch of that perfect eyebrow, so I looked at the list of Health Regulations on the kitchen wall and made my voice harder. This gorgeous ratbag wasn't going to seduce me. I had had enough from the male sex lately, what with Daniel and Darren. George didn't pick up any difference in my manner, which made him very unobservant, very narcissistic, or a sixteen year old boy.

'How long have you been an apprentice?'

'Three months. Worked here for a month for free until she agreed to take me.'

'Vivienne Lefebvre?'

'Yes. I'm going to be very good. And then I'll have my own shop.'

'How long is the apprenticeship?'

'Four years.'

He wasn't volunteering any information.

'How did you get on with the sisters?'

'All right.' He shifted in his seat, a little uncomfortable.

'Very good with Vivienne and not so good with Juliette, eh?' I asked.

He blushed. He looked like Antinous after a hard night fighting off suitors. 'No. Good with Jules, not so…why are you asking me that, anyway? You a cop?'

'No,' I told him.

'Then lay off me,' he ordered. Butter-fed boy, I thought. No one has said anything but 'yes' to him since early childhood. His mother and sisters do all the work and the little prince reclines on the sofa and waits for someone to hand him the remote control. I decided to disconcert him.

'Well, if you wanted to talk to the police, you only had to say,' I said. 'I'll just ring them now. I'm sure that Senior Constable White will—'

'No,' he said. 'Hey, be cool, eh? Ask me another,' he said, leaning back. He was not at ease. His hands, clutching the edge of the metal table, were white to the knuckle.

'Did you ever see anyone interfering with the chocolates?'

'No. I would have said. This is my way out of Cafe Delicious. If I don't work here I'll have to work there. I like it better here. But Selima was quiet. I wouldn't have thought she'd have the nerve,' he said admiringly.

'Do you have any chili sauce in this kitchen?' was the next question.

'No. Only sweet things in here,' said George.

I sent him into the shop and Juliette came back. I asked her the same questions. She told me that she and her sister owned the shop jointly, that George had been a satisfactory apprentice as far as he had gone—and blushed when she said it, looking like the perfect English rose—and that she and her sister got on well with Selima, who was a good girl and very quiet. She came from a Turkish family who weren't very happy about her working in a shop where everyone could see her. She was always picked up from work on Thursdays and Fridays, when the shop closed at nine, by an aunt or cousin who worked in the city. She had never had a sick day or a holiday and had never just not turned up. She had been working for Heavenly Pleasures for seven months and seemed happy in the chocolate trade. To Juliette she had confided that she wanted to go to trade school once she had saved the money and ultimately to become a hairdresser. No boyfriends that Juliette knew about. She had no reason to want to harm the business.

Further, Juliette said that the shop was turning a healthy profit which was split 50/50 with her sister. They had no other siblings and their parents were dead.

I let Juliette go and Vivienne stalked into the room, bumping into the corner of the table and swearing.

'They always make tables just at hip height,' I said. 'Tell me about Selima.'

'I hardly saw her,' snapped Vivienne. 'Front of shop is Juliette's business. Kitchen is mine.'

I asked the rest of my questions.

'George is a good enough apprentice. He'll be better when he spends less time thinking about how beautiful he is. I had to take the mirror off the wall because he'd spend all day gazing into it.' She gestured at a wall with a light patch on it. 'But he's learning fast. He has good hands for sweets. Do you know how we make chocolates?'

I confessed extreme ignorance. Vivienne rose and began to show me round the kitchen. As she did so her voice, which had been strained, dropped to a conversational tone and she was good at explaining things. She had an accent, unlike her sister. It was not like Trudi's, so I assumed it was Belgian. Trudi, it seemed, had spent longer in Belgium.

'Chocolate is a strange substance,' she said, in much the same tone as I talked about yeast. 'In the original bean it is very bitter. In the eighteenth century people used to dry, roast and grind it and make a drink as black as ink, stuffed with cocoa butter and bitter as gall until they added a lot of sugar to it. Then the Belgians—the Swiss have tried to say it was them, and so have the French, but my family comes from Belgium so for me it was the Belgians—found out how to solidify it so that you could make sweets out of it.'

'And you never looked back?'

'No. Chocolate is terribly important. It's the thing which most people would say is the supreme luxury: not like fast cars and cocaine and holidays in Monaco, but a little bit of luxury you can call your own.'

'I was just thinking the same thing. Chocolate and coffee— both bitter beans. Both terribly comforting.'

She gave me the first friendly look I had seen since entering the shop. When you got used to the fact that she was not beautiful despite looking like her sister, Vivienne was not bad looking in a haggard way. She had a very genuine smile.

'Just so. It is curious. There are those who consider that the chocolate-coated coffee bean is the highest of culinary pleasures. We make sweets using only the best couverture, which is chocolate with the highest amount of cocoa butter.'

'What does that mean?'

'The stuff in your cheap Easter egg,' she said scornfully, 'is compound chocolate. It is chocolate with the cocoa butter removed and replaced by vegetable oils. It sets easily at room temperature and is used for children's sweets. This, I think, is unfair to the children but it is cheap.'

'And you wouldn't use couverture for chocolate crackles,' I said. I had liked chocolate crackles. The luxury of a childhood that had not heard of cocoa butter content. Vivienne contrived not to sneer. Just.

'Then there is cooking chocolate, or bittersweet chocolate, an in-between product used for cooking. Couverture is not used for cooking as it burns easily.'

'As in *pain au chocolat*,' I said intelligently. She smiled again.

'Of course, you are a baker, you would use bittersweet in cooking, cakes, and so on. To make sweets we need to temper the chocolate.' She showed me the machine which burbled. 'This melts the block to 45 degrees Celsius, then cools it to 26 degrees, and then raises it to 36 degrees, massages and rolls it. Only then will the couverture set glossy, shiny as chocolate should be. This is our most important trade secret.'

'And I wonder how on earth anyone discovered it,' I marvelled, thinking of all those poor Belgians with notebooks, saying '44 degrees doesn't work, Hans, try 45,' for weeks and weeks. Vivienne shrugged.

'Probably it was done by accident,' she told me. 'Then they back-engineered it. Most important discoveries are done by accident. Lindt discovered conching, by which chocolate is melted and refined and then has more cocoa butter added, which makes chocolate fondant—melting in the mouth as it does.

'Now, suppose that you want to buy a filled chocolate. Here we have fondant.' She showed me the vats. 'In this is just sugar and water, stirred until the sugar dissolves, and then it is flavoured and various things are added'—she did not tell me what these were but every trade has its secrets—'and then the couverture is formed into little moulds, as you see, or rolled and cut, depending on the shape of the sweet. Some of the moulds belonged to our ancestor. This is a tropical truffle, which is rolled and cut like this.' She slapped a handful of fondant onto the table, rolled it between her palms, chopped it rapidly into bits and rolled them in a flat dish full of grated chocolate. She offered me one. I put in into my mouth without hesitation.

Oh, what a burst of chocolate, pineapple, coconut, then the chocolate again.

'Superb,' I said. She smiled again.

'If it is a formed sweet then we make the couverture into the right shape, and then fill the shells.'

She took a big spoonful out of another vat and smoothed it into little round moulds like oven trays, which she had almost rinsed with couverture—the movement was just the same, a sliding swish and a slam as she slapped the mould down onto the table.

'The air bubbles—they must be removed,' she told me as I jumped. 'These must set,' she said. 'But I have some that are ready.'

She dragged a large knife across the mould, levelling the shells. Then she slid a filled mould into a rack which went back under the machine, which capped the sweets with chocolate and, I noticed, stamped the bottom with a grid pattern.

'I cannot give you one of these as it is not set,' she said. 'The liquid fillings are no different. The mould is done the same way and the filling is poured in.'

'Not injected?' I asked. Her lips thinned.

'No. No syringes here. You must look elsewhere for your saboteur. And when your friend finds that girl I will skin her alive. Before Juliette sacks her. I know why she did it,' said Vivienne with a vindictive snap of her teeth.

'Why?'

'Because of my apprentice,' she said. 'She was attracting his attention. Because she is in love with him,' said Vivienne. 'And he wouldn't even look at her.'

Chapter Eight

After that there didn't seem much else to say. Daniel's note said that he would call and ask them to sit through the surveillance tape and identify all the visitors, but that could wait until he got back, if he ever did, and if I ever spoke to him again.

I took my notes and a free box of sweets and went back to my bakery to find that all was well and I had time to consider the history of chocolate. The website Ask Jeeves was, as always, informative. Chocolate was sacred to the Maya and the Aztec. However, I was not going to lightly adopt the preferences of a society whose citizens showed their piety by ripping the hearts out of prisoners on top of pyramids. They made it cold, thick and unsweetened and, frankly, it would need to be an aphrodisiac for anyone to drink the stuff. The name, which I had always wondered about, came from combined words: Mayan xocoatl and an Aztec word for water.

The conquistadors brought it back to Spain and the nobility made pigs of themselves by mixing it with sugar and a variety of spices, worth their weight in gold—cloves, vanilla, allspice, cinnamon. The French court began to drink it. Then the English. Someone, around the seventeenth century, turned it into cakes for easy transport. Probably the Belgians. Except that the inventor of the chocolate bar seems to have been Fry, the English Quaker who got out of brewing alcohol because of its bad effect on the poor and decided to give them something almost as addictive and twice as comforting. God bless his heart. So it was the English. I decided not to tell Vivienne Lefebvre. She might cut off my supply.

I shut down the computer after I deleted a hundred messages about penis enhancers from my email account. Spam. I almost admire their nerve, but not really. I made a mental note to investigate spam filters some day when I had a lot of time on my hands. That is, never.

I decided to wander the halls and see if I could find the small black kitten who, by now, must be hungry and cold and missing her mother. I was feeling rather desolate myself. Like might attract like.

I took the lift to the roof garden and there found Trudi, grubbing up roots and hacking them to bits with a big knife. The sky had, as Mrs Dawson predicted, clouded over and it did look like it was going to rain.

'Hello,' I said disconsolately. 'Seen a black kitten?'

'Only orange one,' she said, raising the knife again. I looked for Lucifer. He was digging industriously.

'He tries to help me,' she said. 'I've got to get these irises back in the ground before it rains. You take little one, eh? And sit in temple.'

I did that. Lucifer finished his excavation and trotted along on his leash, pausing occasionally to sniff at an unusual scent. When we were inside the temple he sat down for a good wash and forgot all about me.

Soot might easily be in the garden. This was, after all, where she had been born. But trying to find her in the thickets would be daunting and she might not want to be found. Lucifer washed very diligently until he got to the hard bit, where a cat has to balance on the tail in order to raise the leg and wash under it. This takes practice. He toppled over and decided to give washing a miss for the moment.

And I didn't even chuckle. Even though he was a very cute kitten and there is something irresistible about the way kittens fall over when learning that manoeuvre. I was definitely depressed.

So when Trudi came back and Lucifer squeaked with delight and ran up her overalls to her shoulder, rubbing his hard little nut of a head under her chin and purring, I went back down, calling for Soot at every floor, listening hard for a mew, and hearing nothing. Nothing like a cat, that is. I met plenty of people. On the seventh floor the door of Pluto, 7B, cracked open and our recluse looked out.

'I'm looking for a kitten,' I explained. It sounded lame, even to me. 'I'm Corinna, the baker.'

'Sorry,' he said politely. 'I haven't seen a kitten.'

'I hope you are feeling better,' I said, seeing that he had a very juicy black eye and one arm was in a sling.

'I'll heal,' he said shortly, and shut the door. So much for him. I worked my way downwards. Jon and Kepler in Neptune, 6A, were either not in or not investigating strange voices in the corridor. Mrs Pemberthy of 5B, Juno, pounced on me on the fifth floor. She was, as always, accompanied by her rotten little dog, Traddles, a creature who combines the charm and appetite of Hannibal Lecter with the appearance of a decayed mop head.

'Kitten? No. There are too many cats in this building as it is. I'm complaining to the residents' council about it. Poor Traddles had his nose scratched by one of your cats, Corinna. One of them has stolen his blue squeaky toy, too. He misses his Squeaky, don't you, darling? And I can only take him for one walkies a day.'

'Hire a walker,' I suggested. Traddles was eyeing my leg with undisguised hunger. Unfortunately he had recovered completely from the pesticide poisoning which had nearly killed his mistress a month or so ago. Mrs Pemberthy squealed and dragged him up into her embrace, from which heights he managed to sneer at me.

'No, I couldn't trust my little sweetheart with anyone but his Mumsie, could I, darling?'

Traddles did not reply and I made my excuses. Cherie Holliday asked me in for a coffee on floor four, where she and her father lived in Daphne. She promised to keep a look out for

Soot and to search her apartment. Mrs Dawson in 4B, Minerva, invited me in to search, as Soot had gone missing on the same night as the bomb threat when all the doors had been open.

'I don't bend like I did, dear,' she said affably. 'You'll need to look under things. Here, you can use my flashlight.'

Mrs Dawson had been reading. She had a large armchair, a footstool, a bright reading light, a small table with a box of chocolates on it, a pile of library books and a good view, as she had said, of the weather. Rain started spattering the windows. She had kicked off her shoes and was wearing her Russian leather boots. A generous wrap patterned with books had been cast aside. I hated to disturb her and said so.

'The poor little creature might be hiding and she will be hungry by now,' she said. 'Search everywhere and I will make us a drink. The nice thing about being a widow is that one always has time for interruptions. Mothers and wives never do, they are always doing two things at once. And that is on good days,' she told me. She went into her kitchen and I searched for Soot.

There were a lot of nooks and crannies and I looked into every one. At the end of my search, I knew two things. One, that Soot wasn't there. Two, that Mrs Dawson had excellent taste and very nice furniture.

I gave her back the flashlight. She gestured me to a chair at the table. Then she poured me a drink from a heatproof jug. I sipped. It was mulled wine, spicy and fragrant. The perfect thing for a cold day. I said so.

'The important thing is to use good wine,' she said. 'What is wrong, Corinna?'

I looked into her clear blue eyes and told her all about Daniel.

'Oh dear,' she said. She sipped more wine. 'The trouble with people who believe that everything is theirs to fix is that they also believe that it is all their fault,' she said musingly. 'He was guilty that he had slept while this girl was in trouble. That's why he was angry. He wasn't angry with you, but himself. He'll get over it. Have some more?' she asked.

I held out my cup. 'Why not?'

My bakery was working fine without me. I wasn't doing anything useful. And it was very good wine. Mrs Dawson didn't say anything else about Daniel. When she spoke again, it was in praise of Jade Forrester, and we had a soothing conversation on her admirable oeuvre, and how on earth she was going to get Avon and Roj together.

I felt much better when I left and descended to the next floor.

Professor Monk in 3, Dionysus, was at home, and agreed to allow me to search his apartment, too. He also had a flashlight ready to hand.

'Leftover from the Blitz,' he explained. 'And reinforced by all those Queensland towns where the lightning was attracted to the power lines. In London you might step on a mine and in Queensland you might step on a taipan.'

'Both deadly,' I grunted, crawling under his Roman couch. No Soot. I gave the rest of the apartment the once-over and found no sign of a kitten. No dust, either. Professor Monk was a tidy man and his cleaner did a good job.

'How about some lunch?' he asked. 'I've got some rather good lasagna from Cafe Delicious.'

'I ought to get back to the bakery,' I said, my will visibly weakening.

'Call Jason and see if he needs help,' he suggested. I did that, from the Prof's un-Roman telephone, which was concealed in a cupboard. Jason told me, with that scornful edge of 'What—don't you *trust* me?' in his voice, that he and Goss were managing perfectly well without me.

So I sat down to a Cafe Delicious lasagna, which was very good, and a glass or two of wine with Professor Monk, the sexiest seventy-six year old in captivity. He talked soothingly about how much he couldn't stand Apollonius Rhodius, a librarian who had written the compilation album Argonautica, about Jason and—duh—the Argonauts.

'The kindest thing I can say about him,' he concluded, 'is that he wore a beige toga, probably with leather patches on the sleeves. His depiction of Medea as a delicate fawn trembling in the pussy willows would sicken both Mills and Boon.'

'Wasn't she a famous witch?' I asked.

'Able to draw the moon down in her hair. And outface giant serpents,' he agreed. 'Not the sort of person to tremble and blush and turn white and go weak at the knees. Can you see our friend Meroe doing that at any time in her life?'

I thought about it through two glasses of mulled wine and another of good pinot.

'No,' I decided. 'Never.'

'My point exactly,' said Professor Monk.

By the time I bade the Professor farewell and descended to the lower levels I was tired but not as discouraged as I had been. Mistress Dread, home from the leather shop for lunch in Venus, 2B, agreed to search her apartment for Soot, who she said would make a nice contrast with her red leather. I already knew that Kylie and Goss in 2A, Pandora, did not have her. I went down to see the boys in Nerds Inc, who lived in Hephaestus. They promised to tell me if they found her as they didn't like cats or indeed mammals of any sort. She wasn't in the bakery and she wouldn't be anywhere near Del Pandamus of Cafe Delicious, because he hated cats. I had searched the whole building and hadn't found Soot, but I had found my self-esteem.

I did a few business things in my own apartment, like ordering the flour and seasonings, checking the GST returns and the invoices from the suppliers, and then went down into the bakery. Goss was cashing up and filling in the bank deposit slip. This involved listing the numbers of notes in each denomination—such as 12 $50 notes = $600; 23 $20 notes = $460 and adding it up at the bottom. This task had always stumped my assistants but now Jason was helping.

'It's a calculator,' he said patiently. 'You enter the number and then you write down the result. Here, let me.'

He showed Goss how to fill in the form and, amazingly, she not only let him explain but filled in the slip correctly. I let her stuff the money into the bag and take it to the bank. Jason shut the shop and said, 'You all right?' and when I said I wasn't, he said soberly, 'You go and get some sleep. You could use a nap. That's what the Prof says. And he'll be back, that Daniel. The dude was just upset that you didn't call him. He always thinks he has to save the world. I didn't mean to get you in bad with him, Corinna, honest.'

He looked so contrite that I hugged him with one arm.

'Never mind, Jason. Clean up and I'll see you tomorrow.'

I got to my apartment, carrying Horatio, who demanded to be carried, some bread, and my notes. I stripped and bathed in scented hot water. Then I lay down in my bed for a few moments just to rest my eyes, and woke only when the alarm went off at four to tell me that I had slept through the whole night and that it was morning once more.

As always, I wished it wasn't. But there it was. Jason was downstairs by the time I had placated Horatio (no dinner! no dinner!) and we mixed and baked and mixed and made muffins. Or, at least, Jason made muffins and I watched. He was making my favourite so far, ginger muffins, and his hands almost blurred as he chopped glacé ginger. I drank coffee and listened to bread rising. This was my life, and it was a very good life, one I had chosen for myself, and I was pleased with it.

The Mouse Police raced out into the wet alley—they would swim rivers for raw tuna scraps—and I watched the dust of the summer being washed away at last. The cobbles were as slick and clean and shiny as Juliette's chocolate. I like rain and I only retreated when it began to drip on me. The overhead balconies tended to collect water and let it go in sudden and surprising showers. Five thirty am and very nice to come back into the warmth of the ovens.

'Shit, it's freezing,' shivered Jason, tucking into his first baguette of the day. I was just shutting the door when Ma'ani appeared and I handed over the sacks.

'Last run,' he said. 'Been a bad night.'

'Oh?' I asked.

'One drowned,' he said. 'Face down in a gutter, poor bugger. Thanks,' he said, and carried the bread away. I was ashamed of my discontent when people were dying in misery. I shook myself.

'Let's do something different,' I said to Jason. 'Let me show you how to stone olives.'

Jason rather enjoyed stoning olives. If you don't need them to stay in shape, you just crush them under a flat blade. It's very therapeutic. We made olive bread, a salty, tangy bread that goes well with Italian cheese and makes the definitive tomato sandwich when the end-of-summer tomatoes are perfectly ripe, with just a smear of olive oil and lots of fresh basil. Otherwise it just reminds people of Venice, which is a nice place to be reminded of.

The rain was really pouring down now. I wondered where Daniel was and if he was getting wet and shut the door. The Mouse Police belted in through the cat-door a moment later, soggy but well fed, and lay down to wash themselves on their flour sacks.

I opened the shop, I handed it over to Kylie, I sent out the restaurant bread by carrier and unlocked the till.

'Since you are taking so much responsibility I shall have to increase your wages,' I told Kylie. She clasped her heavily ringed hands with glee.

'So I can get Tori's collar early!' she said breathlessly.

'Tori's collar?'

'It's a little strip of black doeskin,' she told me. 'With real pink diamonds in it. Well, not diamonds, really, cubic zirconias. But pink ones. Champagne coloured.'

I didn't say a word. It's no business of mine what my staff spend their wages on. Jason was about to hoot with mirth until I stood on his foot. I didn't need dissension in the shop. The doors were open and the people started coming in.

I helped with the first rush, then bagged a few ginger muffins and went back to my apartment for an umbrella. I felt like…well, I didn't know what I felt like, but it wasn't staying in one place. I took my backpack and the Jade Forrester and went out.

Meroe was my first stop. She was serving a nervous woman who seemed, from the ingredients, to be making a love philtre. If not, I don't know what she wanted doves' hearts for. I have always assumed that these were some sort of mushroom. If they weren't, I don't want to know. I had obviously picked up some theory and practice of magic from all those Wiccan magazines. Meroe took the muffins and said gnomically, 'Tomorrow night, full moon,' to me before going back to the artemisia and fern seed.

Was tomorrow night a full moon? I didn't see a lot of nights from the right end. Where was I, in fact, going?

I was walking out of the city along St. Kilda Road before I really thought about it. Flinders Street Station passed. I paused on the bridge to salute one of my favourite views, the rainbow arch pedestrian bridge to Southbank. It is a perfect curve. Such a comfortable shape. It began to rain some more.

Southbank was a maze of interesting shops, museums, art spaces, cafes, restaurants, and of course gaming venues, if you are interested in gaming, which I am not. I stepped down to river level and dived into the covered arcades. It was not too busy, but there was a nice hum of conversation, some very good art works and a pleasant smell of commerce and coffee. The rain drummed on the glass roof. The potted palms waved their fronds in the warm air. I thought of one brand of therapy which I had not tried for my bruised feelings. Shopping.

I prefer to shop with a friend, but it was very relaxing to stroll along, marvelling at the number of shoe shops in the world. Did anyone actually put those misshapen rhinestone-studded pointy things on a real foot? And then balance on that six inch heel? Half the pain in women's lives is due to men but a considerable proportion of the rest is due to shoes, I thought. Deep thoughts for a rainy morning from a woman wearing Birkenstocks. If the Lord had meant us to wear pointy shoes, he would have put our big toe in the middle. I will always sacrifice style for comfort. Actually, it isn't a sacrifice.

I appreciated the Japanese woodblocks and went on, wondering if I really could justify buying, for instance, a flask of White

Linen, a tree made of semi-precious stones, a carved olive-wood bird, or a new pair of gloves. Actually I needed a new pair of gloves. Remembering Mrs Dawson's bitter chocolate glacé kid, I tried on some really expensive hand-stitched Florentine ones and found a pair in bright red which fitted beautifully. And I bought them. I also bought a cat toy for Lucifer and a bag of catnip mice for the others. And a bottle of white lilac bath foam.

Then I took myself firmly to the Art Gallery and revisited some of my favourite paintings. The Tiepolo Banquet of Cleopatra looked well. I bought some postcards and went out into the street where the rain was striking the chestnut leaves with a papery whisper. My hands were warm in my new gloves and the scarlet cheered my heart.

And when I got home there was a police officer waiting for me. Luckily it was Lepidoptera White and I could invite her in before we both drowned.

I watched her boggle at the artfully censored Priapus in the impluvium and then led her upstairs, where I laid down my coat and my purchases and put the coffee on.

'I've heard that there is a problem at the chocolate shop,' she said, sipping her coffee. She took it black with no sugar, which fitted her rather austere character.

'Well, there was,' I responded. 'One of the staff was sabotaging the sweets. But she's run away and now it's all solved.'

'They didn't put in a complaint?' she asked, breaking a ginger muffin and taking a bite. 'For an ex-junkie your Jase makes a very good muffin.'

'Jason. He's not Jase anymore. No, they didn't complain to the police. It would have meant that everyone would know, and I can't imagine that investigating minor trouble in a chocolate shop would be right up there with murder.'

'Hmm,' she said, eating the rest of the muffin. 'Do you know where Daniel is?'

'No,' I said. 'He went to look for Selima. He'll be back,' I said, hoping that he would. 'How did you find out about it?' I asked, not hoping for an answer.

'I hear things,' she said vaguely. 'You went to see Darren the God Boy?'

'Yes, and it wasn't fun. He is a very creepy person.'

'He's got the MAP having kittens. Says he's possessed by the devil. They're very superstitious, prisoners. Nothing much to think about except what they'll do when they get out. Nothing much to do but work on their muscles. Someone attacked Darren and scratched him across the forehead. I'm on my way to ask your witch friend what it means, if anything. Want to come?'

'Why not?' I said, interested. 'Doesn't Sister Mary know?'

'Sister Mary said it isn't anything Christian or Satanic and that he is making it up to get attention. Well, he's got it.' She chuckled as we went out.

Meroe was alone except for Belladonna, who was asleep in a pile of breathing fur on her black-clad knee and consequently very hard to see. Witch and cat were one. I suppose that is how familiars are supposed to be. Bella woke when we came in, sat up and yawned and became discrete; a cat shape with golden eyes and a little pink mouth with teeth.

Meroe does not like Lepidoptera, which is perhaps why Letty White had brought me with her. Letty had once thought that Meroe might be selling drugs. Meroe is not likely to forgive a suspicion like that. We explained what we were doing there.

'Scoring above the breath,' she said firmly. And didn't say anything else. Meroe could be as silent as a granite boulder when she felt like it. Bella yawned again and went back to sleep, vanishing into Meroe's lap.

'Meroe, what does that mean?' I asked.

'An old way of making a witch take a spell off someone was to scratch him or her above the mouth with an iron pin or knife. It was called scoring above the breath.'

'Did it work?' I asked.

'No,' said Meroe. 'But then, the people they were scratching were very unlikely to be witches. A witch would not allow herself to be scratched. Someone, Constable, thinks that your Darren is a witch. And it is someone who has either been reading witchcraft history or has some old family remedy for witches. Which is English. Nowhere else thought that scratching would work.'

'Thank you,' said Lepidoptera, stiffly. We were going out when Meroe said, 'Corinna, full moon. It will all be explained then.'

'Oh, good,' I answered.

I went back to the shop. Senior Constable White paused and asked, 'Can you let me into the building?'

'Of course,' I said, opening the main door into the residence. 'If you see a small black cat, can you catch her for me?'

'I'll try,' she said. I nobly refrained from asking her what she wanted in Insula and went back to sell bread.

Kylie approved of my gloves. The day passed peacefully. Vivienne came, apparently by arrangement, to talk to Jason about a chocolate muffin he was planning. She had a box containing samples of different sorts of chocolate. I left them to their plotting. But I did hear her say, as she went out, 'That is a very good idea, I shall be fascinated to see if it works.'

'Corinna? Can I buy some cream?' asked Jason. I shelled out for the cream and some other ingredients. We closed, cashed up, Kylie went to get Tori's champagne diamond collar and I left Jason the scrubbing and a bonus for getting on with the girls, who could be very trying. He said, 'Ace.'

And because I had been drinking too much lately, I took a thermos of hot chocolate to the roof and sat in the temple, watching the rain sweep over the city and soak the bedraggled kestrel-bait pigeons. From the top of the building we could see the grey curtain swoop across the city, splattering the windows, washing off the bitter city dust. Trudi was sitting there too, with Lucifer asleep under her chin.

'Look at all that good rain,' she said. 'Soaking rain. You can hear plants underground prick up their ears, start to grow.'

'You can,' I said. I shared my hot chocolate with her. Horatio affected not to notice the scrap of orange fur snuggled into the top of Trudi's jumper.

'How are you getting on with Lucifer?' I asked.

'He's a good boy,' she said unexpectedly. 'Helps me dig. Likes the open air. That Traddles, he corners him. When the dog came to attack him, little bit of fur he is, he fluffed up, raised his paw like little lion, ready to fight or die. Brave. You and Meroe, you let me keep him?'

'Of course,' I said. Meroe had been right, as she usually was. Lucifer had found his place. We finished the hot chocolate and Horatio and I went home to read some more of our novel.

But I couldn't concentrate. I retreated to the sofa, flicked on the TV, and channel-surfed until I found a Discovery documentary on Alexander the Great, which might have been quite interesting except I fell asleep.

Chapter Nine

I woke. It was dark. I had heard a noise. I lay still and listened. Horatio was awake, too. I could see his ears moving in the faint street light from my window. He was triangulating for the noise. He was tense, but not alarmed, so the noise was either (1) a rat with a death wish or (2) outside. It came again, a scrunching, scraping noise, not very loud. Nothing in the apartment was moving.

Someone was climbing up to my balcony. Daniel had shown me that it could be done. Up a pipe, quick traverse across the lintel, then reach up…

He was about to get a very nasty surprise. I rose quietly and opened the balcony doors. I stepped between the two pots of Trudi's green leafy things and looked down. I was staring into his face when he grabbed for the rail, slipped, grabbed again, and lost his grip.

Due to previous unpleasantness, I had greased those rails liberally with vaseline. They were as slippery as a budget forecast. I saw him reach this realisation. His eyes widened. He made no sound as he slid, half fell, and then jumped off the wall.

Then he stumbled, got to his feet, ran around the corner and was gone.

'Well, that was interesting,' I told Horatio, who yawned, flicking an uninvolved tail. 'I've never seen him before but I'll remember the face. Pale, blue eyes, quite tall and thin, about twenty. Probably done a lot of climbing. And what do we have here?'

I saw a thin line secured by a grapnel and drew up a supermarket bag. It was heavy. When I opened it and saw the contents I was groping for the phone before my wits had gathered
themselves together enough to panic.

Fingers, do the walking. Horatio and I shut and locked the
balcony door with the world outside and us inside and I went
to the kitchen and put on some coffee. This was bad. What had
I done to attract attention like this? I was drinking my second
cup when Lepidoptera buzzed and I let her in.

'What is it now?' she asked, perilously close to a snarl. I
indicated the bag.

'He was climbing up the wall, but then he grabbed the rail,
and I had smeared the rail with vaseline. So he fell off and ran
away.'

'That was a good idea,' she approved. She stirred the contents
of the bag with her biro. They told a very nasty story. One which
I had been telling myself ever since I opened it. In full, gory,
Tarantino colour.

'I see,' she said thoughtfully. 'We have ropes and manacles to
restrain the prisoner. We have a gun and a couple of scalpels and
a welding iron. And we have a tape recorder. Some of this stuff
might have fingerprints. We'll have to get yours for comparison.
You saw the climber. Describe him.'

I described him. His face was branded in my memory. Letty
White sat down next to me and poured herself some coffee.

'You must have got a shock,' she said, in her dry, exact
voice.

'No, you think so?' I asked weakly. I was too exhausted to
scream at her. Probably a good idea since few police officers take
to being screamed at.

'Why did you grease the balcony railing?'

'Daniel climbed up there one night and scared the shit out of
me. And then told me how to stop anyone getting up again.'

'Where is Daniel?'

'I don't know. He went looking for Selima, the girl from the
chocolate shop who ran away,' I confessed.

Letty White, of all people, patted my shoulder. 'My concern for the present is you.'

'Hey, me too. Why should I deserve this kind of visit?'

'Maybe it wasn't you he was after,' she said. 'Once on your balcony he could make his way right up the building, couldn't he?'

'And the bastard looked strong. Sort of thin, but all muscle. He had to fall about ten feet, and he just stumbled a bit when he landed. Why? Who else could he be after? That's a torturer's tool kit, that bag.'

'Yes,' she said. 'And unless you have some secrets you haven't told me, you haven't got anything worth torturing you for.'

'Fun?' I suggested, then wished I hadn't.

'I don't think so,' she said soothingly. 'I think he was intending to climb higher.'

'Because I'm not worth torturing?'

'Because I found a climbing rope in the alley,' she said. 'You don't need a climbing rope to get to your balcony.'

'Letty,' I said, gripping her wrist. 'You know something about that man in Pluto. You've been involved with him ever since he moved in. Who is he?'

'I can't tell you,' she said. 'But I do think that your burglar was intending to climb higher. Let go of me,' she requested, and I let go. Letty could probably break my grip in any number of inventive, painful ways.

'When I said I can't tell you,' she said, 'I meant it. I really can't. And I'm sorry he's here amongst civilians. But there it is. Don't touch that rail. If we don't find prints on the bag there will be some on the vaseline. Holds a good print, petroleum jelly. Come into St Kilda Road tomorrow and I'll let you know what we find out about the criminal. I'll be around,' she said. 'Call me if you need me. I might as well take a flat here,' she said, taking herself and the bag and line to the door. 'I'm here so often. Call one of your friends, have a nice dinner and take a sleeping pill tonight,' she advised, and I shut the door behind her. With just the suspicion of a slam. I did not appreciate Letty giving me advice on my social circle.

But in one rather large and comforting aspect, she was right. I was not the intended victim. And it was eight o'clock, dinner time. I was just about to ring Meroe, a person who would not be frightened by my burglar, when the phone rang.

I picked it up.

'Corinna?' asked Daniel's voice.

'Daniel,' I answered.

'What is wrong?' he asked, and I burst into tears, hating myself for being so weak. He listened while I told him about the climber, chuckled when I told him about the vaseline and went silent when I described the torture kit. I also told him what Letty White had said.

'Do you want me to come back?'

'Where are you?' I asked.

'Frankston. Selima ran to her cousins in Frankston, but they said that they would have to tell her father she was with them and she left this afternoon. I don't have any more leads. And I'm tired. I think I had better come back and talk to George.'

'Vivienne says that she was in love with him,' I said. 'I asked lots of questions,' I added. 'I know how the shop works.'

'You didn't call me?'

'You didn't exactly leave me with a cordial invitation to ring whenever I liked,' I said sharply. There was a silence. I knew he was still there because I could still hear him breathing.

'Dinner?' he asked.

'All right,' I said. 'But you had better get here fast. I have to go to bed early, you know.'

'On the wings of the wind,' he said, and hung up.

Suddenly I felt immensely cheered. Some sort of reaction, I suppose, to being abruptly woken and then not tortured and murdered. Really improves your day. I cleaned up the kitchen, trimmed some steaks (Horatio appreciates steak scraps, and he had had a shock too) and put some of Meroe's ratatouille in the microwave to thaw. Meroe is a vegetarian but she likes highly flavoured food. If there was a criticism that could be made of her vegetable stew, it might be that she stresses the garlic a tad, but

I don't mind people moving away from me on the bus. Because I rarely take buses. I found the bearnaise sauce, scrubbed, sliced and layered potatoes with milk and cheese for pommes duchesse and took out my best plates and glasses.

I opened a bottle of good red wine. This was a night to appreciate not being dead. Then I had nothing to do, so I sat down to read the business pages. I try to keep up, even though I am no longer the accountant I once was.

The exchange rate was still good, though I wondered, as always, at the durability of the pound sterling, a currency which ought to have been contemplating parity with Yapese stone money or the Flainian pobble bead. I could only assume that Memories of Empire were keeping it afloat. The usual number of bankruptcies. I looked for James but he still wasn't there. Rats.

As I read on, I noticed that the editorial insinuation of unnamed fraud was still there, a trifle stronger. I had been going to call Janet Warren, then realised that I didn't know her new address. But I still had her mobile number and I was about to call it in the scent of almost cooked pommes duchesse when Daniel rang the bell.

He was so beautiful, coming in out of the darkness, smelling of the night. Dark-haired Daniel in the leather coat with his trout-pool eyes. I forgot I was angry with him as he gathered me into a large embrace.

'Ketschele, I was so worried,' he said, hugging me tighter.

'So was I,' I squeaked, running out of breath. He loosened his grip so that I could talk. 'It was horrible and I am very glad you are here. Dinner is almost ready,' I said.

'I can smell delicious smells,' he said. 'You have gone to a lot of trouble for a man who spoke so cruelly to you. That was kind.'

'I am very glad to be alive,' I said.

'And I am a fool,' he said, and kissed me.

We cooked the steaks. Daniel liked his rare, which was nice, because so did I. I wondered how all that blood fitted into his kosher diet, and then realised that I had made a milk dish as well as a flesh dish. Oops. Daniel didn't seem to notice. He piled everything on his plate and ate ravenously for five minutes. When he came up for seconds he looked warmer.

'I was so hungry,' he said. 'And this is so good. Do you want to tell me about your climber?'

'Not yet. Do you want to tell me about Selima?'

'Not yet. Let us reminisce about Paris,' he said, and so we did. The food was very good. We ate it all, Jason's experimental chocolate muffins, which weren't quite right yet—soggy in the middle—but tasted divine with King Island cream.

'I went to the Bourdelle gallery,' I said, and Daniel said, 'You didn't! I've never met anyone else who went there. In Montparnasse?'

'Yes, the original house, with his huge sculptures and that strange Heracles with a bird's beak. It's just round from the Impasse Montparnasse, where one can see how those dead-end buildings worked. And Bourdelle's bequest was…'

'An atelier preserved just as it was,' he said. 'Fascinating. You can imagine the strings of washing across between those windows, where the electric wires are now, and the painters in the garret and the sculptors on the ground floor.'

'And the tough old concierge who kept the door,' I added.

It was one of the most pleasant meals I had ever had. When we had reached coffee and liqueurs Daniel said, reaching for my hand, 'I am so sorry, Corinna.'

'For?'

'For speaking to you like that. I know that I am really sorry, because everyone has already told me what a fool I was.'

'Everyone?'

He took a sip of Grand Marnier, his lips beginning to curve into a smile. 'First there was Meroe, who told me that thinking I was the only person in the world who could rescue lost girls was pure egotism. She recommended a course in Buddhism. And only a rush of business stopped her, I am convinced, from threatening to put a spell on me. Then there was the Professor, who said that you were very downcast and if I was the cause I had better amend it, there's a good chap. Mrs Dawson gave me to understand that she was very disappointed in me as I appeared to be quite a civilised young man, though of course she could be wrong. She also told me firmly that sacrificing others on the altar of our own mission was no way to get to heaven, should I wish to go there.'

'Really?' I asked, not knowing if I felt flattered that my friends wanted to protect me or insulted that they were interfering in my life.

'But the final straw was when I came to the bakery looking for you and you weren't there, but Goss was, and she wouldn't speak to me. And then Jason called me a dickhead. And I am,' he said. 'Forgive me?'

'Try not to do it again,' I said. 'You hurt my feelings. I didn't know if I'd ever see you again.'

'I'm so sorry,' he said, and I fell into his arms and forgave him.

This meant that, although I did get to bed on time, I didn't get a lot of sleep. It was in a mist of satiation and love —those satiny lips, long flanks, strong hands—that I floated down to the bakery at four and Jason said, 'Daniel's back,' and I said, 'Yes,' and we made bread in amiable silence for hours. We completed all the usual breads and Jason retired into his chocolate experiment, scowling. I had tested two chocolate muffins and although they were perfectly good, saleable muffins—indeed, I was intending to sell them—they did not suit Jason. Under that scruffy exterior with trucker's special egg stains on his white apron beat the heart of a perfectionist, so I left him to it and went into the shop to meet Kylie, today's assistant.

She was still worried about Soot, and so was I, but I couldn't think of anywhere else to look.

'I think someone might have found her in the alley and taken her home,' I said as consolingly as I could. 'She didn't have a collar on. And Calico is happy with Cherie and Andy, and Trudi has decided to keep Lucifer. And how is Tori?'

'I bought the new collar and she just sits there and looks so pretty,' enthused Kylie. 'Jason said Daniel's back?' she asked delicately.

'Yes, he's back,' I assured her.

'Good. You, like, belong together. Like Scully and Mulder.'

'Or Buffy and Angel. Dude even looks like Angel,' Jason commented from the door into the bakery. 'She never should have dumped him. How are the choccie muffins selling?'

'Good,' I said. They had been flying off the racks and some people had come back and bought another after eating the first. No one had ever done that with my muffins. Jason wiped his hands on his apron, then ruffled his hair, leaving chocolate streaks on his face.

'They're still not right. I'm going to do some more tryouts. I can pay for the flour,' he said stiffly. 'In case it doesn't work.'

'No, you are not paying for the flour,' I said. 'You may well produce the best chocolate muffin in the world, so go on, try something else. If they are too expensive to sell at two dollars, we can put the price up,' I said, though this seldom works. People expect to pay two dollars for a muffin, whether it is an ordinary blueberry one or a super-deluxe plum pudding muffin stuffed with expensive fruit. Jason went back to the bakery. Kylie and I sold bread. Daniel came in and kissed me on the back of the neck. Kylie almost cooed. She is a sweet romantic girl under all that paint and glitter.

'I'm going back to the shop,' he said. 'I need to collect the tapes and get the customers identified, though that may not be necessary now.'

'You aren't convinced that Selima did it?' I asked.

'I still can't imagine why she would.'

'Not even to attract the gorgeous George's attention? That was Vivienne's theory,' I commented. We were still treating each other very carefully, Daniel and I. Words can wound.

I never believed that coda to 'sticks and stones', not even when my grandma sang it to me.

'Crazy,' said Kylie. 'No girl with a job'd do that. I mean, what does it matter to George that the shop goes under?'

'It matters a lot to George,' I said. 'Because otherwise he's going to be up every morning cooking the trucker's special for Jason. He's a Pandamus.'

'I know,' said Kylie, which was a marginally more polite version of her usual 'D-uh.' 'I talked to her a bit. She was a quiet girl, you know? Real scared of her father.'

'Because?' asked Daniel, alert to any smell of abuse.

'He wants to send her back to Turkey to marry some—erk— old man. And she's said, no way, and her dad's yelled at her a lot. So, like, of course she's run away. I'd run away if my dad tried to marry me to some old man.'

'Who else knew Selima?' I asked urgently.

'Goss talked to her a bit but Cherie knew her better.'

Daniel made a broad gesture and slapped himself quite hard on the forehead.

'Jason, you were right, I am a dickhead. Quick, anyone know, is Cherie home?'

'Haven't seen her go out,' said Kylie. 'Did you call Daniel a dickhead?' she demanded of Jason as Daniel raced up the bakery stairs and thus through my flat and into Insula en route to Daphne and Cherie Holliday.

'Yair,' said Jason, proudly. 'A dude needs another dude to tell him when he's being a dickhead. I'm going back to my muffins,' he said hastily, and Kylie and I were alone.

'Corinna, what's the haps?' asked Kylie. 'Has everyone gone, like, mad?'

'It's a long story and I'll tell you all of it,' I promised. 'It began when I bit into a Heavenly Pleasures chocolate and found it was full of chili sauce…'

I had trailed through the whole story, much interrupted by comments like 'Gross!' and 'Ooh, yuk!' Kylie inspected a sparkling purple fingernail.

'So if it isn't Selima, who is it? And why?' she asked, both good questions to which I presently didn't have any answers.

Business was agreeably brisk. Just as the lunch crowd was rushing away, to be chained once more to their rowing benches, Jason said, 'Aha!' and then, 'Shit, yes!' and emerged from the bakery a strange figure. He had streaks of chocolate through his hair, chocolate all over his apron, and chocolate sauce dripping down his chin. But the light of joy was in his eyes and he held forth a warm chocolate muffin dish in much the same manner as Arthur must have held Excalibur or royal nurses used to produce the heir to the throne.

'Here,' he said. I took one from the tray. It was not very heavy but rich chocolate in colour. It had no icing but a scatter of powdered chocolate on the top. I bit.

Instantly my mouth filled with a rich, full taste. It was, in fact, filled with chocolate sauce. I could not imagine how he had done such a thing. None of that raw cocoa taste, no grains of partially melted compound, no flicker of flour which had marred all the previous chocolate muffins of my acquaintance. It was, in short, a wonderful muffin. I gestured to Kylie to try one, and she squeaked something about her diet as she took it. But she took it. And ate it. And almost swooned.

'Jason, the only thing I could call this is chocolate orgasm,' I told him. 'Now, while you have a shower and put on some clean clothes, I am going to get paper and pen and you are going to write down how you produced this miracle.'

Jason looked down at himself, brushed his hands through his chocolate-stiffened hair and went to have a shower in the little bathroom attached to the kitchen. Presently I also heard the washer going. I wondered whether my laundry liquid, which was supposed to remove all stains, would cope with that much chocolate. If so I ought to write the manufacturer a commendation. Kylie was licking chocolate sauce off her chin.

'He's really good, isn't he?' she asked in a subdued voice. Neither Kylie nor Goss had approved when I took Jason in off the street, a starving ex-junkie with quite a few problems, like bad men trying to kill him.

'He certainly is,' I said. 'The only trouble is that we might find that the ingredients are too expensive to sell them at a profit.'

'Call them "super-deluxe death by chocolate" and make them five dollars,' said Kylie. 'I'd pay five dollars for one of them. If I ate muffins. Which I don't. Unless someone tells me to,' she said, conscious of her devout adherence to the 'famine' diet.

'Wow,' I said, sitting down. Whatever it was that chocolate was supposed to enhance, it had enhanced it.

Daniel came back. Kylie and I sat him down and fed him coffee and one of the chocolate muffins. He reacted in much the same way as we had.

'What a wonderful thing,' he said. 'How on earth did he do it?'

'When he gets out of the shower I am sure that he will tell us,' I said. 'How did you go with Cherie?'

'She didn't want to tell me much,' said Daniel. 'If only I had thought to ask her first before flying off the handle like that. She knows where Selima is, I am sure. Cherie survived very well on the street on her own, you know. I suspect that Selima has told Cherie about her father. But all she will do is get a message to Selima and ask her if she wants to talk to me. That might be enough. But Cherie says very firmly that Selima had nothing to do with the sabotage. I think I had better go on with the investigation.'

'If you still have a client,' I said. 'Juliette thinks this is all solved.'

'Well, if it isn't Selima, then soon Juliette will find out...'

A scatter of footsteps, a frantic woman on the other side of the counter. Juliette, with a handful of chocolates, all of which had been cut in half. They dripped bright red contamination on my clean floor.

'That she still needs us,' concluded Daniel.

Chapter Ten

Daniel went with Juliette, I went into the bakery to hear a lecture on 'the chocolate muffin, its physics and chemistry' by Dr Jason. He was clean and dressed in a clean apron. He had even got all the chocolate out of his hair.

'Trouble with them other choccie muffins,' he said, 'was that you had to use cocoa powder to make them chocolatey because ground chocolate won't melt smooth, or if it does melt, it burns,' he said. 'And muffins have to be done quick, it's no use beating them for long enough to get the chocolate smooth or they go tough.'

'Agreed,' I said. 'Until yours, I have never tasted a satisfactory chocolate muffin. Go on, Jason.'

'So. I thought about how I made my jam doughnut muffins, with the jam in the middle. I thought maybe if I could put chocolate in the middle of the muffin then what I'd have is like your *pain chocolat* or one of them self-saucing puddings. But there the chocolate is dull because it has to cook as long as the pudding or the bread. But a muffin only takes ten minutes. So I asked Vivienne to give me some samples of the different choccies that Heavenly Pleasures makes. The couverture was too easily burned. But the bittersweet was perfect. I made a chocolate sauce with cream to flavour the muffin then I put a glob of it into the middle of each muffin. It holds together long enough to melt just right when the muffin is cooked. And it stays glossy. And it tastes…'

'Ace,' said Kylie.

'Glorious,' I said. 'Write down your proportions and make a copy and put the original somewhere safe. I think you have made a breakthrough,' I told him. He smiled his happy-baby smile, which always tugged at my heart. 'When you move on to your pastrycook's destiny, you can use that muffin as your masterpiece. It's new, fresh, superb, and I bet it isn't hard to make. You've just thought of something which no one has thought of before. A genuine invention and it's your masterpiece. Kylie will help you write it all down,' I told him, as someone cleared their throat meaningfully in the shop. I was neglecting my trade.

The customer, however, was not in a hurry. He was engaged in stroking Horatio, who had actually elevated the royal chin for a scratch, a great mark of favour. That cat gets stroked so much it's a wonder he isn't bald.

He was an ordinary looking middle-aged man in a suit. He looked like someone who didn't wear a suit much. 'Nice cat,' he told Horatio. 'I'm Selima's Uncle Adrian,' he told me. 'Is Daniel Cohen here?'

'Just gone out,' I said. 'You're Selima's uncle?' I didn't mean to sound incredulous, but he sounded Australian and looked fair rather than dark. I really don't know anything about Turks.

'By marriage,' he explained. 'She calls me Uncle. I married her elder sister Mirri. You Daniel's partner?'

'Yes, I suppose so,' I said. The shop was otherwise empty. Adrian settled down for a confidential conversation.

'Look, I know that Selima ran away, and I know why. Her father's an old-style Turkish father and he wanted to arrange a marriage for her. He's an old bloke so he yelled and raved and she got scared. She's the last child at home and all the others got away—Mirri even married a Christian,' he said. 'He hasn't spoken to her since. But her mum sneaks out to visit now that we've got the two kids.'

'So he wanted to make sure that Selima, at least, did as she was told, because none of the others did,' I prompted.

'Yeah. I didn't see her much because the old man kept her on a very short leash. But Mirri, my wife, she thought that Selima had a boy she wanted. She says that women know these things.'

'They do,' I told him, and he smiled.

'Anyway, if Daniel or you find Selima, tell her she can come and stay with us and we won't give her away to the old man. She's a good, hard-working girl. She can see her mum when she comes over to visit the grandkids. We've got room. In fact, I don't know why she didn't come to Mirri instead of going to those bastards in Frankston. They rang up and told the old man that she'd been there and he's breathing fire. Silly old bastard,' said Adrian tolerantly. 'That's how I found out about Daniel, he left them his card. Sel knows the address but I'll write it out.' I pushed over the brown paper bags and a pen and he wrote out an address and a phone number. 'You can call me any time. Mirri's real worried,' he said. 'Bye, cat,' he said to Horatio, and went away, letting his breath out in a sigh of relief as he went.

Kylie was still in the bakery so I leaned on the counter, looking with satisfaction at my denuded shelves. Just enough bread left for the afternoon tea crowd and the Soup Run. And today had brought a reconciliation with Daniel and the invention of a truly new muffin. I felt we should celebrate.

But before I could decide on a suitable celebration, I noticed that the newspaper lay on my counter. Another company crash had made the front page—one of those pyramid ones, where the main losers aren't the expensive executives with their huge houses carefully stashed away in their wife's name, but the small investors, the people with less than a hundred thousand dollars which was all that they had in the world. Their superannuation payout, a redundancy package, even a mortgage on their house—now all gone with the wind, on fact-finding trips to Bangkok resorts and handmade leather suitcases. All gone in speculation on the riskiest Silver River Oil Shares, which might return tenfold or nothing at all. Wicked. People talked about getting tough on crime, when what they meant was getting tough on visible street crime, which hurt and damaged a few, whereas these bastards were hurting, ruining, hundreds or thousands of people and when caught would get a few years in a comfortable low security prison, if that. And come out to find their wife's assets untouched.

The paper was bringing me down—too sad even for a Wednesday—so I folded it up and read my horoscope and the comics. No sense in getting cross about something I couldn't help. But I really must ring Janet Warren, I thought. I didn't have any significant portfolio now, I had sunk all my money into Earthly Delights, but not knowing what the editorial was talking about was still slightly annoying me. Anyway, it would be nice to see Janet again. She had many good points, one of which was that she had always detested James. I rang her mobile and got Janet right away, which always amazed me.

'Janet, it's Corinna.'

'Back from the bread!' she said. She was always good at puns. 'How are you?'

'I'm well, my business is flourishing, and I'd like to catch up with you.'

'Tonight? Only time I have, I'm flying to Singapore tomorrow.'

'All right, anywhere suit you?'

'How about your place? Mine is all packed up. You're lucky you caught me, I'm going to be away six months. Mel is going with me and I was going to be alone tonight—she's gone to say farewell to the girls.'

I gave her the address and hung up. She sounded exactly like she always had. Upbeat, confident, together. Of course, I always thought that being a lesbian gave one the freedom to deal with men on non-sexual terms and a clear-eyed view of their failings. Far too clear eyed for some of her colleagues, who found her strangely impervious to their practised charm.

I looked down at the horoscope. It said 'a good day for charming coincidences' and I laughed.

Kylie came back into the shop. The afternoon tea crowd came in. We sold the rest of the bread and, as an experiment, I put a sign on the remaining chocolate muffins—'super-delicious orgasmic chocolate muffins $5'—and sold all of them. We were in the chocolate muffin business.

From where I was standing, I could see the bakery reflected in the glass on my Hieronymus Bosch painting 'The Garden of Earthly Delights'. Jason was starting the scrubbing and I thought I would go and help him.

'How much did the ingredients of your muffin cost?'

I asked him, getting out the mop and bucket.

'Dollar fifty,' he said. 'I know that's expensive.'

'No problem, we've just sold the rest of them at five dollars each,' I told him.

'Ace,' he said. Then he took the mop out of my hand. "You go and help Daniel,' he told me. 'Me and Kyl can close up. She's even got the hang of the bank deposit.'

Horatio left the shop, which was no fun without devotees in it, and preceded me up the stairs to my apartment, where I had a shower and dressed again, leaving him to catch up on his sleep. I pottered around a bit, making my bed, washing the breakfast dishes, reading the mail—all bills—and then I went out into the street.

Heavenly Pleasures was open. Vivienne was serving in the shop. She pointed to the manufactuary and I went through into that thick, sweet scent. You wouldn't have to eat in this place. Just breathe deeply.

Daniel, Juliette and George were looking at the surveillance video on a small TV and identifying people. Daniel was amending his notes.

'I know that's Mrs Dawson,' he said. 'But who's the man with the eloquent hands?'

'Uncle Max,' said Juliette. The silent film showed the man being given tastes of various chocolates before he selected a box from the stack on the display case. 'He comes in quite a lot. He's got a sweet tooth.'

'Who is Uncle Max?' asked Daniel.

'He's our only living relative,' said Juliette. 'Our father's brother.'

'Corinna thought he was a relative,' said Daniel. 'Relatives never pay.'

Juliette laughed uneasily. 'No, he never pays. But he was helpful when we had all that trouble about the lease last year. It's a forty-year lease and they wanted to cut it short. He went and talked to the landlord of the building for us and he extended the decision on the lease for another twelve months. Uncle Max knows lots of people.'

'Is he a lawyer?'

'No, he isn't anything, I don't think. I never heard he ever had a job. He's always been just Max. He calls himself a gentleman of leisure. He was kind to us when we were children. He used to throw marvellous birthday parties, with magic and clowns and jelly cake. And balloon animals.' It sounded like those parties had been the high point of Juliette's childhood. 'Our father was a very dedicated man, you see, always at the shop, and mother was, well, a bit sour, to tell you the truth. Max always said she should have married him instead.' She laughed again. On the screen, Uncle Max bowed elaborately.

'And this old lady?'

'Comes in every week. Or used to. I haven't seen her this week.'

'What about the guys in the overalls?'

'Don't know them, they look like tradesmen.'

'So they do. And the old gentleman?'

'Henry,' said Juliette. 'He used to flirt with Selima. Perfectly nicely,' she added.

'And—do you see someone outside the shop?' Daniel froze the image. Selima was putting out her hand to touch the window. Another hand met hers, on the outside. A slim Asian man in a suit.

'I never noticed him,' said Juliette. George shrugged.

'Now can we get on with the sweets?' he demanded. Politeness, I observed, had not been amongst George's acquired skills. But it was hard to look away from him, even so.

'Juliette, would you mind if I had a word with George?' asked Daniel, and Juliette, glancing back doubtfully, went out.

'Do you know why I am asking all these questions, George?' asked Daniel.

'Yeah, you want to find out who's sabotaging the sweets.'

'And to do that I have to understand how this shop works,' said Daniel. 'You've been holding out on me, George, and I don't like that.'

I slipped out of my chair and planted myself against the back door, in case George might intend to flee that way. He was looking hunted. But if he ran into the shop, he would have to explain why he was running. He glared at me. I smiled at him. Daniel drew his attention by slamming his hand, palm down, on the table. George jumped. All the beauty of his face had leached away.

'You know something, and you're going to tell me, right now,' said Daniel very quietly.

'All right!' said George. 'I know about that dude. The chink. Came by every day. Selima was stuck on him.'

'What else?' Daniel's face might have been carved out of marble.

'She saw him at lunch. When she went out.'

'Did anyone else know?'

'No,' said George.

'And what did you do with your knowledge of her secret?'

'Me?' asked George. 'Nothing. I didn't want her. I've got...'

'You've got?' pressed Daniel.

'Plans,' said George, and sneered. 'I got my plans. She's not too bad, even though she's older than me.'

'Juliette or Vivienne?' asked Daniel. I contained my shocked gasp.

'Juliette's all right,' said George brutally. 'But Viv knows how to make sweets.'

Daniel lifted his hand and George cringed. That did my heart good.

'If you've lied to me,' said Daniel coldly, 'I shall tell Del Pandamus. And I shall tell Yai Yai. And your life won't be worth living,' he concluded. 'I've finished with you. Come on, Corinna, let's get some fresh air.'

'It is rather stifling in here,' I said.

Daniel packed the tapes into his satchel and we got out into the street.

'Phew!' he said.

'The little monster!' I cried.

'A fine specimen of what they used to call a cad,' said Daniel. 'But I don't think he's ruining the chocolates. Now I need to go and talk to Jon and Kepler.'

'Why?' I asked, almost running to keep up. Everyone has longer legs than I do. 'Because that Chinese boy has turned up at one pm on every tape,' he said, 'and I want to catch him tomorrow. He must work in the city. He's wearing a suit. And if ever there were star-crossed lovers, it would be a respectable Chinese boy and a traditional Turkish girl.'

'If he doesn't turn up?'

'Then he knows that Selima is missing. I don't think we'll be able to find him otherwise. The city is full of well-dressed Asian youths. Are you coming with me?'

'I am,' I said. 'Then I am hoping to decoy you to the roof by luring you with gin and tonic.'

'A wonderful idea,' he said.

Jon answered the door. 6A has a mosaic of a rather contented Neptune, crowned with seaweed and pearls, leaning back in his chariot and ogling a bosomy blue lady who is probably meant to be Thetis.

'We need your help in a rather delicate matter,' I said. He smiled at me. I had never seen him so relaxed. Jon worked for a charity which fed people in all the nastiest places in the world. If it was drought stricken and starving or under a hundred feet of mud, Jon would be there, directing food convoys and arranging to buy local crafts to pay for replanting a forest so the mudslide didn't happen again. Or arranging a water system so the local women didn't have to walk miles carrying it. He spoke eight languages. He was one of the most genuinely kind people I had ever met so this sort of job took a huge toll on his emotions. But he was very good at it, and it looked like it had brought that reward which virtue is always supposed to yield and somehow never does.

Jon's apartment was basically beige, which shows up the fierce colours and strange shapes of the carved masks, painted hangings, woven tapestries and silk fabrics which decorate and occasionally surprise. I had got a real shock from a snarling demon mask the last time I had visited the lavatory.

There was a wave of scent: black pepper, lemon, cumin, garlic. Yummy. Kepler, wearing red silk brocade pyjamas, was reclining on the sofa, which was draped in ikat weaving, staring blankly into space. A chess game was laid out on the ebony coffee table but he was not looking at it. One sensitive hand groped for a laptop and he started to type, still not looking at the keyboard. He seemed to be entranced.

'Come in,' said Jon. 'Kepler will be back with us soon. He's working out a software problem. Glass of wine?'

'Thanks,' I accepted for both of us and took a basketwork chair. 'Is he often like this?' I sipped. It was very good wine.

'Sometimes it can be hours,' said Jon. 'What's the matter, Corinna?'

'We have a Romeo and Juliet story developing under our very windows,' I said, and told him about the Chinese boy and Selima. Jon poured himself a glass and thought about it.

'I gather that the Turks wouldn't accept the boy?'

'Not a chance,' Daniel answered. 'This is an old country paterfamilias here, and the girl has defied him already by refusing to marry the man he told her to marry.'

'And no respectable Chinese family would be happy with a choice of bride from another religion as well as race,' said Jon. 'How sad!'

Kepler snapped out of his trance and shut the notebook.

'What's sad? Why are you telling my Jon sad things?' he demanded of me.

'Life is sad,' I replied. 'Sometimes. We want your help to try and make it better.'

'What do you want me to do?' he asked instantly. You couldn't help liking Kepler. He wasn't in any way foolish, but he did have a quality of innocence. No one else could have carried off those red brocade pyjamas.

'Tomorrow at one I want you to talk to the boy,' said Daniel. 'If I try and catch him he might panic. But you can speak Cantonese and Mandarin.'

'Between us, Jon and I can speak a lot of languages. Very well, we will catch your bird for you.'

'That is a beautiful chess set,' said Daniel.

It was made of glass. The black pieces were a deep green. It was very decorative.

'You play?' asked Kepler.

'A little. But I don't have time for a game today and we are interrupting you. Meet you at Heavenly Pleasures at, say, ten to one tomorrow?' asked Daniel. 'Don't go into the shop. That little ratbag George isn't telling me something, and it might be about Selima or her boyfriend. Thank you,' said Daniel, and we left.

I had the odd feeling that intimacy was closing behind us as we went, like ink colouring water, spreading and deepening, wrapping the two of them together again in their perfect content. They had a rapt closeness which would have made me feel lonely if I hadn't been with Daniel.

We collected Horatio and the esky and ascended to the roof. The rain had eased but it was too wet to sit in the bower. We joined Trudi in the temple of Ceres. There seemed to be a lot of feathers on the floor, which Trudi was sweeping out.

'It is him,' she explained, indicating Lucifer with her chin. He was sitting smugly on her shoulder as if he had just done something really diabolical and the devil was about to call him a good cat and let him eat some sinners. 'He caught pigeon.'

'But he's tiny,' I said. 'How could he?'

'He pounce,' she chuckled. 'Pigeon struts along, then—bang!—Luce jumps on its back. Hangs on. Pigeon takes off, I drag Luce off by lead, otherwise he'd still be flying. But lots of feathers fall off pigeon. Come on, Luce, we go put feathers in compost.'

I dread to think what he's going to be like when he grows up,' I said. Daniel poured me a drink.

'A very scary prospect. Putting that harness on him was a lifesaving idea. Though I wouldn't put it past him to ride his pigeon to the ground safely. What do you have to do today?'

'Go and see Letty White and have my fingerprints taken. She said she might know something about my climber by now.'

'Do you want me to come with you?'

'If you like.'

'I like,' he said, and we drank our drink in silence.

There is nothing to be said for the architecture of the St. Kilda Road Police Complex, so I won't say it. After being searched, stared at, labelled and escorted to the lab to have my fingers stained with black gunge, we found Letty White in her office. It was just a cubicle, but she did have a window. With unparalleled views of sky.

'Miss Chapman,' she said briskly. 'Is this your man?'

She laid a photo on the desk. I sat down in the visitor's chair. I nodded.

'Your uninvited guest was Jim Ronaldson, known as 'the Cat'. For fairly obvious reasons.'

'He's a cat burglar,' I said, getting my breath back.

'He's hired muscle,' said Daniel. 'His father was a climber. I seem to remember he died on Everest. Son took to crime.'

'That's our Jim,' said Letty. 'Rest of the family accepted his father's death, he never did. Nasty record. Children's Court for everything except actual murder.'

'Doesn't he hang out with the Twins?' asked Daniel.

'Yes. Not nice men.' Letty White tucked in the corners of her mouth in disapproval.

'I don't understand,' said Daniel. 'They're guns for hire. Who could have hired them? They cost serious money. Isn't there anything you feel you ought to be telling us?'

'Can't,' said Letty promptly. 'I've asked and they said no. Sorry. But it ought to all be over soon.'

'How soon?' I asked.

'Three weeks. No more. Just keep a eye out for these two, and ring us if you see them.'

She laid another photo down. Two hulking, middle-aged men. They had dark hair and eyes and moustaches and were, as far as I could see, identical twins.

'Caused us a lot of trouble until we found out there were two of them,' commented the senior constable. 'They kept giving each other alibis. Tait and Bull Smith belong to a famous criminal family and they are always armed and dangerous, probably even when asleep. So take care.'

'Thanks a bundle,' I muttered and we left the building, turning in our badges and regaining our possessions.

'This is bad,' said Daniel as we crossed the road to the tram stop.

'No shit,' I agreed.

'But, Corinna, the Twins? They do, as Lepidoptera says, belong to a famous criminal family, but they were thrown out of it some years ago.'

'For?'

'Being too violent. And indiscriminate. Our criminal underworld tries to keep all its little quarrels in the family. It very seldom involves innocent bystanders, because that invites attention and police officers and trouble like search warrants. But the Twins…'

'Don't tell me.' I stepped up into the tram. The light glow of my gin and tonic had entirely worn off and I felt very cold. I found two tickets and put them into the machine, only dropping them twice, which was quite good considering how chilled my fingers were. I had left my red gloves at home.

'All right, but what I'm trying to say is that they are for hire, they are freelancers. Like the Teutonic Knights, with whom they would get on very well.'

'Come in, Georg, let's quaff some of this stolen wine by the bright fire of this massacred village, sort of thing?'

'Just so, ketschele.' His hand was warm in mine. 'And Jim the Cat is a known associate of theirs. They use him to get up to an office, say, and then to open or break the window, get in, and let them in.'

'So you think that our recluse was their target?'

'I can't imagine who else it would be, can you?'

'The only new person is Mrs Dawson,' I answered. 'And we know a lot about her. I'm sure that she could mastermind a criminal family if it took her fancy, but somehow…'

'I can't see her doing anything that tacky,' he agreed.

We got off the tram at Flinders Street. Lately going home had been a whole new world of nasty surprises. I was getting positively superstitious about approaching Insula. But the only person waiting for us when we got there was Sister Mary.

'There you are,' she said, as though we were the people she had always wanted to meet. 'Daniel, can you come to MAP tomorrow? Your old friend Nails wants to talk to you. I'll be there at about ten. And Darren is still causing trouble. I'd appreciate your help,' she said.

There was no use arguing with Sister Mary so we agreed. We might, at least, find out if the Twins and the Cat had anything to do with that fake messiah. Assuming he was talking to anyone, of course.

'Crocodile swamps?' asked Daniel.

'Moat monsters, electric fence, answering machine, deep pit to catch elephants,' I said, and we went in to bar the door and make dinner and then make love and other things that people do when they aren't being interviewed by police or frightened out of their wits by burglars with funny names. Thursday looked like being difficult. I fortified myself against the cold with Daniel, who was always warm.

Chapter Eleven

Four a.m., but for a change I was not underslept, and the coffee tasted unusually good. When I got down the steps I found work had already started. Jason was making a heavy dark Welsh bread called bara brith, stuffed with dried fruit. I mixed the first batches of rye and pasta douro and drank more coffee. I had brought Jason a tray of French bread, bacon, tomatoes and sausages, which Daniel, with a degree of self-sacrifice I would find hard to overpraise, had cooked for us. Jason scoffed the lot in moments.

I ate mine in a leisurely fashion, relishing the different tastes and textures. The bacon was crisp and the tomatoes mushy, just as I liked them. The sausages had been made from contented pigs and the toast was very good. So far, I was enjoying Thursday.

This was not to last. Kylie, who had managed a one-night stand with Jon last month, had just heard about Kepler and Jon, and she wasn't taking it well. She was green today, hair and eyes and all.

'After I put on my best dress for him,' she mumbled. 'I thought we had a thing.'

'You may have had a thing,' I responded, 'But this is another sort of thing.'

'Is it worse being left for a man?' she asked passionately, leaning over the cash register and displaying inches of perfectly flat chest.

'I don't know,' I said. 'It's not nice being left at all: let's not go there, eh?'

'There was this episode of the Simpsons,' she said, and I stopped listening. The habit of anyone under twenty-five of referring any large ethical or moral issues to the judgment of the Simpsons, which no one told the kids was a satire on how not to either have a family or run a uranium plant, is trying to a grown-up mind. I didn't know how much Kylie was actually hurting, so I let her babble on about Homer and Marge, though I would have been happy never to hear those names again.

A curse on the Simpsons. Bring back the sterner philosophers, like Epicurus. Now Epicurus could give Homer Simpson a run for his money, Duff beer or no Duff beer. I had a feeling that Epicureans could hold their drink...

'...and Marge came back to Homer so it was all right,' she concluded.

'Good. Don't judge the entire world by the Simpsons. It's a satire,' I tried.

'What's a satire?' asked Kylie, wide-eyed, and I gave up. We sold bread and muffins until it was time for me and Daniel to go to the prison to talk to his old friend, Nails.

'And he is called Nails because...?' I prompted, when we were on the tram.

'You don't want to know,' he told me.

He was right. Normally a fiend for information, in this case I didn't. Daniel looked gorgeous in a dark blue sweater. I was wearing my prison-visiting black suit.

'This had better be important,' said Daniel. 'I ought to be back at Heavenly Pleasures, or looking for Selima.'

'By the way, I am dining with an old female friend tonight. Can you amuse yourself?'

'Certainly,' he said with a grin. 'I'll go and get Kepler out of bed to replay the game. It was the Immortal Game by Adolf Anderssen, 1851. He had it set out. You looked at the chessmen,' he said, wondering why I was puzzled.

'Only because they were pretty chessmen,' I replied. 'We're here.'

MAP was just as it had been before and we got in with the same walk down the featureless corridor. Daniel was right about the smell. I hadn't got used to it. Halloran was there. He looked worried. Even his nose had gone pale.

'I hope you can do something about this, sir,' he said to Daniel. 'Everyone's jumpy. The place is at boiling point, so it is, and something must be done with that creature, for all the good Sister says that he is faking. And her not a woman I would willingly cross.'

'Hey, me neither,' said Daniel. Nails was brought in after a short wait. He was a tall lad with innumerable piercings and a Celtic tattoo on his arm. I didn't enquire about the rest of him. He seemed uneasy. I personally wouldn't have liked to meet him down a nice sunlit street at noon, much less a dark alley. He was escorted in and sat down.

'Dude,' he said to Daniel.

'Hey,' Daniel replied. 'What's the haps?'

'Dude, we gotta witch,' said Nails.

'Darren the God Boy?' Daniel laughed. Nails didn't.

'I tell you, man, this is serious. He's got everyone spooked. He put the evil eye on Jonesy, and the next day he fell off a ladder and broke his leg. He put a curse on Fats Farren and he fell into the chip maker. He's in hospital.'

'Isn't Fats Farren a child molester?' asked Daniel. 'Are you sure that he fell into the oil on his own?'

'I swear, man, there wasn't no one near him.' Nails leaned forward. 'Listen, someone's going to off him if you don't do something. Or the sister.'

'Look, Nails, everyone listens to you. If you tell them this witchcraft shit is just bullshit, they'll lay off Darren. Who is, and always has been, an extreme nutcase, you know that.'

'Yair,' said Nails. 'I know he's a nutcase. But I ain't got no proof that he ain't doing all this shit. I was in the kitchen when that boiling oil went over and Fats was alone. You gotta do something. If this place goes up, it's hard time for all of us. I just want to get through my time and get home. My old lady's got a new baby and I want to see him at Christmas. Way this is going I won't see my son till he's leaving school.'

'All right,' said Daniel. 'I'll see what I can do. Meanwhile, you keep the lid on it as much as you can, right, Nails? I'm relying on you.'

'And I'm trusting you, dude,' said Nails.

Sister Mary was brought in and Nails bobbed her something rather close to a bow as he was taken out.

Then there was a hissing noise, like an infuriated cat, and Darren came in. Actually he more slithered prone. Even in handcuffs and leg irons he moved easily, sliding across the floor as though he might have had scales on his belly. Sister Mary jumped to her feet.

'Put him into a chair,' she ordered, and two guards, very unwilling to do so, were forced by her imperious will into not only touching Darren but piling him into a chair.

'You pay attention to me!' said Sister Mary. She seemed to grow taller. 'Stop this nonsense immediately!'

'Sssss-ah!' said Darren, recoiling from the cross on her pendant as though he had been blinded. He threw up his handcuffed wrists to cover his eyes. There was a ragged scratch, outlined with betadine, across his forehead.

'Darren, you gotta stop this witchcraft shit,' said Daniel. 'Or someone is going to kill you.'

For a moment I could have sworn the unfocused eyes sharpened and then blinked. Daniel saw it too.

'I know how Fats got burned,' Daniel continued. 'Just takes a bit of fishing line and a wedge to unbalance a pot. Jonesy would have fallen off a ladder anyway, he's fried his brains on speed. But if you don't stop this, someone will kill you dead. And by the way, thanks for the bomb threat, and how did you get in with the Cat and the Twins? They're not your usual company.'

'Ssss,' replied Darren. Daniel glared. Sister Mary glared. I glared. Not that it did any good. Darren's movements were snaky and he was really frightening me. And I'd only saw The Exorcist once. Fed on a diet of horror movies, I could imagine how the prison population was feeling.

'Darren, if you think this is your ticket to a nice safe psych ward, you're wrong,' said Daniel. 'They haven't got a bed in any of the secure hospitals. You've made everyone here your enemy, and you'll have to stay here, and someone will kill you. Have I made myself clear? You think about it.'

'Sssscared you,' said Darren.

'In your dreams,' said Daniel. He got up and called across the corridor. 'Take him away, Mr Halloran.'

Darren hissed and slithered his way out. Sister Mary came as close as she ever did to swearing. 'In the name of the Father, Son and Holy Spirit!' she said.

'I've got a plan,' I said as it burst fully formed into my head. 'Let's get out of here and I'll tell you about it. We'll need to talk to the Prof, Daniel.'

'The Prof?' he asked, baffled.

'Yes, I hope he's home. And we have to get back to catch that Chinese boy. Sister, can you arrange to come back tomorrow, about ten?'

'Yes. But I'm not bringing an exorcist, assuming we have one, which we don't. I'm not bothering the bishop with this nonsense.' Sister Mary was cross.

'No need. You come along with a bottle of holy water and one of ordinary water and I reckon we can expose good old Darren as a fraud.'

'We'll need to have Nails along as a witness,' Daniel was thinking fast. 'He's well respected. You convince him, you convince the prison. Good. See you tomorrow,' he said, and we caught the tram for home.

'What have you got in mind, Sherlock?' he asked. I grinned at him.

'You remember all that witchcraft history which Meroe made me read?' I said. 'There was a famous judge in England called Sir John Holt who single-handedly stopped the witchcraft persecutions there. I'm going to use a Sir John Holt trick on Darren the God Boy,' I said, so pleased as to be bordering on smug. 'And I bet it works just as well for me as it worked for Sir John.'

'I'll be fascinated,' he said. I could tell that he was about to try to tease me into explaining, but it was time for him to go and check out the rest of the customers at Heavenly Pleasures and for me to return to my bakery.

Where things were going well. Jason, I noticed, was wearing a new t-shirt.

'Got it from Chas Li,' he said. 'He came past with a bundle of them. On his way to the Vic market. He's nothing like his brother, is he?'

'No,' I said, thinking of the dreamy Kepler and the bustling Chas.

'I'm going to go over after we finish here and help him with the unloading,' said Jason. 'Catch up with the guys. I'll be careful,' he said, seeing that I looked worried. 'I'm not going back to that life. Sleeping on the ground, cold, hungry, dirty, hustling for a fix. But some of them were nice to me,' he added. 'I want to see how they're doing.'

When he had been a homeless junkie, Jason had hung out near the Vic market, where there was always a meal of sorts to be gleaned from the skips. If you weren't too picky. I worried about this decision. Jason had only been off the gear for a month or so. But if he was going to backslide, then he would, and we'd deal with it when we had to. And one thing I didn't suspect the capitalist Chas to be doing was selling drugs. On a risk/cost analysis, drugs don't cut it unless you are only dealing with a few middlemen. Street dealers get caught repeatedly, because they are on the street. And they have to be on the street in order to deal.

'Okay, but don't stay out too late—I'm hoping for more of your chocolate muffins in the morning,' was all I said, and even that might have been too much. Jason went back to his ovens and I sold more bread. But I didn't have a song in my heart.

At ten to one Kepler and Jon came into the bakery. Kylie saw Jon and scowled, and then caught sight of Kepler and stared.

Her little rosebud mouth dropped quite open. Her eyes were as round as a doll's.

He was a very pretty sight. He was wearing his shadow-grey shantung suit and his long grey-streaked hair was held back by a silver clip. Jon loomed behind him.

'Hello,' I said, leaning over to tip Kylie's mouth shut with a forefinger under her chin. 'Kylie, this is Kepler.'

Kepler held out a hand. Kylie took it, still unspeaking. She wasn't going to say anything, I realised.

'Come along, gentlemen, we need to net our bird. Daniel's at the chocolate shop. This way,' I said, and led them into the alley. Kylie still staring at Kepler's retreating back as we went out.

'You do make an impression,' remarked Jon. Kepler smiled deprecatingly.

'It's the suit,' he said. Jon laughed.

We lurked outside Heavenly Pleasures, one shop along on either side. I was with Kepler, contemplating ladies' underwear, and Jon was stationed near Mistress Dread's, allowing himself to be tempted by a red leather corset with black facings. And spiked nipples. Daniel joined him there.

Time passed. I pointed out the relative merits of black silk camisoles against pink taffeta to Kepler, who nodded. Daniel nudged Jon, sharing a comment on the painful effect of embracing someone wearing that corset. Then, just as I had really run out of things to say about ladies' underwear, in which my colleague could have no interest whatsoever, a slim Chinese boy in a suit slipped between us to look into the window of Heavenly Pleasures.

Kepler said something in a low voice and got no response. The boy was trying to see into the shop between the gilded clouds and cherubs. Then Jon spoke and he looked up and answered in the same tongue.

'Cantonese,' said Jon. 'Come along with me. We need to talk,' he said in English.

'But, sir…' said the boy.

Jon said something imperative, and the boy snapped to it and followed us like a lamb around the corner.

'We need to talk to you about Selima,' said Daniel in English. 'I'm employed to find out what is happening in the chocolate shop and at the moment they are blaming it all on her.'

'It is not her doing,' said the boy sternly.

'We know. Come along inside and we will talk about it. Or would you prefer to go into the cafe? It's all right. We are not trying to kidnap you,' said Jon.

The boy stared at Jon. It was incongruous, I expect, to have heard fluent Cantonese from someone as palpably Western as Jon with his Irish complexion and red hair. But when he looked at Kepler he saw someone not only Chinese but of wealth and status and that seemed to reassure him. He made up his mind.

'I only have an hour,' he said. 'I'm on my lunch break. Can we go somewhere quiet? I'm so worried about Selima.'

'My apartment,' said Jon.

The apartment reassured the boy more. So did the Chinese tea which Jon produced. The boy named himself as Brian Chung, first year accounting student at RMIT, doing work experience with a large city firm. This explained the suit. Eighteen years old. Large family in Frankston. Required to do well and support his ageing parents. Sister doing medicine at Melbourne University and two more at home doing terribly well at school. Other siblings married and in professions. Jon said this was usual.

'The Chinese want their children to have a better life than their parents, like all immigrants,' he said. 'The pressure to succeed is very heavy. Especially when the boys catch the Aussie virus and start being lazy and naughty. Happens to everyone from a strict society who comes here. Because you can't see the rules and they aren't enforced with a big stick, they conclude there aren't any. Until they find out otherwise, they tend to go wild. It wears off,' said Jon tolerantly.

'Yes, it is important that I do well. My dad never gets off my back about studying,' said Brian sullenly. 'And my sisters all get A's without even trying.'

'And then there was Selima,' prompted Jon.

'I met her when I got my sister some chocolates for her birthday,' said Brian, his face lighting up. 'I came back on my next lunch break. She liked me, too. We used to have lunch together every day I could manage it. She's clever. And her dad was just like mine. Then there was trouble at the shop and she ran away.'

'And tried to find you?' asked Jon gently.

'And Mum sent her away,' he said bitterly. 'She came to our house and asked for me and Mum shut the door in her face. And when I got home she screamed at me and then Dad grounded me.'

'That's what she was doing in Frankston,' I said. 'That's why she was there.'

'And those cousins of hers sent her away too,' said Daniel grimly.

'Where is she?' asked Brian, linking his hands in what was almost a begging gesture. 'Please. Tell me.'

'I don't know,' said Daniel. 'But when I find her, what shall I say to her from you?'

'Tell her I still love her,' said Brian stoutly. 'I don't care about any of them—my parents, her parents. Tell her if she runs away again, I'll come with her. I've got a motorbike.'

'Good boy,' approved Jon. 'Now, drink your tea, and leave it to Daniel. If anyone can find Selima, it's him.'

'Did Selima say anything to you about what was happening in the shop?' asked Daniel.

'She liked working there,' said Brian. 'She liked Juliette. She liked chocolate, too. She didn't like George, the apprentice. She really didn't like him. I don't know why. I asked her if he was harassing her, you know, for sex, and she said no. I'm scared for her.'

'Us, too,' said Daniel. 'But I think that she might be safe. Write out your contact details and I'll call you as soon as I can. She hasn't phoned you?'

'Not even messaged,' said Brian miserably. 'I don't know what my mum said to her, but it would have been bad. Mum wants us all to marry people she knows.'

'I'll find her,' said Daniel, and patted the disconsolate boy on the shoulder.

It had been an interesting morning. I could do with less interest in my life.

When I got back to the shop, Kylie had come out of her trance.

'Wasn't he hot?' she asked.

'The essence of hot,' I said.

'It would be like being left for Brad Pitt,' she reasoned. 'Anyone would leave anyone for someone that hot,' she decided.

I was glad that her feelings had not been too badly hurt. Her next comment unsettled me afresh.

'It's a pity he's gay,' she said. 'I wonder…'

'Forget about it,' I advised. 'Lots of pretty men around. You don't want to take him away from Jon, do you?'

I should know better than to say things like that. But anything else I said would only make matters worse. The day went on quietly. We finished up trading to the cheerful strains of 'James K. Polk' by They Might Be Giants, a duo I have loved ever since I heard 'Mammal'. I had made up a tape to beguile the scrubbing. I like music, just not early in the morning.

Daniel and I retired for a nap with a cat or two for company, since we were both going to be up late tonight. Daniel was playing chess, and then going on the Soup Run, and I needed to talk to the Professor and then I was dining with Janet Warren, a notorious nightbird. My naps had greatly improved in quality since Daniel had come into my life. Even Horatio agreed with me.

Chapter Twelve

We got up when it was dark to shower and dress for our various engagements. I wasn't going out, so I put on my purple and gold chrysanthemum gown. Dinner was going to be simple; chicken soup, veal olives from Grandma Chapman's recipe with mixed steamed vegetables, and chocolate muffins for dessert. Janet had always been an uncritical eater. She was built like a box, square shoulders and wide hips.

I fished the food out of the fridge, where it had been gently unfreezing all day. A few weeks ago I had had a cooking binge. Meat is a lot cheaper from the wholesale butcher's and it's just as easy to make three two-person lots of veal olives as one; same amount of washing-up and cooking time. In my kind of cooking, it's the preparation that takes the time. The actual cooking is usually long and slow and needs little attention. Winter brings out the best in the Corinna Chapman cuisine, such as it is. And life is too short to pod peas, unless you like podding peas. Which I don't.

Daniel kissed me goodbye. He was going to play this important game, which he promised to explain to me later in words of one syllable, with Kepler, and then he was going on to the Soup Run. He went out, his leather coat flaring behind him, and I slipped up the stairs to Dionysus, where I caught the Prof on his way out for dinner. He supplied me with what I wanted without asking any questions, and I came downstairs satisfied that I had Darren the God Boy over a barrel.

Then I went back to my kitchen. I got out plates and cutlery, thinking about the sad story of Selima and Brian. I couldn't see any chance of their being happy together. They would both have to ditch their families. The older I got, the more I regretted that I didn't have any family. At least I still had parents, but they were not exactly helpful. They lived in Nimbin in an earth house (with an earth-closet, yuk), made candles and lived on the dole and a more-than vegan diet consisting of windfallen fruit and potatoes that had either committed suicide, leaving signed notes, or died of old age. Which was all right for them. It was their attempt to make me live the same way that had given me frostbite and pneumonia (Mother didn't believe in shoes for children, they break their natural contact with the earth) and nearly killed me (Father didn't believe in antibiotics). If Grandma Chapman hadn't come down like a wolf on the fold and kidnapped me, telling them they weren't fit to have a child, I would probably have died. They might have agreed with Grandma because they didn't have any other children. They sent me presents for Summer Solstice and I sent them aggressively Christian Christmas cards to discourage any familiarity, like them deciding to come and live with me when the weather got cold, something my father had once threatened.

Now even Grandma Chapman was dead. My other grandparents had predeceased me. I probably had cousins but I didn't know any of them. I did, however, have lots of friends. And you get to choose your friends. The doorbell jerked me out of my foolish lamentation on my orphan state. I buzzed my friend inside.

'Corinna!' said Janet bracingly. 'Nice to see you, you've put on weight, it looks good.'

'You too,' I said, hugging her. Her hair was still short and butter yellow, going grey, I noticed. Janet is a mass of muscle and they tell me she dances divinely. She leads, of course. I don't understand why a section of the lesbian culture has taken to ballroom dancing, but there it is. I brought her inside and we sat down on the sofa. She kicked off her shoes and stretched.

'Lush apartment,' she commented. 'Hello, Horatio. You were a mere slip of a kitten when I last saw you, old boy.' She tickled his whiskers. Horatio allowed this liberty, as from an old friend.

'Why are you going to Singapore?'

'I'm a partner now,' she told me as I found the opener and the bottle of the beer she favours. Squire's. To me it tastes like an unexceptionable yeast soup, though I will always be in favour of yeast in any form. To a real beer aficionado, it tastes like nectar. I poured myself a glass of wine. Janet accepted the glass and took a deep, satisfied sip. 'So we've got these idiots on our board who think that buying into a Singaporean bank is a good idea, and I'm out to get the proof that it really isn't.'

'Certainly not,' I said. 'Not unless you want to be taking in washing by the end of the financial year.'

'So, how's your cash flow?' she asked me.

'It's good. No debts, no loans, no trouble. Even my GST is up to date,' I told her. 'Have some of these cheesy things, they're really nice. Dinner in half an hour.'

'Mel moaned a bit about us being sent to a tropical resort,' said Janet. 'She hates hot weather. I promised her an air conditioner in every room, which apparently I've got, and she does need some time to herself to finish her thesis. I'm going to throw a really big party when she finally gets rid of it. I've been living with that thesis for what seems like centuries.'

'The sapphic women?' I asked, remembering. 'In 1920s Paris?'

'The sapphic women,' she groaned. 'In Paris. In the 1920s. Every conversation, every bit of diary or poem or photo or newspaper, every reminiscence of Gertrude and Alice and the ladies of the Closerie Lilas and the Rue Madeline. It's enough to make you turn het, I tell you.' She grinned and took another handful of the cheesy things.

'That'll be the day,' I rejoined. I really had missed Janet. I couldn't imagine why I hadn't called her. Then again, she hadn't called me, either.

'Thought you might want to be alone, lick your wounds, get your new business established,' she said, answering an unspoken question as she always used to. 'Very glad when you finally did phone. What happened to that snake, your ex, what was the creep's name? James.'

'Works for a corporation into high-risk stocks and currency speculation,' I said. She snorted.

'I should have guessed as much. He'll crash and burn, one day soon. Climate's not good for high-risk. People like stuff that will last, at present, even though the returns are lower.'

'So what was that editorial talking about?' I asked. 'That's partly why I called you, I'm out of the loop. I ought to know what they are hinting about and I don't.'

'Just rumours, that's all I know,' she said slowly. 'But there is something big up there, about to fall on us out of a clear sky. The city says that it has something to do with a top accountant in Megatherium being sacked, just like that, turn in your laptop and escorted out of the building by security. No reason given. Name of Benjamin, nice bloke by all accounts. Wife and family in Kew. Rumours are rife about high-level speculation, double books, tax fraud, overextended lines of credit, even money-laundering. I didn't have anything in Megatherium but I've advised all my clients to get their money out now while they still can. But it isn't only Megatherium, though that would be bad enough, God knows. They say there's a bank in jeopardy. We haven't had a bank collapse in living memory.'

'What about Pyramid?' I asked. She snorted again.

'Building society, and under the old rules. Couldn't happen again the way it did before. No, something new and bad is on the way,' said Janet with the relish of any accountant whose advice has been heeded and whose clients are in no danger. 'Now, have I sung enough for my supper? Crack another bottle of Squire's, my dear, and feed me. I'm starving. All this talking is hungry work.'

'Coming right up,' I said.

Dinner was a great success. Janet liked the veal olives, which she said I had cooked for her before. I probably had, it was one of my favourites and froze well. Also, thumping meat with a hammer is very therapeutic if you are in a bad mood, as most of my moods had been before I left James and bought into Insula. When we reached the chocolate muffins she grinned.

'Lucky Mel isn't here,' she said. 'She says my cholesterol's too high and keeps cooking all these healthy meals. Not that they aren't tasty. But choccies of this quality don't usually get into muffins. Your apprentice?'

'His masterpiece,' I said proudly. 'Enough to get him into the guild, I reckon.' I told her about Jason and about Kylie and Gossamer and my plot to eventually persuade them to put on a few pounds. We gossiped about the people in the building, the Prof and Mrs Sylvia Dawson. Janet whistled.

'So that's where she is! How interesting.'

'Why, do you know her?'

'My dear, you really don't read the social pages, do you? Until about six months ago, she was a renowned hostess, did all the big art dinners, very prominent in charity circles. Then she just packed up, sold her house in Brighton and vanished.'

'Why?'

'No one knows,' said Janet. 'Rumour says she had a bad diagnosis, you know. Decided to distribute her estate before she died. So she came here!' she whistled again.

'Well, she must be rich, or she couldn't have just bought an apartment in Insula,' I said. 'And she's very well dressed. But she doesn't look sick. Blooming, I'd say. Takes healthy early morning walks to look at the autumn leaves.'

'Then she must have just got jack of it all,' said Janet. 'Like you did. I can relate to that. Well, it's been lovely,' she said, getting up. 'What did I do with my shoes? Oh yes, there they are.' Horatio was sitting on them. Janet dislodged him gently with one stockinged toe. 'I'm all packed, but there's always something I've forgotten. Goodnight,' she said to me, giving me another hug. 'I'll call when I get home, and perhaps we can have that thesis finishing party after all, eh?'

I saw her out. I did not see hulking identical figures called Tait and Bull or a tall thin man who could not accept that his father had died on Everest. That improved my night. Janet got into her red BMW and drove away, tossing her parking ticket onto the pile on the seat beside her. She parked where she liked and paid for it. It seemed fair enough.

I headed back towards my apartment. I paused near the lift, thinking that I might have heard a faint mew. I stopped and called, but nothing replied. The wind does tend to whistle down the elevator shaft.

I put myself into a lush rose-scented bath, and then into a padded robe which Jon had given me. Daniel rang and asked me if I would like to see the Immortal Game, and I still had some residual anxiety about him, because I said yes. I know very little about chess. But in the cause of love, I reminded myself as the elevator rose, I had once sat through nine hockey games and this couldn't be that tedious. Because nothing earthly possibly could be.

Actually, it was fascinating. No one had ever talked me through a chess game before and the big pieces were distinctive.

'Chess is about war,' said Kepler easily, making room for me on the couch. 'But there are wars and wars. There are wars by attrition, and there are wars won by sudden, brilliant moves.'

'And chess has the advantage of no blood, no death, and no famine,' put in Jon, who could not like war in any other form.

'So here we have a game by Adolf Anderssen which still ranks as one of the best ever,' said Daniel. 'It begins conventionally.'

He moved a pawn to King Four. I know that one. Black does the same, and then white moves another pawn and pawn takes pawn. So far, I got it. Anderssen moves a bishop, his opponent Kieseritsky moves his queen, check. The white king was moved.

Then the pieces began to dance. I was never going to be good enough to really understand what the board was telling me, what it was conveying to the two devotees, Kepler and Daniel. But I began, for the first time, to get a vague idea of how one could call a solution to a chess problem 'elegant'. The centre shifted, a little jerkily, emptied of pieces. Check and counter-check. The black pieces huddled by their king, unable to move. The white pieces ranged all over the board, reckless of danger, sacrificing themselves for a positional advantage. In very few moves—Daniel said there were twenty-two—the black king was trapped beyond rescue and the game was over. Half of white's pieces lay dead on the field, including the queen. But the white king had won the battle.

It was fascinating. At least it was much better than the hockey matches. When it was concluded I excused myself and went back to my apartment. I wondered if Daniel would teach me to play chess. I had always thought it the province of geeks and nerds, but it was really intriguing. Intrigued, I fell asleep.

Friday, and the only good thing about it was that tomorrow was Saturday. I ate breakfast, I read the business editorial with some understanding—Megatherium, eh? I had always heard they were sound, but not now—and fed Horatio, envying him his freedom to just go back to bed. In the unlikely event that reincarnation turns out to be true, I want to come back as a cat. A cat who owns someone like me. Meroe says that I might manage it, as with my karma I might not make it back to human. Fine with me.

When I went down to the bakery I noticed two things. One, it was dark. Two, it was entirely devoid of Jason putting on the first rising of the day. I opened the door in case he had forgotten his keys but no one was there. I hauled sacks and poured water and put on mixers and started everything working. The Mouse Police produced their mouse and rat haul—five of each and a pigeon, which was a real puzzle. I rewarded them, cleaned out their tray and saw them bounce out into the alley to seek tuna.

The day went as it had before Jason had come into my life. I had got used to having him there and I was disturbed. Could something have happened to him? He was still only fifteen. The bread rose. As the time went on I had to make the shop's muffins myself. I made blueberry, the simplest. Even then they would be but poor imitations of those from the hands of the master.

Time ticked on. I began to get very angry with Jason in direct proportion to how anxious I was about him. Bread went into the oven flabby and came out shiny. Megan the courier tootled at the alley door before I was ready for her.

'Just a moment,' I said. 'My apprentice hasn't come in today and I'm behind.'

'Jason?' she said in surprise. 'Here, let me help you with those racks. You read out, I'll check.'

We distributed the bread between all the trays for different restaurants and Megan honked merrily as she gunned her rickshaw engine.

'He really likes being here,' she assured me. 'He'll be back.'

I hoped she was right. And I could still do the day's baking by myself, which was cheering in a way. I had stacked the shop racks before Goss arrived to open the place to the public.

'Where's Jason?' she asked.

'I don't know,' I said grimly, and she didn't ask any more.

I was just resolving to fire the little bastard as soon as I saw him again when Daniel came walking down Calico Alley, with Chas Li at his side. He was carrying something, a mannequin, perhaps, with legs that dangled and a head that lolled.

But it wasn't a mannequin. It was Jason. Daniel put him down on the Mouse Police's stack of flour sacks. He was filthy and moaning.

'What's happened to him?' I asked.

'Too big a hit,' said Daniel. 'Often happens when they go back for a taste. They take the same amount that they took before and their system won't tolerate it. He's been narcanned on the spot. Should come out of it soon. We found him in a skip behind the market.'

'I found him,' corrected Chas. 'But I don't understand. I swear he never meant to get back on the gear.'

'If you look at his arm,' said Daniel, 'you will see the fresh puncture mark amongst all those old tracks.'

Chas stuck to his opinion. 'Yeah, but he came to help me unpack. And he did. I sold all my shirts before anyone noticed

I was there and we took off for some food. Some of the guys he used to know were at the food van and Jason bought them all a hamburger. They talked for a while then he said he had to get back and I thought he left. But one of the losers said something about him, that people had been looking for him, and I got worried so I went searching for him this morning when I had another load to collect. I heard him in that skip. He was groaning. And then Daniel came with the Soup Run and I made him look inside.'

'And I got an ambulance and they gave him narcan. Then I brought him here because I don't want him in hospital.'

'Jason?' I asked, shaking him not very gently by the shoulder. 'Jason?'

His eyes opened a slit and then closed again. He smelt like he had indeed spent the night in a garbage skip. Daniel was looking like a dark angel who finds his charges very obstinately bent on their own destruction.

'He'll be thirsty,' he said. 'Get some water, Corinna, will you? Thanks for coming along, Chas.'

'No probs,' said Chas. 'I'll just go and see how my brother Kep is doing. Then I need to get back…'

'Of course,' said Daniel. Chas went. He stopped at the door.

'Don't be too mad with him,' he said to me. 'He didn't mean to, I'll swear.'

'All right,' I said, and Chas went out, borrowing a muffin on the way.

Jason moaned. I was not feeling sympathetic. But heroin addicts will be heroin addicts and he did seem to be in distress. I knelt down and raised his head on my arm.

'Drink some water,' I said. He drank. I held him until he was steady enough to sit up and take the cup.

'Look at his wrists,' said Daniel abruptly. I looked. They had red rings around them, darkening even as I looked.

I was so angry with Jason that I could barely speak. 'He's bruised all over, to judge from what I can see.'

Daniel said, 'Excuse me,' and caught me by the wrist. 'Struggle,' he said, and I struggled as he tried to lay my arm out flat, endeavouring to straighten my elbow. When he let me go I had red marks on my wrist and forearm in identical places to my narcanned apprentice. I stared at them.

'Jesus, Daniel, do you mean someone did this to him?' My fury with Jason needed another place to go and it had found one. 'Someone held him down and injected him with heroin?'

'At least two someones,' Daniel answered. 'Jason's agile and strong and wary. It would have needed two of them.'

'And you will help me kill them?' I asked politely.

'With pleasure,' he grinned mirthlessly, showing white teeth.

'How much is this going to set him back?' I asked. 'Will he go straight back to what he was?'

'No telling,' Daniel answered. Jason drank the rest of the water and found his voice.

'Sorry,' he said abjectly, and began to cry. 'Sorry, Corinna.'

'That's all right,' I said, patting his hair into which squashed plums had infiltrated. 'It wasn't your fault, Jason.'

'Went there to big-note myself,' he mumbled. 'Show the guys that I could make it. Then they caught me. Two of them. The Twins, Daniel, it was the Twins. And they shot me full of gear and asked me questions, and I told them, I told them all they wanted to know. Oh, shit,' said Jason, and burst into painful weeping which racked his thin body like convulsions.

I let him cry for a few minutes.

'Right, into my bath,' I ordered. 'Breakfast at Cafe Delicious. Stuff those clothes into the washer.'

'You aren't going to sack me?' he asked pathetically, squinting out of his one good eye. There were streaks of dead fruit on his face.

'No,' I said. He dragged me close to hear a dark secret.

'I liked it,' he whispered. 'I liked it. It felt good.'

'Of course it did,' I said. 'That's why you ended up an addict in the first place. That doesn't mean that you are an addict now, does it? Come along, there's bread to sell. Daniel, can you help

Jason? Hot water and the antiseptic soap will make some of those bruises better and there's betadine and the bruise ointment in my bathroom. Bustle along, gentlemen, time's a-wasting.'

For some reason, Daniel hugged me. I went into the bakery and explained what had happened to Goss, who was shocked.

'Have you seen any hulking big middle-aged men with moustaches around?' I asked her.

'No,' she said. 'Moustaches are gross.'

That seemed to dispose of moustaches as a secondary sexual attractant.

'If you do, come and tell me right away. Daniel is looking after Jason and then we have to go to the prison again, though I hope it will be for the last time, God have mercy on us, as Sister Mary would say. Can you manage the shop? I've sent out all the stuff with the carrier. And have you got a big cross and another clunky silver pendant I can borrow?'

'I can manage,' she said. 'I just sell bread until there isn't any left and then I shut up shop. I can even do the banking, now. Is Jason going to be all right?'

'I don't know. As soon as he can tell us a coherent story, we'll call Lepidoptera and he can tell it to her. And the persons who did this to him are going to be really sorry.'

'You go, Corinna!' Goss encouraged me. 'I didn't like Jason to start with but he sort of grows on you. Like I'll get you the stuff,' she said, and went out. Goss and Kylie buy jewellery as some people buy drugs—relentlessly. When Goss came back with a silver cross which would have repelled both vampires and werewolves—a sort of all purpose talisman—I hung it round my neck, along with a heavy Aquarius symbol which I tucked into my shirt. Then I went upstairs to find out how the patient was doing.

Splashing announced that Daniel had inserted Jason into a hot bath. I could smell Dettol. I expected that it would sting but the splashing did not subside. Daniel came out, rolling down his sleeves.

'He's filthy in a way which words cannot properly describe,' he told me. 'His clothes are in the washer even as we speak and

I think we may have to shoot his sneakers before they go out and cause untold harm.'

'Agreed,' I said.

'And as for his state of mind, he just now told me that he was starving hungry, and I consider that a hopeful sign.'

'Good. Get him dried and dressed in his baker's clothes, and feed him a trucker's special. Then leave him in the bakery. Goss will look after him. She's actually sorry that he's hurt, which is more than I would have expected of Goss. I've got to practise my Darren speech.'

'I wish I knew what you and the respected Sir John Holt had in mind,' he said quizzically.

'Sorry. How was your chess game?'

'It's a wonderful game, the Immortal, as you saw,' he told me. 'We had excellent Chinese food which Jon cooked, and next week we are going to play the Evergreen game. Jon, like you, doesn't play chess. Then it was lucky that I was the heavy on the Soup Run last night, because that brought me to the Vic market just in time for Chas to grab me and make me lift the lid off that skip.'

'Meroe would say that it was Meant,' I said.

'Probably was,' he agreed.

We parted. Me to the bakery, he to continue with Jason's ablutions. The morning had been full of incident and it wasn't nine o'clock yet. Mrs Dawson came in, a picture in a dark peach jumper and dark brown trousers. Why hadn't I guessed that she was a society hostess? Mostly because I had never met one before. Now I came to look at her, I could easily imagine her in a tailored gown, making the invited artists comfortable, listening to everyone, intercepting quarrels before they began, even arranging the food and drinks and making sure that vegetarians were catered for and that the cook remembered that Mrs Ambassador Thing was allergic to peanuts. She was born to run a large establishment. Perhaps she had indeed just got tired of it. Her children were grown and gone and her husband was dead. And everyone, without exception, gets sick of artists eventually.

I supplied her with a blueberry muffin and a loaf of rye.

'A fine morning, Corinna,' she said.

'So it is,' I lied. I hadn't even looked at the morning. She patted my hand decisively.

'You should always notice what sort of morning it is, Corinna,' she told me. 'We only get a certain number of mornings.'

That was true enough. Goss and I supplied the early morning crowd. People still bought my muffins, though they wouldn't know until they bit into them that Jason hadn't made them. Then, I feared, they would know. I heard Jason and Daniel go out the back door to Cafe Delicious. A good solid meal inside the boy would make him feel much better. Poor Jason. He had told them everything they asked when they had raped his veins with that needle full of chemical joy. What had they asked? What did they want to know which Jason might be expected to know?

I was getting angry again. I checked the washer. It was groaning. I saw its point. Had they got Jason's keys? He only had the keys to the bakery door and in any case it could not be opened if I shot the bolts. They couldn't copy them because they were security keys which needed the permission of the keyholder—what was I saying? These were people who didn't ask for permission. They took.

No, here was Jason's wallet, his keys and…what did I have here? It was a small tinfoil package. I scrabbled it open. It contained maybe a saltspoon full of white powder. The bastards. They had reawakened an addiction, and they meant him to find this in his pocket, an unbearable temptation. I dropped the foil into a plastic bag and put it in my desk, turning the key in the lock. Letty White needed to see this. And Jason didn't.

Of course, he could have bought it for himself, or some of his loser friends might have given it to him. In any case, it was staying out of his reach. The Twins would keep for the present.

I gathered my big thick book, bound in black leather, and checked that my script was still inside. I was gambling that Darren the God Boy was Latin illiterate, and also that he really wasn't possessed, because I don't believe in possession except as a plot device. And not in the kind of book which I customarily read. I hoped I was right.

Jason came back into the bakery. He was clean and shiny and fully fed and he launched himself at me and gave me one of his lightning, throttling hugs.

'Thanks,' he said. I hugged him. I could still feel all his ribs. It was going to take more than the heroic efforts of Cafe Delicious to make Jason look like Robby Coltrane any time soon. He was vibrating a little, not badly enough to call it a tremor.

'You all right to be left?' I asked. 'Daniel and I need to go to MAP. To disenchant Darren the God Boy.'

'I'm all right,' he mumbled.

'Help Goss,' I instructed, and we went out into the alley, where Sister Mary's small blue indestructible Mazda squatted like a heap of old wreckage waiting for the tow truck.

It was terrifying, driving with Sister Mary. She steered mostly by faith, which was also all that was holding the car together— with perhaps some rubber cement and a few bits of wire.

'I always worry that the car will find out I'm a Jew and divine protection will be withdrawn,' Daniel said as we scooted around a corner.

'Not to worry,' Sister Mary sang out over the crunching of the gears. 'This is an ecumenical vehicle!'

'Falls to pieces in every religion,' I said, reaching for the panic strap. It broke off in my hand.

I was still staring at it as we pulled up outside MAP and got out. Daniel rewired one of the doors, which had fallen off its hinges when he unwisely tried to open it. Sister Mary consulted Halloran, who was waiting at the door.

'All set?' she asked.

'This had better work,' he said, leading us through the security checks.

'It will,' she said. 'I have perfect faith in the Lord and Corinna. In that order.'

More than I did, but I kept my doubts to myself. Sister Mary had the two bottles I had asked her to bring and I had my script and my bible. Thus equipped, we went forth to do battle with the devil.

'They've had him to the hospital for tests,' said Halloran as we walked along the Kafka corridor. 'Nothing at all wrong, they say, no brain malfunction, no epilepsy.'

'The malfunction is in his nasty little mind,' Sister Mary said, 'not in his soul. Is he still being a snake?'

'Yes.' Halloran led us into a larger room, which had a video screen and another no smoking sign approximately the size of Texas. Perversely, as soon as I saw that sign I longed for a cigarette. I was still addicted to nicotine; ought I to throw nasturtiums at poor Jason? I gave up smoking, he could give up heroin.

There was a table in the middle of the room. It was of lightweight plastic, presumably so it would not cause damage if someone threw it. I put down the book, the bottles of water and the silver cross.

Nails was brought in and a guard sat him down near the wall, where he could see anything that went on. I did not speak to him. He didn't speak either, except to say, 'Dude,' to Daniel.

Sister Mary took a deep breath and so did I.

We heard the hissing before he came into sight. Well, well, Darren the God Boy had removed most of his clothes and was now patterned everywhere he could reach with the half-moons of his own fingernails. They looked disturbingly like scales. He slithered as though he had no bones, sliding along the floor. The guards, thoroughly unnerved, lifted him into a chair where he slumped, hissing occasionally and flicking out his tongue. Sister Mary made the sign of the cross.

The effect was instant. Darren reared up like a cobra about to strike. From somewhere inside him came a voice, a treacly voice, most unlike his own.

'Who comes here?'

'One who is not afraid of you,' said Sister Mary, and I believed her.

'I have taken this man for my own,' said the thick voice. 'Because he is worthy.'

'You've got to do something about your hiring protocols,' I said, and the strange eyes turned to me. He moved his whole body to turn his head, as though he really was a snake. I splashed him with the contents of my bottle of water, which had been marked 'spring water'. He laughed.

Sister Mary began to pray. 'Veni Creator Spiritus,' she said, and Darren writhed and struggled, until the guards brought leg irons and handcuffs and secured him to his chair. She sprinkled him with water from her bottle, marked 'holy water', and he twisted and writhed. I dropped the silver cross over his head and he screamed until I took it away. I palmed it and replaced it with the Aquarius symbol. He screamed again.

Then it was my turn. 'Gallia in tres partes divisa est,' I said. Darren shrieked and the voice begged for mercy. 'Arma virumque cano,' I added. Darren executed a spectacular writhe and screamed, 'No! No!'

'Si vis pace bellum para. Caveat emptor,' I finished, and first Daniel and then Sister Mary began to laugh. She laughed so hard that she had to sit down. Then she reached for the holy water bottle and took a gulp. Halloran looked shocked. Nails, who was not stupid, looked as though enlightenment was about to dawn on him.

'Give it up, mate,' Daniel advised Darren. 'You are so entirely sprung that I doubt anyone in the world has ever been that sprung before. The first water that Corinna splashed on you. That was real holy water. Got that? The stuff in the water bottle was genuine holy water and you laughed it off. The stuff in the holy water bottle was spring water, and I could do with a swig too, Sister.'

'The words?' asked Nails alertly.

'Sister Mary was praying,' I said. 'I was saying that Gaul was divided into three parts, that of arms and the man I sing, that if you want peace prepare for war, and that the buyer should beware. So unless someone has elevated Julius Caesar, Virgil and the anonymous writer of Latin maxims to sainthood, he is faking. And we have proved it,' I said, looking into Nails' cynical eyes under the perforated eyebrows. 'He reacted identically to the cross and the Zodiac sign. We've got him, haven't we?'

Nails stood up. He did not speak to me but to Daniel. 'Dude,' he said. 'You got a real bright old lady. And a nun on your side. Remind me not to give you any shit.'

'I'll remind you,' said Daniel.

We hadn't been looking at Darren. We turned at a thud as he fell to the floor.

'Oh no, not again,' exclaimed Sister Mary. 'Darren, don't you learn?'

'That looks genuine,' observed Daniel, as the chained body jerked and whimpered. 'Yes, foam coming from his mouth. Get something to put between his teeth. And call the police surgeon. It looks to me like Darren is having a real fit at last.'

'God have mercy on him,' said Sister Mary. And meant it.

They carried Darren out. 'Are you convinced now, Halloran?' Sister Mary demanded of the guard.

'Oh yes, Sister, God love you, I'm convinced. You've been on TV, did you know?' he told us. 'Closed circuit. Whole prison's been watching. The heat'll go out of this now. Thank you,' he said.

Sister Mary offered us a lift home in her ecumenical machine, but for some reason we preferred to walk.

'Sooner or later even the Holy Spirit will desert that heap of rust,' I said, fitting myself under Daniel's arm.

'And then there will be a little sighing noise and nothing left but a pile of red dust,' he replied. 'Nails is right.'

'In what?'

'I have got a very bright old lady,' he said, and kissed me, in Spencer Street, in full daylight. And I kissed him back.

Chapter Thirteen

I went back to Earthly Delights. Daniel went to lurk in Heavenly Pleasures and check out the customers. Trading was good but we ran out of bread early.

'See?' said Jason. 'You need me.'

'I know that,' I told him. 'How do you feel?'

'Buzzed,' he said frankly. 'I'm going home for some sleep once I've cleaned up. I never slept in a skip before, not even when things were real bad.'

'Nothing to recommend it?' I asked as lightly as I could.

'Nah. Cosy, though. But there were rats.'

He showed me a wound on his hand where he had been nibbled. T.S. Eliot rose into my disgusted mind. 'I thought I was in rat's alley, where the dead men left their bones.' I was suddenly so angry with the Twins that I could have killed them. Jason backed away a pace.

'I'm going to call Letty White and you will tell her all about it,' I said. 'I know you don't like cops but if Chas hadn't found you, Jason, what would have happened next? You know that market well.'

'They would have emptied the skips,' he said, going pale. 'Into them trucks which crunch the rubbish to mush.'

'Quite,' I said, and left him to drink coffee while I called Senior Constable White. I had words I wanted to say to her. She knew that we were in all likelihood harbouring someone in our building whom lots of people—people with serious money—would like to remove. Permanently. Before he could, as it happened, testify? Janet Warren had told me about a top accountant who had been abruptly fired and made to turn in his laptop. What if he had taken all the company records with him on floppy disks? If our recluse was this accountant, then Letty was deliberately exposing us to danger. Why wasn't he in a proper witness protection program, hiding in Shepparton under a false beard?

She came, listened carefully to what Jason had to say, and made copious notes. I shut the shop and sent Kylie and Jason to do the banking. When the door was closed and the shutters down, I opened the drawer and gave Lepidoptera the plastic bag with the foil in it.

'That was in Jason's pocket,' I told her. 'No reason to think that he put it there. Now, Senior Constable White, I've heard an interesting story from my friend who is an accountant and I'd like your opinion of it. Shall we go up to my apartment?'

'Here's good,' she said, leaning on a mixing tub. 'Tell me.'

I told her everything Janet Warren had told me. At the end of it I said, 'And I've just denatured Darren the God boy.'

'I heard. Good work,' she approved.

'He's sick, so Daniel couldn't talk to him. But I don't believe he had a lot to do with what's been happening here. Someone has been trying to find something, if not someone. The bomb threat got us all out on the street in our jammies with everything we hold most dear. The Prof took his Aristophanes translation, his life's work. Kylie and Goss took their make-up. Cherie Holliday took her father and her Pumpkin bear. I would have taken my Grandma's bluebird brooch and my photos if I'd had the time. And my pasta douro yeast. Are you seeing a pattern here?'

'Go on,' she said evenly.

'Our Mr Recluse was found in the alley after the bomb threat, all beaten up and robbed,' I said. 'Someone searched him rather roughly for something they meant to find. And I don't believe they found it, did they?'

'Maybe,' she murmured. 'Go on, Ms Chapman.'

'I think that they are still looking,' I said through my teeth, 'because my apprentice was assaulted, forcibly injected with heroin, and bled of everything he knew about this building and the people in it. Then they threw him in a skip as though he was garbage. So now these two gentlemen know all that Jason knows, and Mr White is still here and still a threat, and what are you going to do about it? Is he the accountant who was sacked from Megatherium? Did he take something away with him—proof of fraud, perhaps? And if so why isn't it in a safe in that ugly police building? What are you doing about protecting us?'

'I can't answer any questions,' said Letty White. 'Except that you are not alone. You are never alone. You might not see your protectors, but they are there. Jason was out by himself. We are keeping an eye on him now. He's safe enough.'

'That isn't an acceptable answer,' I seethed.

'I know,' she said sadly. 'But it's the only answer I can give you.'

'I just had a horrible thought about why the proof isn't in a safe in St. Kilda Road,' I told her

She looked at me. I thought I saw a faint nod of the head, but it could have been a trick of the light. Then she gave me a half-salute and was gone through the bakery into the shop.

I kicked the mixing tub hard enough to hurt my foot. Anyone who thinks of the terrible buying power of illegal drugs doesn't usually consider how much more money might be in corporate crime. One gigantic shipment of heroin might coin a million or so in a very hazardous operation with a good chance of total loss. Bleeding a corporate account might return you a million every day until you are caught. Vast, impossible sums of money change hands, all electronic and therefore somehow unreal, every trading day, through company transfers, currency futures, and the stock exchange. And Mr White's proof, whatever it was, floppy disks perhaps, was still here because that vast buying power could also buy—a police officer? That was a nasty thought. No wonder Lepidoptera looked pained. The same would apply, of course, to bribing a bank officer who cared for a safety deposit.

And this state of affairs had almost got my Jason killed. It was the skip which made me most angry. They had thrown him away as though he was rubbish.

Jason came back into the shop, ran water into his bucket, and started the cleaning. This was therapeutic and I joined him. We scrubbed vengefully. When he was mopping his way out I heard him singing a little song. I had heard it before. He had made it up himself. Jason's song had caught my attention because of the last line. It had a sort of boppy tune.

'I travel along,' sang Jason. 'Singing my song. You may say it's wrong...' There was a pause as he emptied the bucket down the drain.

'Bugger yer,' he concluded. And laughed. Then he gathered up his clean clothes, gave me a casual wave, and went back to his hostel to get some sleep.

I had to tell someone about Mr Recluse, and Daniel was my best bet. Meroe had tried to understand the share market once and it had given her a headache. But I could go and tell her about Darren, so I went to do that.

<>◇<>

Meroe had been delighted by the disenchantment of Darren, though she was most pleased, I think, by the fact that I had actually read all that witchcraft history which she had given me.

'If I could find a picture of Sir John Holt I'd put it on the wall,' she said. 'That was well done, Corinna. The last thing a place like a prison needs is a witchcraft panic. Now, Bella,' she said to her black cat, 'you take care of the shop for me.'

She put the black cat down on her chair and Belladonna curled up into a black cushion. Meroe began to unpack several boxes which occupied the space behind the curtain.

'I've found out something about our recluse,' I said. She put her finger to her lips, turning away from the door. Then she laid a hand on my arm and conducted me out into the street.

'Walls, as the Professor would say, have ears. What have you found out?'

'That he might be a sacked accountant.' I told her the whole story as Janet had told it to me. Meroe shook her head.

'That man has shutters behind his eyes. That could be it. He is certainly afraid. I shall enquire of the spirits. Nothing to be done right now, Corinna, but beware of speech. Speech is silver. Silence is golden,' she said.

Hungarians. They do have a streak of paranoia. I took my leave very quietly and went to Heavenly Pleasures. The shop was busy. Juliette whispered that she had removed all the boxes and refilled them, so that no nasty surprises should be expected. I didn't tell her that this would not make a shred of difference if her stock was contaminated. I went through to find Daniel sitting behind a screen with a notepad on his knee, recording the customers. Behind him moulds banged on the metal table with unnecessary force. Vivienne didn't like having people in her kitchen, even gorgeous dark handsome men like Daniel. She was relieving her feelings by scolding George, who, today, could not do a thing right.

'George! That is a milk mixture!' she yelled. 'George! Get the pralines off the heat! George, you clumsy idiot, clean that up at once!'

Mutinously George got the mop and bucket to clean up the toffee he had spilled when Vivienne had shrieked close to his ear. Was he really confident of being able to marry this woman? And who would want to, when she was prone to moods like this one? I moved gently away from anything she might throw and leaned on the wall behind Daniel.

'Darling,' called a rich, deep voice from the shop. 'Vivi, you aren't going to come and throw something at your old uncle for old time's sake?'

I peeked out and saw an elderly gentleman in a coat with an astrakhan collar, smiling fondly at Juliette. She was dimpling. Vivienne came out of the kitchen and threw herself into his embrace. He patted her back with his beautiful, elegant hands.

'Darling, you're having a bad time,' he said consolingly. He had the most chocolatey voice I had ever heard and eyes that twinkled with benevolence, like Father Christmas. 'Come along. Let Uncle take you out to lunch, Vivi. You let your apprentice alone. He'll be all right if you stop screaming at him. Come along, get your coat, it's cold out there,' he said, and got his way.

Vivienne collected her coat and allowed him to lead her out into the street. Behind me I heard George say something fervent in Greek. Daniel chuckled.

'No, she isn't, and that's not a nice thing to say about a lady,' he said. 'Especially your employer.' I heard George swear. He obviously didn't know that Daniel spoke Greek. 'That was the magic man?' Daniel continued.

'Yes, Uncle Max,' said Juliette. 'He comes in and takes one of us to lunch sometimes. We can't both go, of course. He's our only relative and I don't know what we'd do without him when Viv gets into one of her moods. George, can you manage with what work you've got?'

'Yes,' said George, who had clearly decided that silence was indeed golden, and went back to filling moulds with pineapple cream. Daniel stretched a hand back to pat the only bit of me he could reach, which was my hip. I wriggled.

'I'm going to be here all day,' he said. 'Have you something else you want to do?'

'Am I putting you off?' I asked.

He said, 'I don't like people standing behind me,' and of course, an ex-soldier wouldn't. I did have something to do, as it happened.

'I'll be back in Insula,' I said. 'Dine with me?'

'Delighted,' said Daniel and I went out, taking and paying for a small box of chocolates on the way. I needed to talk to Cherie Holliday, because she probably knew where Selima was, and it was time we got this sorted out. If Selima didn't want to talk to Daniel, perhaps she would talk to me.

Cherie Holliday lives with her father in Daphne, number 4A, opposite Mrs Dawson in Minerva, 4B. I could hear Gilbert and Sullivan's 'Ruddigore' from 4B and something raucous and heavily accented from 4A. I rang. Cherie answered. She was wearing an apron and was more than a little floury.

'Oh, Corinna, good, come in and help me. I've done something wrong with this dough,' she exclaimed.

The upper apartments have bigger kitchens than mine and this one had seen some hard service since Holliday went off the booze and started cooking again. When he moved in, his fridge had contained nothing but frozen dinners and bottles of Stoli. Now the kitchen had ropes of hanging garlic and chilis, a lot more pots, and that scent of dishes having been made and dishes in prospect which every working kitchen gets. Cherie clicked the CD player off with her one clean finger.

She was attempting to make bread, and it wasn't going well. The dough slumped, grey and depressed, at the bottom of the bowl. I poked it. It wasn't absolutely chilled so it might be salvaged.

'I wanted to make coffee scrolls because Dad likes them,' she said. 'But it isn't rising.'

'Yeast is a plant,' I said, falling back into my instructor's manner. 'It needs heat to grow, just like a sprout or a blade of grass. This environment is too cold, so it's sulking. Have you got an electric blanket on your bed? Go and turn it on full.'

Cherie came back. 'You're going to put dough in my bed?'

'Not like it is,' I explained. 'Got a big new plastic bag? Good. Now, shove the whole thing, bowl and all, into that bag, Leave it some room to breathe, and then put it into your bed. Give it ten minutes and we shall see. Got the icing sugar and the coffee? If that dough is cactus, we can make another lot. Why don't we tidy the kitchen a bit while we wait?' I asked, picking up a dish cloth. There was flour on every conceivable surface.

'I dropped the box,' Cherie told me. 'It spreads a lot.'

'Believe me, I know,' I said. 'Lucifer tore open ten kilos of the stuff and I thought we'd never get him clean, or the bakery either. How is Calico?'

'She stays in the parlour while I'm cooking,' said Cherie. I had always thought Calico to be a sensible cat. 'She doesn't even seem to miss her kittens,' said Cherie.

'Cats are very sanguine,' I said, wiping flour off the stove.

'What does that mean?'

'Optimistic,' I said. 'Expecting the best.'

'But what can have happened to Soot?' asked Cherie, clutching her dustpan to her bosom. She had more bosom than Kylie and the gesture was very affecting.

'I don't know,' I said. 'Sometimes you never know the end of the story.'

'Yes,' she said sadly. Determined, abused, dark-haired Cherie had run away from a father who did not believe her to find herself a new name, a job and a place to live. She knew all about what can happen to stray creatures in the city. Her eyes clouded over for a moment. 'So she could be dead.'

'We didn't find a body,' I reminded her.

'She's only a little cat. There mightn't be much to find.'

'True, but cats have a way of not dying,' I said, truthfully.

'Then where is she? Is Soot another story we don't get to hear the end of?'

'Tell me about Selima,' I said, changing the subject before we both burst into tears. 'Will she speak to us?'

'You, maybe,' she replied. 'There was this boy.'

'We know about the boy. Jon talked to him. Rides a motorbike. His name's Brian.'

'You know a lot,' she said suspiciously.

'It's Daniel's job. He's a private investigator. Mine too, I suppose. Ask her if she'll talk to me. Tell her her job is safe and her boy still loves her. Is she safe where she is, Cherie?'

Cherie wrung her flour-covered hands.

'I don't know where she is. I took her to the hostel where I lived when I was…you know, before I found Dad again. It was all right. Not flash, but cheap and safe. But she left there. All I've got is a phone number and mostly the phone is switched off. But I'll keep trying.'

'And I'll put her back on the Soup Run's watch list. She must be somewhere.'

'I suppose.' Cherie didn't sound convinced.

'Now, go get the dough, and let's see how it looks,' I encouraged.

The dough was rising. It wasn't the best bread dough I had ever seen, but it would do. I watched as Cherie kneaded it and then put the dough back to rise again in its flat rectangle, ready to be filled, rolled, cooked and iced. Anyway, whatever the standard of cuisine, Andy Holliday would eat those rolls as though they were manna. He had lost his daughter for years and then found her again.

'Where is your father?' I asked.

'He went out to his AA meeting,' she said. 'He's trying really hard. Falls off the wagon a lot,' she said indulgently. 'But not hard. He hasn't been real drunk since I came home. He might even make a social drinker, that's what Alateen say. They say he might not even be an alcoholic.'

'Good,' I said. 'Don't forget to call me if you can find Selima. It's important. No one is accusing her of anything.' I said.

'Cross your heart?' she asked me, half playfully, half serious.

I crossed my heart, and left her to finish cooking. One thing amused me. After eating those coffee scrolls, Andy would really appreciate my bread.

And back I went to my own apartment, feeling at a really loose end. I knew what was before me. At a loose end, I go out, or stay in and read, or possibly cook. At a very loose end, I channel-surf cable until I find bad sci-fi. At a really loose end, I do the mending.

I dragged out the sewing machine, worked out what had gone wrong with it last time—never put the machine away unthreaded, Grandma Chapman said, and I always did—found the scissors and a reasonable match of thread, and got out the rubbish bag full of mending. I would keep the rubbish bag for the things which, on later examination, I might find not worth the effort.

This certainly applied to the replacement of the zipper in an old pair of trousers which were too tight anyway. I found a crochet hook and hooked up the threads in the elbow of a rather nice plum-coloured jumper which Horatio had beguiled a cold day last winter by unknitting. I meditated on the maxim that it is always harder to create than destroy, and how well this applied to ravelling up an unravelled piece of knitting. I managed to tie off most of the ends eventually and laid it aside to wash. Had it really been that long ago since I did the mending?

Well, it was going to get done. I could do nothing about all the problems I faced until there was what the Prof calls a *novus actus interveniens*—a new thing happening—so I repaired tears, sewed up hems, replaced buttons and patched holes. I put on a talking book to listen to, one of Jade Forrester's early romances. Horatio took up his resting position on the already mended clothes, as having me continually dragging a dead garment out from under him interrupted his repose and his dignity.

Generations of women had sewed as I was sewing, listening to someone read aloud to them from, say, the novels of Sir Walter Scott. They were much better needleworkers than me, but then, I couldn't stand Walter Scott. Not even Rob Roy. Walter Scott. Now there was an idea. I thought about it as I sewed.

There is a comfort in mending which is not present in making. The garment is useless as it is, but with ten minutes work it will be wearable again. I stitched pieces of elastic into my apron strings, so that they would not snap under the strain. I repaired my favourite silk jacket, the lining of which had been lightly shredded by Horatio, who liked the sound of silk tearing through his claws. He only likes to shred really thin silk, so the brocade and embroidery had survived. I threw out a couple of socks which I couldn't really have been meaning to reheel. I sewed up the split back seam of one shirt and the split side seam of another, which I am ashamed to say I had kept wearing for months after I had begun to feel a breeze around my midriff. I harvested safety pins, straight pins and several staples from my makeshift repairs.

I threw out three pairs of de-elasticated knickers. I mended a hole in a trouser pocket through which I must have lost a small fortune in change. I contemplated the hardest task, which was putting a very careful patch on my favourite throw rug. It had fallen too close to a candle one night, but luckily had not caught fire. How on earth was I going to fix this? I stared at it as the copious blue folds fell around me. I really had missed that rug. The reader went on through an intensely romantic passage and I sighed, got up and made myself a cup of coffee. I brought it back into the parlour, thinking.

Aha! A solution! I shortened the whole thing by a hand's breadth and made a new hem, which solved the problem of not being able to match the material, and gave me back my mohair rug. I rehooked a bra. I sewed up a pillowcase.

The day was getting on. Usually doing the mending produced results faster than this. I put on the lights and continued. New buttons on my old red jacket. Throw out six pairs of laddered tights. Dismiss any idea of fixing that extremely old t-shirt with holes in. Perhaps Chas Li would sell me another one.

Then there was really nothing left. I shook the bag. It was empty. A large pile of resurrected clothes lay ready to be washed and worn again. Horatio yawned, showing the points of his ivory teeth in his red mouth, like a small, bored vampire.

Well, there was still Buffy. If all else failed, I could watch TV. I shoved all the washables into the washer, and fed the Mouse Police while I was there. I put the dry-cleanables into the dry-cleaning pile, which I would convey to Mr Hong of the One Hour Dry Cleaners eventually—certainly before next year. I dislodged Horatio and took the rubbish bag into the spare bedroom, along with the sewing machine and all the supplies.

Nothing, not a phone message, not a ring at the door. My never-fail method of making something happen had entirely failed.

Still, I had done all the mending. Glowing with conscious pride, I went to inspect the fridge to see what I had to offer a man who had been sitting in a chocolate shop all day. Something with a strong taste. A pasta sauce, perhaps, with garlic and herbs.

If I had time I could make chicken with a hundred garlics, a dish never forgotten. For that I needed a chicken. Which I had. And—oh dear—a chicken brick. A terracotta casserole with a tightly fitting terracotta lid in which the baked chicken steams and becomes so tender that it can be eaten with a spoon. And I knew I had one somewhere.

Daniel came in to find me in the midst of every dish, slide, pot, saucepan and casserole I owned, which meant that I was surrounded.

'Hello,' I said. 'I'm looking for a pot.'

'You seem to have been very successful,' he replied.

'Another pot,' I told him. 'I was going to cook chicken with a hundred garlics but I must have put it away right at the back of…aha!'

It was a good day for Aha!. I had had occasion to say it several times. I dragged out the chicken brick in triumph and then looked at the time. Six. Far too late to start that dish. I had to soak the brick overnight so that it wouldn't crack in the oven, something I had temporarily forgotten.

'But I can make it tomorrow,' I said, getting up. 'Let's just stuff all these back in the cupboards.'

'You've been doing enough cooking,' said Daniel, kneeling down to help me. 'This looks like a nice pot. I'll have this one.'

We shoved the others, clanging, back into their homes. Daniel put his pot on the table and produced a shopping bag. It seemed to contain mostly onions.

'Onion soup?' I asked intelligently.

'Good guess. I've brought the baguette from the shop, and I've got gruyère cheese, and all I need now is a sharp knife, a chopping board, and a little cognac.'

'For the soup?' I asked, finding the bottle. He poured himself a glass.

'First, for me,' he said. 'Then for the soup.'

He looked tired and discouraged. 'We don't have to cook,' I said. 'We can order a pizza, or any other sort of food.'

'You don't trust my cooking?' His mouth quirked at the corner.

I kissed him. There were dark shadows under his eyes. 'You look worn out. I thought you might like to rest rather than chop onions.'

'I like chopping onions,' he replied. 'And right now I'd like to make onion soup for you.'

'Good,' I said. 'I'll get out of your way and work up an appetite.'

Horatio had already voted with his paws. He doesn't like the smell of onions. I joined him on the couch with the blue mohair throw rug and we turned on the television. The finance report came on.

'The All-Ords fell three points today,' said the smiling presenter. 'The price of oil is making all the markets jittery.'

Well, something was making the Australian market jittery. Usually stable stocks were rising and falling and even the staples, the blue-chips, were looking a little battered. Janet Warren had been right, as was her habit. Something nasty was afoot.

I thought of telling Daniel about it, but it would require too much explanation. The market works on sandbox politics, and something was making the children nervous. The approach of a big bully? Or a thunderstorm?

Coincidentally, the weatherman, after reminding us all to save water, told Horatio and me that a storm front was approaching. Hail, lightning, rain. Abandon any garden parties. Bring in the washing. I had known that from the way Horatio had been washing his ears and whiskers in an irritated way, as though they had developed a kink which would not be smoothed. He reacts the same way to the Grand Prix.

Delicious smells were wafting from the kitchen. I switched to the sci-fi channel and an old episode of Star Trek came on. Captain Kirk on a desert planet, having to reinvent weapons from whatever he could find. Being Captain Kirk, he found out how to make a cannon. I'm glad that sort of thing doesn't happen to me. I would be reduced to throwing stones. James

Tiberius Kirk, given enough time, could have knocked up a small thermonuclear missile...

I was almost asleep when a thud rocked the whole building. It was followed by a boom.

Doing the mending had worked. A bit late, but it had worked.

Chapter Fourteen

I joined my lover in the kitchen. Daniel took the pot off the heat, turned off the gas and said, 'What was that?'

'Thunder,' I suggested. My voice, I was proud to say, did not shake much.

'Not thunder,' he said. 'I've heard thunder and that wasn't it.'

'And you've heard explosives and that was it?' I asked.

'Yes, and it came from above us.'

'Mr Recluse,' I said. 'We'd better—'

'Call the cops,' he said. I grabbed the phone. Letty White said she would be right down and not to do anything until she got there.

I marvel at her confidence, really I do. I called Meroe. She was uninjured but Belladonna had fled into the linen cupboard and was staying there, it seemed, for the duration. I called the Prof and he said that he had heard noises above him and was going up to investigate, and then he hung up before I could tell him what Letty had said. Damn. We'd have to go up and I didn't want to, but Trudi was up there too and she might be hurt. When the cops came the first thing they would do would be to throw everyone out into the night again.

'Daniel, Professor Monk is already on the way up, don't you think we had better go and help him?'

'Come on,' said Daniel.

Horatio did not seem to be perturbed at all. He was a deeply philosophical cat. And once I got up he would be a deeply philosophical cat in sole possession of a mohair throw. He knew where his priorities lay.

I grabbed a blanket and a first aid kit and went to the door as Daniel held it open for me. 'We'll have to climb,' he told me. 'The lift well might have been damaged.'

'Lead on,' I said.

Stairs. I am not built to climb stairs. But Insula is not a high building. I struggled on behind Daniel, sparing an occasional glance for his perfectly formed attributes. Up to the second floor, where we collected Mistress Dread. In plain clothes she favours a Country Road look and is called Pat, but that doesn't make her any less formidable. Kylie and Goss, for a miracle, actually went back into their apartment when Daniel told them that he'd come and get them if anything interesting happened. Up to the third floor, where we saw no one. The Prof had climbed up to the top and the other apartment, Mars, is unoccupied. Up to the fourth floor, where Cherie and Andy joined us, along with Mrs Dawson in her Russian boots. To the fifth floor, where Mistress Dread very kindly stayed with Mrs Pemberthy, who was having hysterics. Mrs P is slightly scared of Mistress Dread, and she is the only person (apart from Mrs P) that Traddles doesn't even try to bite. Going up to the source of the explosion might be a brave act, but staying behind with Mrs Pemberthy was a lot braver. We owed Mistress Dread a favour.

I flagged. I was out of breath. When we got to the sixth floor, Jon and Kepler were out and all was quiet. And thus to the seventh floor at last, seconds before I contributed to those statistics on coronary heart disease and overweight people. Trudi and the Prof were standing at the door of Pluto, heads bent as though they were listening.

'I can't hear a sound,' said the Professor.

'I hear…something,' said Trudi. Lucifer abseiled down from her shoulder and trotted to the door, bouncing up and down on all four paws and mewing. We all listened. The building, shocked awake by the noise, was settling again. Faint creaks and thuds sounded as the walls settled into their accustomed places. I heard the storm break outside with a whoosh of cold hail like small shot. Then I thought I heard something else. A very small, sad sound.

'Yes,' said Meroe. 'Open the door at once. Trudi, do you have your keys?'

'I get,' she said, and went up into her apartment on the top floor.

'But wait, do we have any right to open someone else's door?' asked Andy Holliday.

'He can complain to the police who will be here any minute,' I said. 'Meroe, are you sure?'

'Yes,' she said. Witches have very good ears and (as she would say) other ways of finding things out. When Trudi came back with the keys she slipped the card through the lock and the door sagged on its hinges and fell open.

And a very small, very thin black kitten tottered out, climbed the Professor as if every movement hurt, and nestled in his bosom as though she had been looking for him all her short life. He cradled her in his beautiful long hands.

'Hello,' he said to the kitten. She put out a little pink tongue and licked his thumb. Then she closed her eyes and gave a short purr.

From that point, of course, the Professor was lost. He was one of the Chosen Ones. Meroe gave Soot a fast examination.

'She's thirsty and hungry and cold,' she said. 'Let's take her down to your apartment and get her some warm milk. Where on earth have you been, Soot?'

'Her name isn't Soot,' I heard Professor Monk say as Meroe led him away. 'Soot is the name of a large hearty dog, not a delicate cat. Her name is Nox, because she came at night.'

Where had Soot—sorry, Nox—been? And where was Mr Recluse? We ventured into the apartment. The smoke was clearing away. Mr Recluse lay by his wrecked bed, perfectly alive and bound up like a mummy. The safe was blasted open. The whole apartment looked like it had been hit by a—well, a bomb. Every drawer had been pulled out, every cushion ripped, every cupboard emptied. The Paul Klee lookalike sculptures lay twisted on the floor. Not much appeared to have actually been broken. But everything that could hold something quite small had been searched.

'Dear me,' said Mrs Dawson. She took up a handy carving knife in a tea towel and began to saw at the knots. All we could see of poor Mr Recluse were his eyes, which were wild with terror.

'And that's the answer to the riddle of where Soot has been all this time,' said Daniel, pointing. The elaborate iron grating which covered the heating and air conditioning vents was twisted and bent.

'It is? She's a pretty small kitten but she couldn't slip through the gaps in that,' I said.

'She must have rushed into the open vent in the cellar when the bomb scare happened,' he said. 'And then couldn't find her way out. Probably lived on condensation and mice.' Daniel sniffed. He looked at the grating without touching it.

'They must have put a tiny charge on the grating,' he gave as his opinion. 'Then followed it in, overpowered Mr White, tied him up and ransacked the place.'

'They did a good job,' I said, gazing at the ruin.

'But they had him at their mercy,' said Cherie Holliday. 'Why didn't they kill him?'

That girl watches too many episodes of those tough American cop series where they deal with fifteen dead bodies in the first ten minutes.

'Because they still don't know if they've got what he has hidden,' I reasoned. 'So they don't dare to kill him yet.'

'And they might still be in the vents,' said Andy Holliday, putting an arm around Cherie. He would certainly rather die than lose her again.

'I don't think so,' said Daniel. 'But here comes the cavalry.'

'You are all in very big trouble,' announced Letty White as she stalked through the door. Since she looked like she meant it, and she had a large number of people in white coats with her, we left. Mrs Dawson had got Mr Recluse free, however, and was helping him to sit up. I saw her pat him on the shoulder, and then we were firmly ushered out and the damaged door was closed.

We still didn't know whether the lift was safe, so we left Trudi with an excited Lucifer and trailed down the stairs, shedding people as we went. Mrs Pemberthy had conquered her hysterics and Mistress Dread (I must remember to call her Pat when she is not wearing fishnets, a corset, and brandishing her whip) was waiting on the landing.

'All right, Corinna?' she asked, as though exploding safes happened every day.

'All clear,' I said. 'Alive and unharmed.'

'Good. I didn't want to miss Movie of the Week,' she said, and joined us as we went down. We left Mrs Dawson, Andy Holliday and Cherie on four. We called in at Dionysus on three to see how the kitten was coming along.

'Nox drank a lot of diluted milk, peed very politely in the sink, then ate half a tin of salmon which I was keeping for my evening sandwich,' Professor Monk told us. He opened his hands to show us the sleeping kitten. 'Then she had a quick wash and brush up and now she is asleep. Meroe has gone to bring me a litter tray and some real cat food. Is she not exquisite?' he asked.

She was. She was as black as Belladonna, and one day she would be as shiny. She opened one eye, feeling our stares, then snuggled into the Prof's hands and went to sleep again. She was tiny and dusty and starved, weighing in at perhaps three ounces on the old scale, but this kitten, one felt, had the same strength of character as her brother Lucifer.

We went on. Pat stayed to explain to Kylie and Gossamer. Daniel and I got back to my apartment to find that Horatio had managed to gather the entire mohair rug under and around himself but otherwise nothing had changed. It was strange, somehow, to see all my ornaments and books in their accustomed places. To have the house smell of onion soup and white musk bath oil. With all that devastation upstairs it seemed unnatural. I was vividly reminded of having locked myself out of Grandma's house when the door slammed after me while I was pegging out a tea towel. I could see the kitchen through the window, my cup of coffee still steaming on the table, and all inside bright and warm, while I was stuck outside in the cold, wondering where I had last hidden the spare key.

'Where were we?' I asked.

'Onion soup,' said Daniel, and went back into the kitchen. I joined him and poured myself a glass of cognac. Letty White was going to be very cross with us. I mentioned this to Daniel.

'Better, then, that she should be cross with people who have recently eaten French onion soup,' he said, stirring. I couldn't argue with that.

The soup was terrific. It was a robust soup with onions and cognac and cheese. It warmed the drinker down to the toes. Perfect for a traumatic night. Which wasn't over yet. It was lucky that it was Friday, because I had a feeling that I wasn't going to get to bed by my usual eight o'clock.

The storm arrived and decided that it liked it here and was going to stay. Wind howled. Rain drummed on the indestructible green things on the balcony, which meant that it was coming from the southwest Antarctic ice shelf and would be freezing cold. Daniel and I settled down on the piece of sofa which did not contain Horatio and watched Buffy DVDs, still unnerved by the night's events and knowing that at any moment Letty White would come knocking at the door.

'God help all those sleeping out tonight,' murmured Daniel, drawing me into his embrace. I leaned my head on his chest. I could hear his heart beating. It was a very soothing sound. The rain clawed at the windows, but it couldn't get in.

The doorbell pealed, and Letty White stomped in. Her wrath was apparent, though a little jaded by having delivered the same speech to at least five people before us, assuming she began at the top of the building.

'I can't trust you for a moment!' she began hoarsely. 'There could have been a bomb in there, or a couple of armed men.'

'Except that you told me that we are always protected,' I replied. 'Never alone, you said. So I assumed that if there were any armed men or bombs, there would also be large, heavily armed police officers in flak jackets. And as for trust, Senior Constable, it goes both ways. We went to rescue Nox, whom I'm sure you will have met by now.'

'The Professor showed me,' she said. 'It looked like it hadn't had a decent meal for a week, granted. But you still should have done as I told you.'

'But I didn't. So let's consider this chewing out at an end. Have you had any dinner? How about some French onion soup? Some coffee?'

For a second I thought she was going to fly right off the handle and have us arrested, but suddenly she let out a breath and deflated.

'Yeah, all right,' she muttered. 'Soup sounds nice. I've been living on junk food. Also some real coffee. The Scene of the Crime Officers are going to be hours.'

Daniel went into the kitchen to heat up the soup and toast some more baguette. I fetched some coffee and watched Ms White drink it. She cupped both hands around the mug as though she was cold. I dislodged Horatio from some of the rug and cast an end around her shoulders. The wind howled outside.

'They got in through the heating ducts, as you saw,' she said. 'And got out through them, as well. There's a door to the cellar which has a padlock on it, but padlocks don't stop people like this.'

'How is poor Mr White?'

'Scared silly,' she said. 'As he has every right to be.'

'Here's some soup,' said Daniel, carrying in a tray and putting it on her lap. 'Why not just eat it in peace, and we'll put the DVD back on again. You don't need to talk to us,' he said gently.

We sat there watching Buffy with Letty White, something I would have wagered good money against us doing, though I am not a betting woman. Horatio nestled close to her and purred affably. Buffy ran before were-hyaenas through the dark zoo. After a while I saw that Letty was watching the screen as well.

The episode finished and Daniel got up to take the tray.

'How about a muffin?' he asked. 'We've only got blueberry left. And some more coffee?'

Letty accepted. When we were all settled again, she began to talk.

'You know I can't tell you any more about the man in the apartment, but I can tell you that the burglars were looking for computer records. They were in the safe. Now they've got them, they shouldn't be back. That's the only reason I'm leaving the man here.'

'So they've got the floppy disks,' I said.

'They were in the safe and they are gone.'

'So now it all ought to be as calm and bright as a Christmas carol,' I said suspiciously.

'Just like a Christmas carol,' she said, unwrapping her rug and pushing Horatio gently aside. 'Thanks for dinner. I'm glad you found your kitten,' she said, and we let her out into the cold hallway.

'Did you believe a word of that happy ending?' asked Daniel.

'No. You?'

'No,' he said, putting an arm around my shoulders and drawing me into the apartment.

'If they have found what they want, they'll come back and kill him,' I said slowly.

'And if they haven't, they'll come back and torture him to find it,' said Daniel.

'Nothing to be done about it tonight,' I said. He kissed me with his satiny mouth. We watched more Buffy, and then we went to bed.

◇◇◇

Ah, Saturday. Not only did I get to go back to sleep, but I had Daniel. He slept very neatly, mouth closed, eyelashes like a sooty fringe-line on his smooth cheek. He woke while I was watching him.

'Hey,' he said, gathering me into his embrace. I like being gathered. I snuggled like Nox had into the Professor's hands. Outside the storm was raging. I drowsed, warm and cosy and safe.

When I woke to the scent of coffee it was ten in the morning and time to be up and doing with a heart for any fate. I did not feel like being up and doing, but I got up anyway. Horatio had deserted me for the kitchen, where there might, if he played his cards right, be food. I padded down to the bakery to feed the Mouse Police and put my washed clothes into the dryer. All seemed calm down there. No water had come into the bakery, though it was still blowing a gale outside. I wandered up again and found that there were croissants as well as coffee and sat down to enjoy them in warm silence. Bliss.

By eleven we were talking again. Daniel fed another one of the silent surveillance videos into the machine and watched it on fast forward, making pencil marks on his notes. I did some light cleaning. Then I sat down with him to watch.

'These are the customers who come in at least once a week,' he said, showing me a list. There were more than twenty names on it. 'None of them, as far as I have found, have any reason to ruin the sisters. It has to be one of these possibilities. A random madman, someone trying to use the shop as a distraction or a prelude to poisoning, an extortion attempt, or an inside job.'

'There isn't a lot we can do about a random madman,' I commented. 'There never is. If it was an extortion attempt, we would have expected a ransom demand by now, and they all swear there hasn't been one. Someone who was intending to frame Heavenly Pleasures for poisoning their spouse would have done it by now.' I had not wasted that time spent reading true crime, no matter what my teachers said.

'Explain,' he demanded.

'Well, assume you want to poison someone. You somehow get into Heavenly Pleasures and inject some of their chocolates, then you put them back into stock. Then you send a box of

Heavenly Pleasures chocolates to your victim. Meanwhile the shop innocently sells some poisoned ones to totally unrelated people. Your poisoning looks random and the only person blamed is Heavenly Pleasures.'

'Nasty,' he said. 'This actually has happened?'

'Twice. Once in America and once in England. Cordelia Botkin and Christianna Edmunds. Both ladies decided that the way to demonstrate to their lover that he should leave his wife and marry them was to remove the wife. They hit on a remarkably similar method. They bought chocolates from a shop, then took them home and doctored them. Then they took them back and exchanged them. An additional wrinkle, in the case of Miss Edmunds, was to get a street kid to return them. She would then give him a chocolate or a penny and thus she had never even appeared in the chocolate shop.'

'Clever,' he said.

'But elaborate. Elaborate schemes usually come undone in one way or another. Both ladies sent the poisoned chocolates to their victims. But, of course, this long-distance murder is prone to error. They got a few visitors and the maid, but not, as it happens, the wife. Several other innocent bystanders were poisoned by the chocolates they had planted in the shops. And when the chocolate shop was suspected, they wrote indignant letters about public healths standards to the police.'

'How, then, did they get caught?' asked Daniel. There is nothing sexier than a man happy to listen to a lecture.

'Miss Botkin, because she drew attention to herself, and a shrewd policeman began to ask questions about sweet consumption in her household. In Miss Edmunds' case, the last street kid whom she had sent on her errand was cheated of his reward. She didn't have a penny on her and wouldn't give him sixpence. He was so angry that he followed her home. Then, when a reward was offered, he could lead the police to her house and expose the whole scheme. Little ratbag cleaned up,' I commented admiringly.

'In crime, it is good to be generous,' he said.

'When driving a stolen car to a bank robbery, fasten your safety belt and do not exceed the speed limit,' I said solemnly. 'That's good advice, that is.'

'So it is,' he agreed.

'But the Christianna Edmunds method couldn't work in Heavenly Pleasures,' I said. 'No one would put returned chocolates back into stock these days. It's illegal under the Health Act. I'm amazed they did it in the old days.'

'Well, I've done some technological things to the boxes and the packing—UV light sensitive markings,' said Daniel. 'That ought to show us how the chocolates are getting back into Heavenly Pleasures, if it is an outsider doing a modified Christianna. But let us now consider the insiders.'

'Viv, Juliette and George?'

'And Selima. And probably Uncle Max. Isn't he the definitive Uncle Max? I had an Uncle Max like that.'

'Half your luck,' I said.

'He used to arrive in just such a coat with an astrakhan collar, I swear, pockets full of chocolates. There must be a factory somewhere, turning out affable elderly gentlemen with beautiful smiles and rich voices.'

'They probably moonlight as Father Christmases,' I agreed.

'Just so,' said Daniel. 'Now, what do we know about the personnel?'

'Juliette and Vivienne are orphans, and Uncle Max is their only relative. They own Heavenly Pleasures fifty/fifty. They get on all right—would you say all right?'

'Viv is sensitive to Juliette's beauty, and envious. But she is the chocolate maker, so she has status. Juliette can't help being beautiful, doesn't flaunt it in Viv's face, and actually runs the shop, does the accounts and the ordering; Viv needs her. They, in fact, need each other. They get on as well as such sisters usually do. Now, think about George.'

'I don't want to,' I said.

'I know. Detectives have to be brave. According to what he revealed to us of his own rat-infested little mind, he has designs on Vivienne. But she doesn't seem to like him, certainly does not seem to be attracted to him.'

'Whereas he flirts with Juliette, we've seen him. But in that sort of boy, flirting would be a reflex, something he does without thinking.'

'I don't think George does anything without thinking,' said Daniel.

'All right, but perhaps Viv is just keeping him as her own secret. Treating him like a dog in the shop and kissing his feet afterwards—erk, I wish I hadn't said that. But it is possible, no?'

'A horribly compelling idea,' agreed Daniel. 'What could upset this arrangement would be if either sister had a boyfriend. Does anyone know? You hear all the gossip.'

'Nothing,' I confessed. 'They don't have a lot of time away from the shop.'

'But Selima found a lover while working there,' Daniel said, 'Just by looking through the window.'

This was true. We watched the strange jerky images in silence for a while. 'There is also the inheritance.' I had an idea. 'What if one sister tried to edge out the other? Viv, say, decides that she doesn't need Juliette anymore?'

'I suppose they have left their halves of the shop to each other,' said Daniel. 'I'll find out. I've located an old friend of Viv's who wants to talk to me. But not today. Today we are relaxing and theorising. I'm too prone to go off like an overloaded firework and you could do with some rest.'

'That's true. What do we consider next?'

'We look at who benefits from the crime. The shop is flourishing. The sisters must be making a fortune. There is the shop and the fittings,' said Daniel.

'But their ingredients are very costly,' I objected. 'One slab of that seventy per cent cocoa butter couverture costs a king's ransom. Vivienne told me they only use the best and it's very pricey. One of Jason's superlative chocolate muffins, for instance, costs a dollar fifty to make. Compared to sixty cents for an ordinary one, which I sell for two dollars. They would be managing well, but not making obscene profits. The fittings might be very valuable. Some of those chocolate moulds are antiques. Collectors pay a lot for stuff like that. But the shop's on a lease. I don't think they have a huge capital.'

'Someone said something about the lease…' Daniel concentrated. 'Yes. It was renegotiated. Who owns the building?'

'Some consortium. It's very rare, these days, for a single person to own a building. That one has a lot of offices above and the shops below; they might have different owners. I could find out.'

'Find out,' he requested. 'Knowledge is power.'

'So I am told.' I leaned against him. Horatio leaned against me. There was a lot of leaning going on.

'What we have is a lack of knowledge. We don't know how, we don't know who, and we don't know why,' said Daniel.

'That about sums it up.' I was about to untangle myself and go and investigate possibilities for lunch when the doorbell rang. Daniel opened the door. There was Cherie Holliday, holding a mobile phone.

Chapter Fifteen

'Selima?' I asked, taking the phone. Cherie nodded. Daniel came inside. I grabbed the opportunity to talk to the lost girl.

'Hello,' I said into the phone. 'How are you?' The voice was trembling. She said, 'Please come and get me! Cherie says you're kind and clever. Please.' Then she gave me an address. As I was about to tell her we were coming, the phone went dead. My idea bloomed in my head. If only it worked. It had to work. I gave the phone back to Cherie.

'We need to go and get Selima,' I said. 'Can you come?'

'I'll just tell Dad and put some shoes on,' she said.

'You, too?' asked Daniel. I found my backpack and my shoes and stood up. Daniel looked grim. I must have matched him.

'Coats,' I said. 'And you might bring a blanket and a thermos, Daniel. And the address of her sister's house.'

'Bad?' he asked.

'Not good,' I told him, as he shrugged into his leather coat and helped me into my guaranteed-against-all-conditions-including-blizzard lumberjack's jacket. I had, of course, always wanted to be a lumberjack. Actually I had bought it because it was big enough for me and a couple of jumpers. And a small family, including dog, to be truthful. 'Call your taxi,' I told Daniel, 'and then I need the phone again.'

Shortly, Cherie came back in a waterproof coat and shoes and we went out to meet Daniel's taxi. It was driven by an old mate of his called Timbo, a young man of such extreme reticence that I had only found out his name after about three journeys. He was agreeably plump on the Coltrane model, with a head of rich curly brown hair and gentle brown eyes like a cow. He was a very good driver. And at least he didn't want me to agree to some lunatic political theory in order to get me to my destination alive. I have agreed, in my time, to some very odd statements from taxi drivers. My favourite was probably the one which posited that Phillip Ruddock had been kidnapped by aliens, who had left an android in his place. Can't argue with that. Later contemplation had informed me that by the Asimov Three Laws of Robotics, it couldn't have been an android. They are not allowed to harm humans.

I was talking urgently on the mobile phone as we got in— Cherie and me in the back seat and Daniel next to the driver, standard distribution—and Timbo took off gently. He treated the car as though it was a loved domestic pet, never stomping hard on its pedals or wrenching it around corners. But before I had folded the phone and looked up, we had passed Footscray and somehow found ourselves on the Geelong Road. We were heading out of town.

'Where are we going?' asked Daniel.

'Werribee,' I said.

'Which is where Selima is?' asked Cherie.

'Yes. Damn this rain! It all depends on him getting there in time.'

'Are you going to explain?' Daniel asked a little acidly.

'After I make another call,' I said, flipping open the phone.

Cherie and Daniel exchanged a glance. I had better start explaining soon. The rain swept the road, blurring headlights, greasing the surface until even the obliging Timbo had to slow to avoid sliding off the road altogether. People behave oddly in rain. Especially Melburnians, who ought to be used to it. They speed up in order to get home faster because driving in the rain is dangerous. This means that some of them, of course, never get home at all. Several of these had come to grief. We crept past a Turner painting of disaster; throbbing red and blue lights, angled cars, the woop-woop-woop of the ambulance sirens, all blurred and drowned in rain.

'Not far now,' I said.

'Where are we going again?' he asked.

'To a wedding,' I said. Fortunately—since he could have reached over the seat to strangle me—I began to explain. 'Selima was very shocked when first Brian's mother and then her own cousins rejected her. She could have gone back to the hostel, but she felt so worthless and badly used that she was easy prey for the old men when they found her. They explained that now she had been out of her father's house for a night, she was tainted and no one would believe that she had not been with a lover. They said that she would be an outcast. They would have told her that the only way to retrieve her own and her family's honour was to go on with the marriage her father had arranged for her.'

'But the husband is in Turkey,' Cherie objected.

'Here she can marry by proxy,' I said. 'Then they can send her to Turkey to complete the bargain. It's a good deal for them. Turkish women in Turkey are considerably more advanced now and not many of them would allow an arranged marriage like this one—not educated girls in a secular state. They can't be forced to marry anymore.'

'So he'd be getting an educated young woman at half the price?' Cherie asked, disgusted.

'Exactly. Remnant migrant populations can stagnate, hanging on to the ways of the old country, even after the old country has moved on; just like their language goes out of date. There wouldn't be a lot of old Turkish patriarchs left in Turkey as strict as this one.'

'Which is why all his children left him,' I said. 'One by one.'

'He'll die alone,' said Daniel. 'And then, with any luck, his breed will be extinct. He's a tragic figure, in a way.'

'Hah,' said Cherie, which rather summed up my view as well.

'So what have you arranged, puppet-master?' he asked, using *Blake's 7* slang for a psy-corps expert. I grinned at him as Timbo negotiated a sweeping turn and we began to edge down a side road, just before we got to Werribee.

'Is anyone following us?' I asked.

Cherie and Daniel peered into the downpour.

'Can't see anyone. But not likely to, unless he's driving a tank with fog lights.'

'Never mind. On we go. Timbo, keep the engine running. We might have to leave in a hurry. I think—yes, that must be the house.'

It was a large brick house on an unfenced block with a paved yard behind and a carport big enough to take three or four cars. In this a marriage feast was being held. We stopped in the street, just able to see that at the back door a pavilion had been set up, decked with fine cloth and glittery with Christmas tree lights sputtering out in the drifting rain. A band was tootling and banging. The party was all male. I wondered where all the women of the house were. A beast of some sort twirled slowly on a spit. The scene looked innocent and charming, if you didn't know that it included another sort of sacrifice apart from that poor mammal.

I stared past the festivities. An old man sat on a decorated chair next to the house. There was another chair beside him, which was empty. Timbo eased the car forward a little and I could see into the side window. There I saw a girl in beautiful garments, red and gold, with a red veil over her black hair. She stared straight ahead, seemingly in a trance, or perhaps drugged. Two old women were tending her, tweaking the veil into place, painting her hands with henna, attaching heavy earrings to her ears and a tinkling chain of coins across her brow.

Selima looked out into the rainy darkness with a blank expression which caught at my heart. Daniel had his hand on the door handle when I said 'Wait a moment, Daniel.'

'Give me a good reason,' he said angrily.

'If we take her away now she will be shamed. She has agreed to this. Whatever unfair tactics were employed to make her agree, she has agreed. While there is a chance of solving this another way and letting her make her own choice, I want to leave it to her.'

'All right,' he said grudgingly. 'I trust you.'

He gave me his beautiful smile and took my hand.

The music skirled and hooted. Elderly gentlemen danced creakily in the rain. They, at least, were having a good time. No one challenged us as we sat silently in the car on the edge of the road. The rain rained. The party went on. I tried to get a good look at the proxy groom, but he was too heavily bearded to see much of his face. Inside, the old women assisted the bride to her feet. Something was about to happen.

Cherie Holliday was silent, absorbed in the scene. We were simultaneously cut off from it and inside it, both part of the picture and observing it from the outside. We could hear the band and smell the scent of roasting meat, but we were not members of the wedding party. Just when my nerve was about to crack, the two old women led the bride out of view, and a moment later she appeared at the back door. She moved like a sleepwalker. The proxy groom stood up and held out his hand. The girl flinched and tried to run back into the house but the old women restrained her and turned her to face the man again. This was horrible. I wondered if either of the women was Selima's mother and how she could do such a thing to her daughter. But I suppose it had been done to her in her turn, when she was a nervous seventeen year old, given to an older man. He held out his hand again and this time, Selima took it.

There was a roar of engines from behind and, with a swoosh of mud, a big red motorbike slid into the backyard, demolishing several strings of lights. The rider was dressed in black leathers, his full-face helmet visor down. He skidded to a halt, engine running, and waited, one booted foot on the ground. He was a figure full of threat and mystery, utterly unexpected, an intrusion from another time or planet.

There was a moment when everyone held their breath. The old men stopped dead in their tracks. The music died. Nothing happened except the rain rained and the spit turned. Cherie

Holliday grabbed my hand so hard that her nails cut into my palm and I didn't care. The rider raised his visor and turned his face to the wedding.

Then, in a jingle of ornaments, Selima gave a cry of glad recognition and relief, ran to the bike, leapt on the back and put both her arms around the rider's waist. And with a swoosh and a roar, they were gone.

And so were we. I had just enough time to see a strange little picture of the two elderly women, arms around each other, laughing until they cried, as Timbo turned the car and we were out onto the highway again.

'Young Lochinvar is come out of the west,' I said to Daniel, with great relief.

'You are a genius. Pure genius, Corinna. Marriage by capture is part of that culture which those old men were exploiting,' he said. 'In the old days it would have been a horse but this was more efficient.

'Here we are,' I said. 'Get that blanket, Cherie, she will be freezing.'

The medieval pair were waiting in the shelter of a closed petrol station. Brian had taken off his helmet and Selima was kissing him and laughing and weeping. Her thin silks were clinging to her beautiful plump body and she was shivering with cold and tension. Her crimson veil was wrapped around the black leather of his jacket, making a hotly erotic, terribly touching picture. His gloved hands clutched her bare shoulders. She was slick with rain and oil and flushed with the wind of her escape.

'Meet you in Essendon,' I told him, as I wrapped the blanket around Selima and started to lead her to the car. She leaned out of the wrapping to kiss Brian again, full on the mouth, then allowed herself to be conducted into the warmth of the back seat between Cherie and me. Brian looked dazed and elated. Daniel gave him a hug and came back to the taxi, and Timbo slid us gently into gear.

'He'll meet us at your sister's place,' I said. 'You can't ride all that way in those clothes—and without a helmet.'

'Did you do this?' demanded Selima fiercely. I nodded. Selima reached out, grabbed me, and kissed me hard. Then she kissed Cherie and Daniel. She was wet and bare and scented with a heavy, flowery, musky oil, very erotic in that enclosed space. Cherie and I wrapped her up in the blanket again and produced a thermos of chicken soup. That should dampen the atmosphere a little, I thought. Nothing less sexy than chicken soup.

Selima drank soup and slowly stopped shivering, losing her manic edge. 'I thought I was lost,' she said wonderingly. 'I thought there was no way out.'

'Ah, but you had right on your side,' I told her. 'With right, there is always a way out. Have some more soup.'

'I haven't been eating,' Selima commented. 'But that only made me more a proper trembling virgin. Those old women prepared me like a...like a chicken trussed for baking. They never took their eyes off me. But luckily they didn't know about mobile phones and I managed to ring Cherie from the loo. Is this legal?' she demanded of me.

'Oh, yes, you are now married by custom,' I said. 'But not by law. See how things with Brian work out,' I said gently. 'Then you can decide if you want to be married for real. But your father can't do anything to you now.'

'He'll be so angry,' said Selima.

'No,' I said. 'Remember, you behaved properly. It isn't your fault that you got captured. They treated you like a possession. The possession isn't at fault if someone steals it. I doubt your father will even have to return the presents.'

'It wasn't presents,' said Selima. 'It was money. Quite a lot of money.' Then she asked, 'Where are we going?'

'Your sister Mirri,' I told her. 'Unless there is somewhere else you want to go?'

'Oh, no, Mirri is a darling, I just couldn't get her involved. I'm in enough trouble as it is. I'll probably be arrested soon.'

'Why?' I asked.

Selima put down the cup and sighed.

'No reason not to tell you, you rescued me. I was stealing from the shop.'

'You were? How?'

'I'd slip a fifty dollar note out of the till when we were making up the bank deposit slip every day,' she said. 'It was easy enough to do. The money never got onto the docket so no one knew it was missing.'

'And why were you doing this?' I asked.

'George,' she said with infinite distaste. 'I gave it to George. It was his idea.'

'What did George have over you?' I asked.

'Brian. He knew about Brian and he said he would tell my father. Which would mean that I would lose my job because Dad would never let me leave the house again. And I would have to run away, which would bring disgrace on my family.'

'George,' said Cherie with disgust. 'Why did he make you do that? Can't just be for the money.'

'He hates Turks,' said Selima, surprised that we didn't know this. 'He's always talking about the land his family lost in the Exchange of Populations. I've met the rest of the Pandamus family and they don't think like that, not even their Grandma. But George thinks that the Turks cheated them and he hates Turks. And me,' she added. 'He liked making me steal.'

'What a charming young gentleman,' said Daniel. 'I shall have a word with George. I don't think he'll trouble you again. Do you have any idea about the contaminated chocolates?'

'No,' said Selima simply. 'I can't imagine who would do that.'

Then she closed her eyes and abruptly fell asleep, leaning her decorated head on my shoulder. Timbo made his first and only comment for the night.

'That was sweet,' he said. And so it was.

When we got to Essendon Brian was already there, taking off his helmet on the porch. Mirri and her husband Adrian were waiting with a proud child carrying a brass tray of Turkish delight . When we got Selima out of the car Mirri gave a cry and embraced her.

'My little sister!' she sobbed. 'Married! Come in, come in,' she urged, and we all trooped into the house, where a pair of little girls pounced on Selima in her finery and hugged her around the knees, crying, 'Lima! Lima!'

'Sit down,' ordered Mirri. She was an older version of her sister. Seeing Brian standing hesitantly in the doorway, she dragged him inside, streaming water, and hugged him. 'Coffee,' said Mirri firmly. 'So you did it,' she said to me. 'Thank you.'

'My pleasure,' I said politely. I was so gratified. It had worked.

Then we really had to sit down and drink Turkish coffee and eat rahat lokoum while Selima was removed, stripped, dried and inserted into some of her sister's clothes. Brian took off his leathers and was revealed as an ordinary young man in jeans. The occasion, however, was not ordinary. We had pulled off an authentic medieval rescue. We drank the coffee and became a little hilarious.

The children were delighted with Selima's wedding finery. One put an earring into my hand and I wondered that the girl's earlobes hadn't been permanently stretched. It was made of solid gold and weighed accordingly. I was about to say that Selima could live for quite a while on the proceeds of her jewellery when I asked her, 'Do you want to go back to Heavenly Pleasures?'

Selima, now clad in a dark red tracksuit, shuddered.

'Not while George is there.'

'Good. I will arrange a glowing reference and you can get another job. You can stay here, and your father has no power over you,' I assured her.

'The old bastard,' commented Mirri. 'If I'd known this is what he was plotting—to sell my sister—I would have strangled the old beast myself.'

'No need,' I said. 'Selima? You make your own decisions now. No one else can tell you what to do. Now, we have to go. Goodnight,' I said to Brian. 'The same goes for you, you know.'

Brian ducked his head. 'I know,' he said. He looked older. More mature.

Timbo was waiting for us. We took him some Turkish delight. He scoffed it joyously all the way back to Insula. Thus in a mist of powdered sugar did we return from Young Lochinvar's wedding. And we were all so tired that we went straight to bed.

Sunday morning dawned cold and rainy. At least the dams would be filling. I got up and made breakfast. Out of the window I saw Mrs Dawson in a bright red slicker and her Van Gogh umbrella issuing forth, presumably to go to church. No one else was stirring. I made a stack of rye bread toast, found the cherry jam, and kissed Daniel as he wandered out into the kitchen, following the life-giving Arabica scent.

We ate in silence. Horatio begged—well, firmly requested—a dab of butter. The rain scattered across the windows. I read the newspaper, remembering the crossword collective in Vertigo and wondering how anyone could be expected to know as much as the compiler required.

Then I drifted on to think of Selima and her romantic escape. She was stealing from the shop but she wasn't sabotaging the chocolates. I decided to do a vigorous rummage amongst the inhabitants of Insula to gather some gossip. Someone must know something about the chocolate shop sisters.

Meanwhile, poor Mr Recluse was out of hospital and up there in that ruined apartment, and we probably ought to do something about him as well. Since he wasn't a criminal or a serial killer but a person wishing to be of value to the state, he deserved our support. While we had him. I hoped the Twins had not found what they wanted from him, though if he had it, they would have located it in that devastating search.

The cherry jam went very well with the rye toast and the paper was no more distressing than usual. I hoped that Jason had managed a day without going back to his old habits. I knew where he lived but I couldn't think of a way of checking up on him without looking like I was checking up on him. Which might be enough to drive him back on drugs because he would think that I didn't trust him. Those visitors to the Royal Family thinking that court etiquette was tricky were on safe ground compared to me dealing with a teenaged boy.

Daniel left to talk to Viv's old friend, and I continued with my advanced toast-study until I was interrupted by a phone call. It was Meroe.

'Mrs Dawson has spoken to Mr White,' she told me. 'You know, I really find it hard to call Mrs Dawson "Sylvia". She is going to help him clear up the mess in his apartment. Can you come too?'

'Certainly,' I said. 'I'll bring bread and cheese.'

Chapter Sixteen

'I'll bring tea and some cleansing incense,' said Meroe. 'Mrs Dawson is asking some of the others as well. She told me that she would provide the champagne. I do like her,' said Meroe. 'Ten minutes? Oh, and the lift is working. Trudi spoke to it.'

I was very glad to hear that. I put on jeans and an old t-shirt and tied up my hair in a scarf. I assembled a basket of bread and a few cheeses. And a big jar of homemade chutney. Grandma Chapman's Gentleman's Relish, no finer to be found. The only difficulty in making it was standing by until it suddenly went from highly spiced vegetable stew to your actual chutney, which happened in seconds and was not a good idea to miss.

We could have a ploughman's lunch. And I didn't have to carry it up the stairs. I wrote Daniel a note and left it in the middle of the kitchen table, under the cat.

One thing was clear. Mr Recluse no longer had anything to hide, or he wouldn't be allowing us into his apartment to handle everything he owned.

When I got into the lift it collected Cherie and Jon on the way up.

'Kep's still asleep,' Jon told me. 'He was up all night working on a virus problem from India. It's the Pakistanis, apparently. They hate India and spend a lot of time trying to ruin their computer systems. He'll be out for hours. He works very hard, when he works.'

'And Dad's making this special stew,' said Cherie. 'It's got a million ingredients.'

'What sort of stew?' I asked. She was tying a scarf around her hair as she thought.

'French word. Casserole? No, that's not it.'

'Cassoulet,' I suggested.

'Yeah, that's it. You have to cook a lot of duck pieces in salt first. But it tastes real good. Worth the mess. Calico is helping by eating all the bits of leftover meat. She almost got away with the duck,' Cherie laughed. 'She was sitting on a chair and the duck was on a tea towel which was hanging over the edge of the table. Calico just stuck a claw into the tea towel and reeled it in and the duck was moving very slowly across the table all by itself, before Dad worked out he wasn't seeing things and grabbed it back. She was pretty pissed, but he gave her some insides. That's the only trouble with cooking. All those heads and legs and guts and things.'

'You must at all costs avoid eating Asian food in Asia,' Jon told her as we got out of the lift. Mrs Dawson was already there, attired in a big cook's smock and holding a broom in the manner made famous by the Roman legionary. She smiled on us.

'There you are,' she said. 'This is very nice of you. Now, Corinna and Cherie, if you please, can you begin with the kitchen, and Jon can help me stand furniture up again.'

'Perhaps it would be better if Jon and I did the furniture,' I suggested. 'We're closer in height.'

Mrs Dawson paused, making perfectly sure that I was not in any way suggesting that she wasn't able to stand a wardrobe up by herself if necessary. I wasn't, so she smiled and agreed.

We started in the bedroom, heaving the bed base back onto its legs and the mattress back onto the base and untangling the linen. Jon rehung three pictures which had been taken off the wall, presumably to examine the backs. This seemed like a good time to start my enquiries.

'Do you know the ladies from the chocolate shop?' I asked, handing him a pillow to reclothe in its case. The bedclothes must have come with the apartment. The sheets were thick Egyptian cotton and probably antique. The blankets were pure wool and the spread was a hand-pieced Amish quilt in the pattern called wedding ring. I had investigated quilting, and decided that I would need to have a neat mind and be able to sew straight seams, neither of which is amongst my accomplishments. Jon had certainly made his share of beds. His had hospital corners, which he flicked under with a knife-edged hand like a martial arts person.

'I've met them,' he said. 'I don't know them well. In fact, I met Vivienne in Sydney last year. Just in the crowd. But she seemed to be having a very good time.'

'At the Mardi Gras?' I asked.

'Yes. I was surprised. Don't know why I should have been. But she might have been there just for the parade, you know. Lots of straight people go to Mardi Gras. It's a good show. You take that side of this wardrobe, Corinna. Heave on three. One, two, three.'

We stood the heavy wardrobe back up and replaced the few clothes which Mr Recluse had brought with him. Good, if boring, clothes. Three pairs of shoes. Two pairs of pyjamas. The usual underwear of the gentleman. Working together, Jon and I had transformed the bedroom from a fine imitation of Cologne Sacked by the Goths to a place where someone could actually sleep. Nothing was broken.

'They seem to have been fairly neat,' said Jon.

'If by neat you mean that they didn't piss on the wall or dance on the sheets with muddy boots, I agree. They were looking for something.'

'They surely were. Well, this is nice.'

The police must have taken the remains of the sheet with which Mr Recluse had been secured. We went into the dining room where we stood a table back on its legs, put the chairs under it, and replaced the tablecloth, the cork mats with views of London, a vase, two strange sculptures made of flat lead and plastic slugs and wire (one of which had a brass segmented fish hanging from it) and all the pebbles and shells from a dish of objets trouvés, collected circa 1920 by some bush child who had just encountered the sea.

Two glasses had been smashed and ground to powder and I went into the kitchen to find the vacuum cleaner before someone got a cut foot. It was an old model but it whirred efficiently. There wasn't really room for us both in the small dining room, so Jon took over and I selected my next interviewee. Meroe was ladling spilt rice into a rubbish bag.

'Do you know the chocolate shop ladies, Meroe?' I asked, holding the bag so that she could tip using both hands.

'Thank you, Corinna. Terrible jangle of vibrations in here, I feel quite dizzy. Juliette and Vivienne? Not really. Neither of them were interested in the occult. They make very good chocolates, though. Reach over, if you can, and get me that dustpan? Isn't it lucky that most of Mr White's supplies were frozen? This rice must have been here since about 1960. Even the weevils have interbred and become extinct.'

She replaced the canister in the line on the shelf. 'But I did see the young girl, Selima, was it? She came in and asked for a tarot reading. It was interesting.'

'What did it say?'

Meroe looked at me with her dark, reproving eyes. 'You know I can't tell you that.'

'Suppose I asked if it referred to anything other than her guilt at being a thief and her love for a young Asian man?'

'Ah. No, except that she was very angry with her father. You have spoken to Selima, then? I was concerned for her. How is she?'

'Rescued,' I said. 'A very dramatic escape. Very Walter Scott. And I don't even like Walter Scott. Some of these saucepans are collector's items,' I said, picking up a beautifully enamelled skillet and clanging it back into its cupboard. 'You all right in here?'

'Yes, I'm throwing away all this stuff. The fridge, fortunately, was not unplugged, though it was searched. I'll put the kettle on when I am done.'

'I'll be in the parlour.'

Mrs Dawson was replacing books in the bookcase while Mr Recluse sat on the couch, looking at a pile of cushions with ripped covers. 'If you have a needle and thread I can cobble up those seams,' I told him.

'In my bag, Corinna dear,' said Mrs Dawson. I found a darning needle and that chameleon thread and sat down on the floor. Mrs Dawson had also supplied a strong pair of dressmaking scissors and a thimble.

'Can you talk while you are sewing?' asked Mrs Dawson.

'Yes,' I said, taking up a sadly torn raw silk cushion and turning the cover inside out. I could hear the neat thud of books slotting home into their places.

'Then perhaps you can tell me what is going on in the police investigation,' said Mrs Dawson.

'Not a lot,' I said, stitching. 'You would know as much as I do. My police person isn't saying anything about who Mr White is or why he is here,' I added, looking up from the seam I was making. 'But she did put a time limit on his danger—three weeks.'

'Ah,' said Mrs Dawson. 'How annoying.'

'In return, can I ask a question?' I put down the mended cover, reunited it with its cushion, and handed it to Mr White. He still hadn't said a word.

'Certainly.' Mrs Dawson finished with the books, levered herself to her feet, and began to replace ornaments on the mantlepiece. The blown-open safe was ruined, revealed against the far wall of the parlour behind a big picture of remote brown moorlands with a brown stag and a brown sky. I took up another ripped cushion. This one was blue Thai silk.

'Do you know anything about the ladies—no, the whole staff—in the chocolate shop?'

'Juliette is a sweet child with a thin streak of anger somewhere inside her—one feels these things. Vivienne is a strong-minded woman prone to moods, possibly hormonal. George is an insolent brat who will come to a very bad end, if I'm any judge. And he will deserve it. Selima is a downtrodden girl who might do almost anything if pushed far enough.'

Now that was a bundle of news. Mrs Dawson was a very acute observer. I reminded myself not to take her lightly—not that I ever had.

'Selima ran away, but she's safe now. It was a very impressive rescue. Of the four, who would you say would be likely to sabotage the chocolates?'

'None of them,' said Mrs Dawson decisively, righting a terracotta statue of the Infant Samuel Before Eli and clearly regretting that it hadn't been broken. 'Juliette and Vivienne need each other. George is a bad-mannered narcissist but he needs his job. So does Selima.'

'I came to the same conclusion,' I said sadly, fixing another cushion and reaching for the third. Mrs Dawson picked up glasses from the lounge chair and dusted each one before she put them on a silver tray much in need of a good polish.

'I believe these are Venetian glass,' she said. 'Not one broken. Remarkable. Daniel?' she called. 'How are you getting on with the bath?'

'I think I've got all the glass out of it,' said Daniel, who must have removed Horatio from the table and found my note. He had come in without my hearing him. 'I'll just do a last run-over with a piece of Blu-Tack and that should do it. Luckily it was a fairly thick tooth glass, not a fine champagne glass.'

'Then Mr White can have the bath he so desperately wants, and we shall prepare luncheon,' decided Mrs Dawson. Jon gave Mr White a bath towel and his slippers and Daniel yielded him the bathroom. Mr White plodded inside and shut the door.

'Chatty man, isn't he?' I said. Mr White made me really uneasy.

'He was in shock, so they gave him a sedative in hospital,' said Mrs Dawson. 'It hasn't worn off yet. Jon, can you open the champagne? I think we all need a drink.'

'First we cleanse the violence and fear,' said Meroe. Kylie and Goss, clearly by arrangement, came in at this point. They set up a lot of candles at different points of the room and chanted while Meroe lit her incense and opened windows. Daniel, Jon,

Mrs Dawson and I stood in the middle of the room. I swear some of the nervous energy that had been making me jittery seemed to lift or be soothed. The incense smelt of Orthodox churches. Meroe put on a CD of sweet, soft music. I drew a deep breath. So did Jon. He, of course, is more used to this sort of thing than I am. Daniel took my hand. His hand was cold. Mrs Dawson preserved her social smile, as I was sure she could do through tidal wave, earthquake, nuclear attack, or someone using the salad fork for their fish course. They made hostesses tough in the old days.

'Thank you, dear, very effective,' was all she said when Meroe had concluded, blown out her candles, and dismissed her hand-maidens. Jon opened the bottle of champagne and we all drank out of the Venetian glasses, which were tinged faintly green and so thin that I was afraid I might bite a piece out of the rim. As should have been expected, it was very good champagne.

Then Meroe and I went to assemble lunch. The apartment really did feel different. It also smelled very nice. We had lovely things to eat. Meroe's organic leaves and herbs, the last of the cherry tomatoes, baby cucumbers, three different cheeses, four different sorts of bread and the Gentleman's Relish. Meroe had managed to save the salt. We made a salad dressing from her superlative herbal vinegar and cold pressed virgin olive oil, and found that there were enough plates, bowls and cutlery to supply an array with a five course dinner. I sliced busily with one of those invaluable breadknives which have been in the kitchen for decades and are sharpened to a streak.

'This looks like lunch,' I said, piling the leaves into a Chelsea salad bowl which was probably worth the purchase price of Earthly Delights. Meroe gave me a strange look.

'It is lunch, no?' she asked.

We announced to the bubbly-bibbers that they should come and serve themselves as there wasn't enough room for us all to be seated at the table. I selected seed bread, blue cheese and salad and took the couch, where Daniel and Jon joined me. Mrs Dawson and Meroe sat down at the table.

We could hear extensive splashing from the bathroom. A damp but clean Mr Recluse emerged, padded into his bedroom, and came out clothed and in his right mind. He took Mrs Dawson's hand.

'I can't believe that you did all this for me,' he said to her. He had a nice voice, quite deep. An Australian accent.

'Nonsense, dear boy,' she said briskly. 'Do get yourself some lunch and join me at the table. These dissolute creatures are used to eating from plates on their knees but I haven't got the knack.'

The dissolute creatures grinned and stuffed their faces. I went back for some pasta douro, cheddar and Gentleman's Relish and found that it was just as good as I remembered. I was hungry and the food was vanishing fast.

'Now,' said Mrs Dawson to Daniel. 'Tell us the tale of how Corinna contrived Selima's escape.'

Daniel let her refill his glass and told the company of the wicked bargain for Selima's virginity, the dancing old men in the rainy back yard, the arrival of the leatherclad motorcyclist and the way Selima had leapt to horseback with a shriek of delight and had been borne away, her red veil streaming and all her ornaments jangling wildly, to freedom and peace. It was a good story and he told it well.

'One touch to her hand, and one word in her ear,
'When they reached the hall door, and the charger stood near,
'So light to the croupe the fair lady he swung,
'So light to the saddle before her he sprung!
'She is won! we are gone over bank bush and scaur,
'"They'll have fleet steeds that follow" quoth fair Lochinvar,'
Mrs Dawson quoted, clapping her hands. 'Oh, well done! Is the young man a worthy knight?'

'He is a very good, solemn, devoted student who would never hurt her,' said Daniel. 'As to whether it will work, well, one never knows that. Perhaps his glamour will fade when she isn't in fear of betrayal by that cad George all the time. But perhaps not,' he said, smiling at me. 'Sometimes lovers who come in out of the dark and the rain, stay.'

'So they do,' I replied.

Unexpectedly, Mr White clapped me on the shoulder. 'That was a good plan,' he said. 'But you took a chance! What if the boy hadn't come? Chickened out at the last moment? Fell off his bike on the wet road?'

'I'd have thought of something else,' I said equably. 'Quite fast. We had a getaway driver. By the way, how did you meet Timbo?' I asked Daniel.

'I helped him to get his licence back,' said Daniel. 'He's a very good driver. Not one of his mates' robberies failed because Timbo was driving the getaway car. They got caught because they were stupid,' said Daniel. 'He got a light sentence because he was so young and clearly not involved in any of the plotting.'

'Oh,' I said. Still, Timbo was a very good driver.

'Well, I have an appointment this afternoon,' said Mrs Dawson. 'Let's just clear up the dishes and we'll leave poor Mr White to get some sleep. No, dear, let Daniel do it,' she said as Meroe began to get up. 'And I shall help him.'

'Do you play chess at all?' asked Jon of Mr White.

'Just enough to be worth beating,' he replied, yawning.

'You will be welcome to try Kepler's skills,' said Jon. 'Your bed's all made. Get some rest, eh?'

Mr White went into his bedroom. When the dishes were done—there was no dishwasher, of course—we took our leave. My basket was quite empty of bread, which was gratifying. I took the relish back. From his taste in frozen dinners, tending to the macaroni cheese as it did, I didn't think Mr White was likely to eat it.

'You spoke to Viv's friend,' I challenged when Daniel and I were back behind closed doors.

'Certainly,' he said. 'A nice girl whom you would be delighted to take home to mother. Her name is Kat and she is about your admirable shape, with long black hair. She's a travel agent. She and Viv met at—'

'Mardi Gras?' I said. Daniel's eyes opened wide.

'However did you guess that? Have you been taking witch-craft lessons from Meroe?'

'No. Jon told me he met Viv there.'

'Ah, inside information,' said Daniel.

'Best kind.' I sounded smug even to myself.

'So it is. Kat really admires Viv's skills and her conversation and stays out of her way when she goes berserk, as she calls it. They have no plans to set up house together. Kat told me that Viv was too exciting for close quarters. But they have got plans to travel together—Kat gets all kinds of discounts—when George is experienced enough to make chocolates for the shop every day for two weeks. Juliette and Viv have an agreement about that, according to Kat. They already shut the shop for a week in the middle of summer, after the Christmas rush. Kat doesn't know Juliette very well, but says that Juliette is not interested in men, though not in the same way as Viv. Juliette had some sort of heartbreak and she is still recovering.'

'Do we tell them about George and his blackmailing Selima?'

'Oh, I think we should. They won't sack him but it ought to wipe the smile off his pretty face,' said Daniel consideringly.

'And Viv isn't going to fall in with his matrimonial plans,' I realised, giggling. 'He's wasting his powder and his shot on a lesbian. Oh, poor George,' I said, with studied hypocrisy.

'And the ladies will have him over a barrel in dealing with the next girl who works there,' said Daniel, breaking into an evil grin. 'I think that George's life is going to be really unpleasant, and it's no more than the little rat deserves. But that still doesn't get us closer to the problem,' he said, allowing the grin to fade.

'Never mind. Tomorrow I'm going to find out who owns that building and talk to the landlord. You go over those customer videos again. And we wait for events. We are going to solve this one,' I told Daniel.

'Perfect faith,' he said in reply.

'Perfect love,' I finished the quote, and took him off to bed.

We got up about six and decided to ask the Prof if he felt like some company for dinner. He did and we went up to order pizza from Pizza Deluxe, who make amazing meals and also deliver. I love their barbecued chicken pizza. Daniel loves goat's cheese and sundried tomatoes. The Professor prefers seafood.

Professor Monk has lived alone since his wife died. He sold their house and furniture and had Roman items made for his Roman apartment. I wondered how Nox was coping with her change in circumstances.

I should have known. Tent to castle, cats are adaptable. When we came in she was sleeping, in a small night-black ball, in the exact centre of a soft Pompeiian red cushion.

'She picks her backgrounds,' he told us. 'She seems to like contrasts. I nearly sat on her when she was reposing on the black cushion, so now she avoids it.'

'Where does she sleep?' I asked.

'Right next to my face, under my chin,' he said. He seemed younger and his complexion was pink. 'She curls up quite confidingly, sure that I am not going to roll on her.'

'She'll get out of the way if you do,' I told him 'Cats have very fast reflexes.'

'I tried to persuade her to sleep in a rather nice cat bed which Meroe lent me, but she did not fancy it. Now, Daniel, if you would be so good, could you order the food? I'd like my usual seafood, and I'm sure that Nox will like it too.'

Nox woke while I watched, put out two tiny front paws, stretched elaborately, then trotted off the cushion and leapt onto the Professor's lap. There she sat up straight in the pose made fashionable by the Egyptian Goddess Basht, tail curled around paws, perfectly self-possessed. Daniel ordered the food and held out a hand to her. She allowed her ears to be gently handled, rubbed her chin against his hand, then lost interest in him, diving onto Professor Monk's wrist and growling ferociously as she disembowelled his hand with kicks of her back feet. He freed himself with some difficulty and put Nox on the floor, where she found that I had shoelaces and began to drag them out of my shoe. She was fascinating to watch, so we watched her.

Time passed in ritual acts of kitten worship. The creature had already put on condition. Her coat was beginning to shine. A few more square meals and you would never be able to guess she had spent more than a week trapped in the air conditioning.

But when the food came and the flat boxes were opened, Nox was transformed into a predator. She stalked the Professor's seafood pizza, pinned it down under one paw, and began to tear and guzzle hot clams off the top with every sign of enjoyment. She was so completely focused he was able to detach a piece of pizza, put it on a plate and put the plate and Nox on the floor without disturbing her concentration.

'She was hungry for a long time,' he said. 'I'm sure she'll learn table manners when she is a little older.'

I wasn't so sure. I suspected that when Nox grew bigger the only part of the pizza which the Professor would be allowed to keep would be the box. If he was lucky. As we ate we discussed the position of Mr Recluse, who seemed a nice man, or more of a good bloke, perhaps. I asked Professor Monk if he knew the chocolate shop ladies.

'No,' he said. 'Well, not really. I only know them through their Uncle Max.'

'And how do you know Uncle Max?' I asked, picking a string of cheese off my lip. Pizza is not a delicate dish. Nox tore off a prawn and wrestled it into submission.

'Oh,' he said vaguely, 'I've seen him around. Got talking to him in the shop, in fact. Have gone out for a drink with him occasionally when I met him in the street. I think he lives around here. An unhappy man. Probably drinks too much. Likes to gossip. He's very proud of his nieces. I get the impression that he and his brother both fell in love with the same woman, and she married his brother, that is, the ladies' father. Perhaps he never found anyone he liked as well. That can happen,' said the Professor, a little sadly. Though Professor Monk had a wide female acquaintance, I doubt he would ever find anyone who suited him as well as his deceased wife. They had been married for more than forty years. You can share a lot of jokes and memories and quotes and heartaches in forty years. You don't replace that overnight.

'But we need some wine,' said the Professor. He put his plate carefully on the table, and went to bring us a glass of his favourite red. As soon as his back was turned Nox left her denuded slice and made a wild dive for the table. I fielded her in mid flight.

'You haven't eaten all the anchovies yet,' I reminded her, and put her down next to her plate again. She gave me a Meroe look but inspected the pizza for more tidbits. Daniel laughed.

'Cats aren't the only ones with fast reflexes,' he said.

The Professor came back in with three glasses.

'You haven't eaten my dinner,' he said to Nox. 'What a good civilised kitten you are!'

Nox purred. I didn't say a word.

We had to leave early because the next day was Monday and it was back to the bread. As we went out I saw Nox scale the Professor, occupy his lap and begin an elaborate wash.

'There's a man who is firmly under paw,' said Daniel.

'And loving it.'

Chapter Seventeen

Ah, Monday. I was rather looking forward to getting back to making bread, the weekend had been so full of incident. When I got downstairs Jason was there, pouring flour into the mixer. He was properly clad and shod and was singing his little song under his breath. Everything all right with Jason, then. I supplied a small snack in the form of several cheese rolls with Gentleman's Relish and we began the day's work in perfect harmony.

Rye bread, pumpernickel for a special order, pasta douro, wholewheat. Bread for all nations. Jason knocked off for a proper breakfast at Cafe Delicious and returned to compound a revolutionary raspberry muffin for the paupers to go with the chocolate ones for the working rich. The bakery smelt like heaven. I got a strong whiff of it as I let the Mouse Police out into the alley.

It had stopped raining for the moment. I took a deep breath of the rain-rinsed air. Mrs Dawson came past in her red slicker and bought rye bread.

'I'm glad to see that you are noticing the weather, Corinna,' she remarked. 'I believe that it is likely to remain fine for a couple of days. You learn a lot about weather if you see both dawn and sunset,' she said gnomically, and walked off briskly down the alley. She did not step aside when Ma'ani, intent on the last Soup Run, loomed over her. She just looked at him. He got out of her way.

It was a brisk day. Both sorts of muffins sold out. Bread went off to its proper destination. Kylie came in to serve. Pretty soon I was able to leave her with the shop and go in search of corporate information. It was not hard to find. The city real property directory told me that the whole building belonged to Lucinda Three, a shelf company if ever I'd heard of one. Further research online led me to believe that Lucinda Three was an offshoot of a rather big property trust called Reliable Properties. I always suspect anyone who needs to call their property 'reliable' so I did some more digging and finally came up with a board, noting down the names of the members. And, of course, the name and address of the landlord. I did not reel in shock, only because I was sitting down. I should have known. Something shonky going down in my neck of the woods, and who is going to be involved in it?

Why, James, of course. My very ex-husband. The last person in the world I wanted to meet, with the possible exception of Osama bin Laden. The man who quite recently had attempted to make me sell my apartment in order to buy into the company that was going to pull Insula down. That James. My gorge rose. However, I needed the information and I wasn't going to get it any other way. I picked up the phone.

Actually, it was not so bad talking to James once I had got over the initial revulsion. I invited him to lunch at a very expensive Italian restaurant he favours, the Venetian, which has a $30 lunch special. Which was all I was intending to pay. I said to Daniel, who was watching videotapes with Horatio, 'I'm taking that creep James to lunch, expect disgusting revelations in about two hours,' and he nodded. I dressed carefully in my black trousers and white shirt and black jacket, which made me look approximately legal. I put the corporate search printouts into my briefcase, which increased the resemblance.

Then I stalked off through the lunch crowd to find the person who had done so much towards ruining my life. It wasn't James's fault that I wasn't a blubbery mess in a crimplene tent, baking cakes for the children's school and unable to form an opinion of her own, despised by all. That's what James wanted in a wife and he had tried very hard to mould me to fit. Eventually I had broken my dependence and walked out but he had done me considerable damage and I hadn't forgiven him yet. This is why Meroe says I'm not doing too well in the karma department.

He was there, sweating slightly. He had lost more hair since I had seen him last and he looked puffy around the eyes, slack around the jaw and red-veined around the nose. This cheered me considerably (I'm going to come back as a cockroach, I just know it). I joined him at his table. A half-empty bottle of wine was already there. I was at least two glasses behind him.

'Corinna,' he said. 'Nice to see you. Have you lost weight?'

'No,' I told him. 'I like me as I am. Have you ordered?'

'I was waiting for you,' he said. This was a change. Usually James would only be half civil at a restaurant if he got to control the whole production.

'Tell you what, I'll have the pasta alla puttanesca and the steak,' I said to the waiter. 'Rare, if you please. James?'

'I'll have the soup and the steak, rare as well,' he murmured.

'What's the matter, James? Business gone bankrupt?' I probed.

'No, business is good. I've got a new development opportunity in your area,' he said eagerly. 'Just around the corner from you in Calico Alley.'

He was actually going to tell me about it without being asked. Heaven was being kind to Corinna today. Cross examining James was always a bloody business.

'Really? So you are Reliable Properties?' I asked.

'Just took the portfolio over. Apartments,' said James, sketching luxurious accommodations for the rich and famous in the cold air. 'Gut the building and construct luxury apartments.'

'What about the tenants? There are tenants, I assume?'

'All sorted out,' he said confidently. 'We've got a lot of capital available, I was able to make them very good offers. You interested?'

'Maybe. Who did you deal with from Heavenly Pleasures? I asked idly, tucking into my hot, spicy pasta.

James told me. My heart went cold. But I let him keep talking, through a glass of wine and a very good steak with pepper sauce. Then I had another glass of wine. So did James. He was well fed but his huckster's energy had suddenly deserted him.

'What really is the matter, James?' I asked, disposed to listen. After all, he had saved me hours of research. His lip quivered. I couldn't help noticing that it had a blob of pepper sauce on it.

'It's Yvonne,' he said.

'Your wife?'

'Yes.'

'The one who wears frilly blue pinnies, makes sponges and stays home with your children?' I asked.

'Yes. But now she doesn't want to. When this baby is born she wants to get a nanny and go back to work.'

'What did she do before she met you?' I asked.

'She was a merchant banker,' he said. 'Very good at her job. But she wanted to have children. I thought she was happy,' he said. 'She was always there when I got home to make me a drink and ask about my day. She always got up to the baby and let me sleep through. I never had to hire a cleaner or eat takeaway meals. And now she says I'm exploiting her!'

There was really nothing I could say to James which might have got through to the selfish, irresponsible sod. So I laid some money on the table, patted him silently on the shoulder, and took my leave.

On the walk back I considered what he had said. James wouldn't lie about it, he had no reason to lie. But it made me feel nauseous, and I wanted to know what Daniel had found out. Before I landed a bombshell like this one, I wanted to be sure of my facts.

'Hello.' I kissed Daniel on the neck, under the growing-out bristle of his short haircut. 'Disgusting revelations coming up.'

'I've got one too,' he said. 'I think. Look,' he said.

I sat down in his embrace and watched the video.

'Do you see what I see?' he asked.

'Slow it down, frame by frame,' I demanded. My eyes were having difficulty with the lack of contrast. Then I saw what Daniel wanted me to see. Oh dear.

'What shall we do?' I asked.

'We wait for the final piece of proof,' he said gloomily. My black angel was not pleased with humanity today. 'Then we tell them.'

'I agree,' I said. 'I'm going to help Jason with the scrubbing. Back soon.'

There was no need to help Jason. The bakery was so clean you could have eaten your dinner off the floor, though in that event the Mouse Police would have claimed it first.

'You got enough sleep?' I asked him delicately.

'Yeah. I'm going to see a drug counsellor Sister Mary put me onto,' he said. 'Every Saturday morning. It's still there, Corinna. I thought it was gone but it isn't. The little voice that says "get a fix". So I'm going to see this bloke until it shuts up.'

'Did you go out and score on Saturday?' I asked.

'No,' he said.

'On Sunday?'

'No,' he said.

'Then you aren't going to do it today,' I said.

He thought about this. Then he said, 'Yeah. Yeah, that's right. See you tomorrow,' he added, and went out.

The shutters were up, the Mouse Police were drowsing, and I was possessed of a furious energy. I went back to my apartment and scoured my kitchen, banging my pots until they rang, sloshing water over the floor. Then I shifted into the parlour and vacuumed my carpet within an inch of its life. I beat cushions as though they were personal enemies. Dust and cat fur rose in clouds.

Daniel and Horatio prudently withdrew to the balcony, where it was cold but peaceful. It took four hours for the fury to be exhausted and by then the apartment was shining and I was filthy. I went to take a long bath with chestnut essence.

Horatio and Daniel crept back. Daniel sat on the edge of the bath and said, 'Feeling better, ketschele? My mother used to clean like that when she was angry.'

'Better than hitting things,' I said, sinking into the hot foamy water. 'It produces a clean environment to be miserable in. And actually I do feel better. I hate meeting James. He reminds me of what I used to be like.'

'And that was?' His hand slid into the water, caressing my breast.

'Frumpy,' I said. 'Convinced I was ugly. Ashamed.'

'You were being what he told you to be,' he said. The hand slid down further. 'Briefly. Then you remembered that you were strong. And confident. And beautiful. And you are.'

This time I got out of the bath first. I had just cleaned that bathroom.

◇◇◇

I woke slowly, aware of being clean and safe and embraced by a man I loved. That hadn't happened to me at all before I met Daniel and I still wasn't close to getting used to it. The phone was ringing. I picked it up, much against my inclination.

When I heard what the frantic voice at the other end was saying, I sat up. 'We're on our way,' I said.

Daniel read the news in my expression.

'All right, Corinna,' he groaned, swinging his legs out of bed. 'Let's get this over with.'

We dressed, took the bag of equipment between us, and went soberly down to Heavenly Pleasures. Juliette was in tears. Even Vivienne was disturbed.

'We'll have to close,' wailed Juliette. 'Who could be doing this to us?'

'I can show you,' said Daniel. 'Bring me the contaminated box. Set up the TV, George,' he ordered. George did not protest but did as he was told. Daniel put the poisoned box down on the metal table and fished out what looked like a flashlight from his bag.

'I marked all the new boxes,' he said. 'I marked them in ink which can only be detected under ultraviolet light. This is a UV light.'

'Like the ones in discos,' said George.

'Just like that. You've seen how they make a white shirt glow? This is the same thing. The trouble with this case,' said Daniel, 'is that no one seemed to have a reason to destroy your business. You might have your disagreements, and I have things to tell you about George's nasty little games, but fundamentally you need each other. Neither of you were thinking of marrying and thus threatening the partnership. Selima had nothing to do with this. So, not only who, but how? If your kitchen was clean, how did the contaminated chocolates get into your stock?'

'I don't know,' said Juliette, blowing her nose.

'It was a puzzle,' said Daniel. 'There. See the mark? It's an aleph. You can check it here, in my notes. This box was on your counter two days ago. This box has been taken out of the shop, the sweets have been doctored, and it was returned without you noticing.'

'How?' asked Vivienne, sharply.

'I'll show you how,' said Daniel. 'Run the tape, Corinna.'

We watched as several people came into the shop. Then in came an amiable old man in a coat with an astrakhan collar. He laughed as he waved his hands around, flirting with Juliette.

'No,' said Vivienne.

Daniel had a point to make.

'Watch it frame by frame,' he instructed. 'Watch the left hand. The right is waving in the air—classic magician's misdirection. Didn't he do magic tricks at those great parties he threw when you were children? And the left hand comes up out of the pocket and—it's almost too fast to see, but you can see it—puts a box into the pile on the counter. This box,' said Daniel, 'which was returned by a customer because of the soy sauce in the chocolate cream. Shall I show you the film again?'

'Yes,' said Vivienne. She sat down and watched it narrowly. Then she sighed. 'Why?' she asked.

'You make a profit because your rent is so low. High rent: no profit. He had a very good offer for the rest of the forty-year lease from the landlord, who wants to gut this building and turn it into apartments,' I said. 'He could have taken the money and run. And you would have been so discouraged, you would have given up the business without a fight.'

'It would have worked,' said Juliette, breaking out into fresh tears and leaning unconsciously on Daniel's arm as she staggered to her feet. I waited for jealousy to return so that I could fling it out. But not a green flicker. The hours I had spent recently receiving ardent proofs of Daniel's affection had paid off. I wasn't jealous anymore.

'What are you doing?' asked Juliette of her sister. She had a mobile phone in her hands.

'I'm calling him,' she said, pressing her speed dialler. 'I need to see him and ask him why he did this to us.'

'Don't,' moaned Juliette. Vivienne ignored her. George made a move towards the door and I caught his arm.

'No you don't,' I told him. 'Not unless you want your uncle Del and Yai Yai to know what you did to Selima. I don't want to be here, either. But we shall see it through, George. Have a seat,' I said. And we waited, for an agonising half-hour, until we heard the cheery voice at the door and Uncle Max swept in.

'Darlings!' he said. 'Why so glum?'

'Why did you do it, Max?' asked Vivienne. He was about to shrug his shoulders when she went on, her voice grating 'We've seen the video. That was a marked box you put back. We've heard about your deal with the landlord. Why did you do it, Max? All we ever did to you was to love you.'

'This is between us,' he said softly, making a gesture to exclude Daniel, George and me. I think he was still trying to win. He thought that he could play upon the ladies' emotions, if there were no witnesses.

'No,' said Vivienne. 'You tell us, Max. Or I call the cops.'

'There's forgery,' I said helpfully. 'He must have forged your signatures to a power of attorney to make that lease deal with Reliable Properties. James is an idiot but he's not a bloody idiot. And then there's criminal damage, trespass to property…'

'All right,' said Max. 'Enough. I did all those things. But I had cause. My brother and I were close as peas in a pod. But when he died, to whom did he leave his business? To his loving brother? No, to two girls.'

'He left you a lot of money,' said Vivienne through stony lips.

'Money, pah! He gave you the inherited moulds and trays, the expertise. Me he never offered to teach. I was just Max, silly Max, idle Max. Angry Max,' he said. His kindly eyes glittered with malice. 'You were so proud of your sweets, boasted of your skill. I thought, I'll show you. Then I'll get the money, open my own shop, and you can come work for me. I'll be the boss as I should have been. Now. Call your police,' he challenged. 'When it gets into the papers it'll finish your shop forever.'

'Oh, Vivi, what shall we do?' wailed Juliette.

Vivienne was already dialling. Max crumpled and Daniel got him a chair.

Then we all went down to the police station. Again. Daniel handed over his video and his marked box, and I gave them the papers relating to Reliable Properties. I flirted with the idea of handing George over also, but this might well have been a lesson to him that long-held hatreds, in the end, hurt the hater. It might persuade him to forget about the Exchange of Populations at last. Or not, of course.

The police car took the two very distressed sisters home and Daniel and I caught a tram back to the city. It was a new one, which whooshed instead of clacked. I was running out of tickets and reminded myself to buy some more next time I was passing a Met shop.

'I'm getting tired of that police station,' was all Daniel said. 'How about a nice dinner tonight? My shout. What about staying on this tram and going to that wonderful Japanese restaurant in Carlton?'

'Yes,' I said, utterly exhausted. I felt better after some toki teriyaki and a lot of green tea. But we took a taxi home and I fell asleep on the way. I woke long enough to brush my teeth and then fell bonelessly into bed.

Chapter Eighteen

I didn't wake until the alarm exploded and a brand-new Tuesday was vouchsafed to us.

I never liked Tuesdays, but this one went gently along, without nasty surprises or bombs or revelations that kindly uncles have been harbouring a grudge for the last twenty-five years. In fact it was a nice day, soothing and calm, just what I had in mind. Daniel slept in until noon, joined me for an early lunch, and we went to a movie. An old movie. We went to see *Bladerunner* at the Astor. We can almost recite *Bladerunner.* Then we dined frugally on Thai food (well, lavishly, actually, there is no way to dine frugally on Thai food, the Thais would be insulted). Daniel went to play his chess game with Kepler and I put myself to bed, early, sober, and alone except for Horatio.

Wednesday proved to be as anodyne as Tuesday. I baked, I swept, I sold bread, I visited the Professor and Nox, I drank gin and tonic in the garden with Daniel. No one tried to burgle the building or kill Mr Recluse. He kept himself to himself, but now nodded pleasantly if we met him in the lift. Mrs Dawson wore a gorgeous woven stole to astound the morning; a goldy green background patterned with firedrakes.

The chocolate shop remained closed. I didn't see how the sisters could possibly ever forgive us. We had taken away their Uncle Max. I didn't hear what had happened until I joined Jason—for a change—at Cafe Delicious. I was there partly to buy some lunch before all the moussaka was gone and partly to watch him eat his trucker's special, always a spectacle, though not for the faint of stomach. And of all people behind the counter, there was the beautiful George. He scowled at me. Jason bristled up in my defence, which was sweet of him.

'You got a problem?' he asked George in a menacing undertone.

'No, no problem,' said George, backing away. Jason returned to his half-demolished meal.

'Three portions of moussaka to take away, please,' I asked, leaning on the counter. 'So, what are you doing here, George?'

'They haven't worked out what to do, the silly bitches,' said George.

Hoping for his reform was going to be one of those long-term projects. Then he yelped as Del, in passing, boxed his ears for 'using words like that in his cafe where customers might hear, you want me to tell Yai Yai?' George shook his head.

'You mean they haven't decided whether to stay or move their shop?' I asked, watching him parcel up my moussaka very inexpertly.

'Nah, whether to stay in partnership. Jules didn't know that Viv was a les.'

'Neither did you,' I reminded him. 'Why should Juliette mind about Vivienne's sex life?'

'I dunno, why ask me? All I know is I'm back here until those...' Del Pandamus, cleaning tables within hearing, raised an eyebrow and George continued: '...ladies make up their minds. They're pretty pi...dark with you, too.'

'I know. I can understand that. Thanks George. Hope it works out well for you.'

Yeah,' he muttered. I paid for the moussaka. I was leaving as George said, 'Corinna? What happened to Selima?'

'She's well and happy,' I said, not wanting to disclose any more. Was George suffering from remorse at last? Stranger things had happened, though to be that strange they had to be reported in *The Fortean Times*.

'So she won't be coming back to the shop?' he asked.

'Why, do you miss her? Want to apologise?'

'I miss something about her,' he said. The little ratbag. He meant the money!

'I've told the sisters about your blackmailing her. Your little extras are off the menu, George.'

'Shit,' he swore, and Del clipped his ears again.

In all, George was not getting any more than he deserved. He was like the puddin' thieves in *The Magic Pudding*. 'Puddin' thieves don't suffer from remorse. They only suffer from blighted hopes and suppressed activity' as Bill Barnacle had said.

I went back to the bakery and made caraway seed rye bread. I love the taste. Jason, refreshed by enough food to stuff an elephant, made muffins. It was a nice day.

It segued into a nice afternoon and a nice night and so the evening and the morning passed away until it was Thursday again.

Thursdays were always busy. We made double rye, wholemeal and pasta douro and armloads of rolls, baguettes, half-baguettes, petits batons and shells for a restaurant order. It was a society wedding reception, I believe. By the time we had loaded all the trays for Megan's rickshaw—she had to make three journeys—and stocked the shelves, Jason and I were more than a little pooped. Thus we were pleased that Goss needed some pocket money and joined Kylie in running the shop. They worked well with one another. I heard them chatting happily to the customers as the crowd ebbed and flowed.

It struck me that, in a few months, provided Jason was okay and the girls didn't get that soap opera job, I might actually be able to leave the shop for a couple of days and go on holiday. I hadn't had a day off since I started Earthly Delights. It was an intoxicating thought. Should we go to Sydney for the theatres and the harbour views? Or would I prefer a snug little cottage somewhere down on the Ocean Road, with a spa and no neighbours?

No contest, really. Now to find out when I could extract Daniel from his detective profession. He came in chuckling.

'What's funny?'

'Darren the God Boy. He's in hospital.'

'Oh? Why? Did someone attack him again?'

'No. They'll have to leave him there until his condition stabilises. Corinna, he's a real epileptic now. No doubt that he was faking before. No doubt that he's really sick now.'

'That's very…karmic,' I said. I really couldn't think of another adjective. 'We must tell Meroe.'

'You do that. I'm going to do some routine investigations. Back three-ish.' He kissed me and I took Meroe some of the Royal Wedding bread, which was, I have to say, the epitome of the baker's art. I had made traditional wedding breads, plaits and twined wreaths, glazed with egg so that they shone beautifully. And Jason had learned to make the flat woven baskets which people would either eat or take home to lacquer, depending on taste. I preferred to eat them.

Meroe was wearing her usual black skirt and top, but was also draped in a night coloured stole in which—somewhere—Belladonna slept.

'What's wrong?' I asked, putting down the bag.

'The tides of fate are moving,' she said darkly, staring into a crystal ball held between her hands.

'Yes,' I said. 'Aren't they always?'

'Death and darkness,' said Meroe, making her meaning clear.

'Any advice for the endangered?' I asked. No harm in asking, after all.

'Beware of a great fall,' she said.

'As the eggs said to Humpty Dumpty,' I added.

'Swords,' she said, breaking into clear speech. 'Swords everywhere. Nothing more can I see,' she said, wrapping a cloth around the crystal ball and putting it back in its box. 'Hello, Corinna. Oh, how lovely! You've made Hungarian wedding bread!'

These sudden shifts of mood are hard to keep up with. I had gone abruptly from conversing with the Sybil of Cumae to everyone's grandma. I didn't mention that most wedding bread is much the same and sat down on the visitor's chair to tell her about Darren the God Boy. Belladonna emerged from the black folds and began stropping her claws on Meroe's chair and the atmosphere lightened. She agreed that Darren's affliction was, indeed, karmic in nature, thanked me for the bread, and I left before the Sybil came back.

And, a little shamefaced, I admit, I went up to my apartment, found my Swiss army knife, and put it in my pocket.

Because I had to do various business things that afternoon I did not change my clothes. I was watching Daniel make his own version of puttanesca sauce and talking about this and that when there was a loud ringing at the door. I opened it, and there was a man with a gun. It wasn't a big gun. It was one of those skeletal things and you could see through the stock. This did not make the sight any better.

He was a thickset man with a big moustache. One of the Twins, Tait or Bull. He growled, 'Come on,' and gestured with the gun. I was out onto the landing very quickly. He might not realise Daniel was there if he didn't call out to see who was at the door.

He did. He came out of the kitchen and saw the Twin. And he joined me on the landing.

'This isn't a good deal, Bull Twin,' said Daniel.

Bull said nothing. He just pointed with the gun, and we began to walk up the stairs. And as we walked we collected more people. Kylie and Gossamer, scared to death. Thank God the Professor wasn't home. Meroe was out. So was Mistress Dread and Mrs P. Jon and Kepler were at home, unluckily. Nerds Inc. obviously hadn't answered the door and the Pandamus family always went out for dinner at the Thai place on Thursdays. Cherie was home, Andy was at his AA meeting. We plodded up and up, urged on by the man with the gun. It was surrealistic, horrible, tiring.

When we got to the top we had added Mr Recluse, Mrs Dawson and Trudi to our congregation. We went out into the garden where an identical man with a similar gun was waiting. Tait and Bull. Dull-eyed and armed.

'Cops have this place bugged, you know,' remarked Daniel to Tait.

'Not the garden,' he replied. 'Our employer's got contacts. They didn't bug the roof. Sorry about this, Daniel.'

'This isn't going to work,' he said urgently. 'You're the fall guy, you know that? Who's going to do time for this? Not your employer! Don't do it. Take the guns and just go down the stairs. We won't say a word.'

For a moment there was real doubt in those sullen dark eyes. But then Bull yelled at him to get his arse into gear and he shook his head. 'Got to tie you up,' Tait said, picking up a piece of cut rope from a pile of them. 'You sit down, Daniel. You shut up. We know what we're doing.'

Daniel didn't say another word. Tait bound his hands behind his back, and then mine. Tightly. He moved down the line of people, Trudi, Mrs Dawson, Cherie, Jon, Kepler, Kylie and Goss. They made us sit down on the wet grass. Mr Recluse he took by the shoulder and dragged him into the middle of the lawn, where he could see all of our faces. I was fighting down panic. I hate to be tied. Long ago James had laughingly looped my hands in my pantyhose and tied them to a bedhead and I had fought hysterically to get free. Daniel leaned a shoulder into mine and whispered, 'Calm, ketschele, calm,' and I struggled to breathe. Breathe in, breathe out. Breathe in, breathe out.

I needed a cigarette. I also needed to pee. God, I was so scared. Two armed men and me with…with a knife in my pocket.

I had a knife in my pocket. The tides of fate indeed. Now I just had to work out how to get to it without being detected. I whispered my news to Daniel. He kissed me on the neck and turned a little away from me, feeling for the blade. No one was looking at us. All attention was focused on the Twins.

'The disks we got out of your safe,' said Twin One. 'Been decoded. Aren't the right ones.'

'Aren't they?' asked Mr Recluse.

'Where are the real ones?'

'They are the real ones,' insisted Mr Recluse.

'Nah,' said Tait. 'You've got the real ones somewhere. So we're gonna start shooting these people, until you tell us where they are.'

Kylie shrieked in terror. Bull menaced her with the gun until her cry died away into sobbing. I could see Goss leaning close to her.

'And I'm telling you your boss got it wrong,' said Ben White stubbornly. 'You've been through my apartment. You've searched it to the bones. If there was anything there, you would have found it. And you did bloody find it,' he said. 'You call up your bosses and tell them to use the password tiger, that's t-i-g-e-r, all lower case. You do it now.'

I had to hand it to Mr White, he was doing well. Bull flipped open a mobile phone. I was aware of Daniel swearing in Hebrew under his breath. The weight of the knife was gone from my pocket and in a moment I felt the cold blade slide through the ropes. The relief was so great that I almost fainted. I kept my hands behind my back, accepted the knife, and felt for his bonds. I paused several times, when a Twin's gaze swept over me, but I cut through them at last. Daniel took the knife and started work on Trudi. I couldn't see any sign of Lucifer, which was fortunate.

Bull was waiting for a reply from the phone. Ben White was standing with his legs well apart, arms folded. Trudi was free and working on Mrs Dawson when the reply came through. Bull scowled and flipped the phone shut.

'Didn't work,' he said to Ben White. 'Who's gonna be first? What about this nice little chick?'

He hauled Gossamer to her feet, grabbing her by the shirt, which tore. She kicked him in the shin. He let go of her, howled and hopped.

Then Trudi sprang up and started to throw flowerpots. Her aim was good. The Twins were hit with terracotta shards and blinded with potting mix. I screamed to the others, 'Run, girls!' and threw myself aside into the bushes. I wasn't going to leave Daniel. Jon, somehow, had freed himself and Kepler and was on his feet. Cherie grabbed Kylie and Goss and dived for the lift. The door hissed shut and it clanged into action. Bull fired at it but they made lifts solid in the old days.

Three pawns off the board. This was turning into the Immortal Game.

'Give it up,' said Daniel quietly. 'The cops'll be here in a moment. Ditch the hardware and get out of here while you still can.'

'Still got you,' said Tait. 'Still got her,' he pointed with the gun to Mrs Dawson, standing straight as a reed. Trudi was somewhere in the undergrowth like me, lurking. 'Still got them,' he said, indicating Jon and Kepler. 'Boss says he'll send a helicopter for us.'

'You're dreaming,' said Daniel scornfully. Bull fired a shot at him. It howled past. Daniel did not move. I wished that he wasn't so brave.

'You,' Tait beckoned to Kepler. 'Pretty boy. Come here.'

I believe he picked Kepler because he could not imagine that anyone dressed in red brocade pyjamas could be dangerous. Not even as dangerous as girls, who kicked. Kepler walked across to Tait and stood next to him. I was glad that I could not see Jon's face. Check.

'Now, tell us where the disks are.'

'There are no more disks,' said Mr White.

'Look, give us a break,' said Tait 'You left our employer's business, you handed in your laptop, you turned over all your records. But there's a committal hearing on Tuesday and you're the main prosecution witness. You know that we have to kill you, but the boss needs to know where your records are.'

I noticed that he knew all the long words which related to criminal law.

'You've got them,' Ben White insisted. 'But you don't need all these people. You just need me. Let the others go and I'll tell you everything.'

'So, there are extra records?' said Tait.

'Yeah, all right, there are extra records,' sighed Mr White. 'Let the others go and let's get on with this, it's a cold night.'

Trudi touched my arm. 'What to do?' she asked.

'I have no idea,' I said. 'Can you reach the stairs?'

'Girls will have called cops,' she said. 'If I go for stairs, I'll be seen. Door's shut.'

'Then we wait,' I said.

'For what?'

'A great fall,' I said. Meroe had been right about the swords. Maybe she was right about this, as well.

'Where's Lucifer?'

'Fell off my shoulder,' said Trudi. 'Somewhere here.'

The night was getting darker, as nights have a habit of doing. I was chilled to the marrow and wet from the shrubs. Tait took Kepler's arm and shoved the gun into his face. Check again.

'Where are the records?' he screamed at Mr White. Down in the street, sirens sounded. Cherie had not wasted any time. The cops were on their way. I felt frantic and helpless. I began to make my way towards the group. I would, I realised, much rather die with Daniel than mourn him.

Looking up, I saw the nearest tall building's windows lined with fascinated faces, and I hated humans more than I have ever hated them before. What would the poet say? 'Butcher'd to make a Roman holiday'? They would make a sideshow of our death and even now, I would bet, someone up there was on the phone to a radio station, as a special reporter, talking about the showdown on the roof. I worked out that if I crept along behind the bower I could get to the temple of Ceres under cover, so I did that. In fact, I castled.

Tait shook Kepler. Jon cried out, 'No!'

Kepler smiled seraphically, said something in a language I did not know, and leaned into Tait's hold, turning him so that his back was toward the other gunman. Then he did something complicated with one hand and a flying foot, and the gun shot out of Tait's grasp and fell off the roof. Jon joined him in holding Tait, both of them sheltering behind him.

A knight's move. Bull had fast reflexes. He grabbed Mrs Dawson. She was so small that he had to lift her almost off the ground to bring the gun to bear on her. A pin.

It was a perfect Mexican standoff. In the movies this always ends with one side or the other giving up, but Jon and Kepler were not letting go of Tait and Bull was hanging on to Mrs Dawson. I hoped she wasn't too terrified. She was an old lady, after all.

I got to the temple of Ceres. Big deal. That meant I could straighten up from my terrified crouch, but it didn't do me a bit of good. There was nothing in there I could use as a weapon. Trudi always put her implements away. I cursed her neatness. I longed for a spade or a rake. I could just hear the good meaty smack a spade would make, colliding with the back of a Twin's thick head. Then I stepped on something that squeaked and almost had a heart attack. It was Traddles' missing toy, a blue dog bone with a noise-maker inside it.

I grabbed it gently. No one had heard the noise. Daniel was talking.

'Look, guys, this hasn't worked,' he said reasonably. 'Killing us is only going to get you life, instead of the eight years or so you'll get for false imprisonment and assault. You haven't hurt anyone yet. Why take it any further?'

'You know how much we're getting paid?' asked Tait. 'Ten big ones.'

'Not from that company, you aren't,' said Mr White. Tait scowled.

'What d'ya mean?'

'I mean that that company hasn't got a pot to piss in. They don't have a brass razoo. They are broke. Bankrupt. They owe gazillions to their creditors, who will be lucky if they get five cents on the dollar.'

'Oh, jeez,' said Bull. 'I said we ought to get it in advance!'

'That would have been wise,' said Mr White. They thought about it. This took time. Mrs Dawson shrugged herself disdainfully out of Bull's loosening grip and reached behind her, as if to stretch her back. She hadn't shown the slightest sign of fear. If this was a chess game, she was queen.

'Nah,' decided Bull. 'I say you're lying. Boss said he'd send a helicopter for us. Give us the records or I kill the old lady.'

Just then we all heard the clatter of an approaching helicopter. Bull said, 'See! I told you this deal was all right!' and raised the gun to Mrs Dawson's neatly coiffed head. I refused to close my eyes. I was going to witness what happened next.

What happened next was that I threw Squeaky at Bull and he flinched, and Mrs Dawson produced a small gun from behind her back and shot Bull in the wrist. Blood flew. The gun fell. She stalked him across the roof.

'You cannot say that I am not a patient woman,' she said to him. 'I have listened to you for long enough. Now you will get down on your knees or I will shoot you in the leg. This is my own gun and I am quite used to firing it.'

Daniel followed her as Bull backed across the garden. Trudi rose from the undergrowth. I grabbed the fallen gun. Kepler and Jon threw Tait to the ground and bound him with some handy rope which he had thoughtfully brought with him. Mrs Dawson looked like a small, immaculately dressed figure of retribution.

'This is my son,' she said. 'My own son that you have been trying to kill. Helicopter or no helicopter, you are going to jail for a very long time.'

They had almost run out of roof. Bull was witless with shock. He backed one step too far, caught his heel on something, and fell off the roof. Far down, we heard a horrible splatting thud which I do not wish ever to hear again.

'Oh dear,' said Mrs Dawson without a trace of emotion in her voice.

Trudi dived and grabbed and hauled up a small orange furball on a string. He had been dangling eight storeys from oblivion by his lead, over which the dead man had tripped. It had been hooked on a flower pot.

'Mrrow?' said Lucifer. Trudi caught him up and hugged him. I hugged Daniel, Jon hugged Kepler, Mrs Dawson hugged Mr White.

There was a lot of hugging to be seen from the helicopter, which was hovering overhead. I looked up into its glaring searchlight, wondering if it was staffed by bad guys humming

'Ride of the Valkyries'. But it was marked in stylish blue and white and was, of course, Daphne, the police helicopter. Check and mate.

Chapter Nineteen

It was a long night. We had, fortunately, been filmed by a concealed video unit as well as by an enthusiastic amateur in one of the overlooking buildings so we didn't have to go over the facts too often. Jon and Kepler held hands in stunned amazement that they were both still alive. Mrs Dawson surrendered her gun, pointing out that she had a licence for it and she wanted it back in due course. Her son Ben sat beside her, looking very proud and vaguely embarrassed, as grown-ups rescued by their mothers often are. Mrs Dawson insisted that the interviews took place in her apartment, and kept Daniel busy opening more champagne. To celebrate, she said, life and the joy of being alive. I got rather drunk on relief and champagne in equal proportions.

Large men in vests had ker-thumped through Insula, seeking any more assailants and finding none. The only other arrest was made by Letty White, who recognised a notorious rapist who had jumped his bail in the crowd which gathered outside. She had brought him down with one ferocious tackle, described by a large sergeant as 'ouch'. Trudi had found the gin and shared it with Cherie and Andy, who fell right off the wagon again. The Professor, coming home from his dinner date, had been appropriately horrified. Tait had been taken away, weeping for his dead brother. Further revelations were expected in the papers. Especially about who had told him that the roof was not bugged.

Kylie had been visited by a doctor who had prescribed sedatives and a night's sleep for herself and Goss, and I told them that they deserved a day off. I left a note for Jason in the bakery that he had a day off, too, and to come and visit after noon. I put a note on the shop door saying 'Closed for Repairs. Open Again Monday'. No customers would have been able to make their way to Earthly Delights, anyway. There was police tape saying 'Crime Scene—Do Not Cross' all over the place.

Then we trailed home and went to bed. I couldn't sleep, and lay awake looking at Daniel and pondering how much more, now, I had to lose. We had come very close to the edge of disaster. If Mrs Dawson hadn't been so unexpectedly armed....Finally I resorted to a sleeping pill and did not wake until Jason, agog, rang the bell at noon on Friday.

Then we went through it all again. Jason was disappointed that he had been left out of the action. When he went off to spend an afternoon playing video games, I called around. Everyone was all right. The girls were still sleeping. Mrs Dawson and her son were having afternoon tea. Trudi was in, reading bulb catalogues and playing with Lucifer. The Professor and Nox were taking an afternoon nap. Meroe was with Cherie, concocting hangover cures for Andy. Jon and Kepler were staying in bed until further notice.

The police were leaving, taking their tape with them. I said to Daniel, 'What about a little celebration? Saturday night? Tonight everyone will want to stay in and do comforting things. But we do need to talk this over. For one thing, I want to know where those disks were, if there were any disks.'

'It'll be too cold in the garden,' he said.

'What about the atrium?' I asked. 'We can put a cover over the glass door. It's big enough for all of us and Horatio can stare at the fish. He likes staring at the fish. Everyone can bring their own chair and Trudi has a trestle. We can order in the food from Cafe Delicious and Del and his family can come as well. They close at three on Saturdays.'

'A good notion,' said Daniel. 'Tell you what,' he added, noticing that I was yawning again, 'you go and have a little nap, and I'll organise it.'

I woke in the late afternoon, profoundly grateful that we were all alive. Daniel had gone out and left me a note saying that there was goulash in the oven and I wasn't to do anything. I had a bath in voluptuous lilac foam. I dressed in my purple chrysanthemum gown. I hugged Horatio, who allowed me this liberty as cats do when you really need to hug them. Then Daniel came back.

'All set,' he said. 'With food and wine and one nice surprise —I hope.' He wouldn't tell me anything about the surprise and I didn't feel like teasing him. I felt like sitting on the couch in the warm darkness, watching the whole *Star Wars* trilogy until I fell asleep again. So we did that. The Empire rose and fell, and eventually the Jedi returned, and when I woke again it was Saturday.

It was a lazy day. I read a book, finished it, and read another book. I didn't feel like exerting myself. I felt fragile, breakable, and unwilling to let Daniel out of my sight. He felt the same and came in and watched me take a bath.

Meroe called and offered me some of her herbal tea and I drank it. It tasted like cut grass. She informed me that the tides of fate had now rolled on and that our prospects for the future were very bright. In view of her accuracy in telling me about swords, I was prepared to believe in this one too. She told me that she had also dosed Kylie and Gossamer with the cut-grass tea. Kylie had originally been intending to ask her father to find her another place to live but had now decided to stay. She and Goss had spent the previous night on the phone to all their friends and this had effectively worn out their shock. And they hadn't seen Bull die, of course.

Meroe was on her way into the street, to incense the pavement where Bull had landed and make sure that his spirit wasn't hanging around. I told her I thought this was an excellent idea—the last thing we needed was the ghost of a thug haunting the place—and could I help? But it appeared that she had to do this sort of thing on her own.

The day passed with agreeable slowness. I knew that everyone was doing the things that made them feel better. Those who were not making love were making soup or planning gardens or reading detective stories or watching TV or eating macaroni cheese. Insula was comforting itself for its exposure to violence and sudden death. It was as though the building, also, needed soothing. A car backfired and we all, as it were, jumped together.

By seven, the trestle table was up and draped, with one of those frightful Klee sculptures in the middle—Ben White's joke, I fancied. The glass door to the street had been covered with some of Jon's Javanese fabrics, figured with gold-edged flowers. Del Pandamus and his entire family, including a reluctant George, had brought enough food for an army and many bottles of ouzo. Each Pandamus carried a folding chair, from a big canvas one for Del to a tiny pink armchair for their youngest, Chrysoula. She had yet to be talked out of wearing her fairy dress which her grandma had made for her.

Jon and Kepler brought a folding bamboo loveseat. Daniel and I carried down a variety of seats for various people. We also had a crate or so of wine. The Professor was not there, which was odd. I wondered if he had received an invitation and Daniel assured me that he would be along, so I stopped wondering. Instead I took a piece of spanakopita and a glass of red and greeted the girls, who had dressed in their best: glittery dresses held up by witchcraft or faith, sparkly make-up, and uniformly golden hair. Chrysoula identified with them immediately, informing me that they were all fairies together. Andy raised a glass of sparkling water; he was off the booze again. Cherie was actually wearing a non-Goth dress, something in dark blue which fell elegantly to the floor. She had Pumpkin bear with her. He always came to these parties.

Mrs Dawson made an entrance. She was wearing a dark chocolate dress in heavy satin, very plain, with a huge gold brooch on the shoulder—some sort of stylised lion. It looked like it had come from an archaeological site. Ben White was with her, hovering at her shoulder, handing her a glass of champagne and a plate of those moreish nibbly meze things which Greeks do so well: pickled eggplant, vinegared octopus, barbecued quail, lamb kofta. Daniel joined me at the table as I gathered a zucchini patty, a mushroom cooked in red wine and a ball of labneh with a piece of flat bread. Yum.

'Is this a scotch egg?' asked Andy Holliday suspiciously.

'No, it's kibbeh. You'll like it,' Daniel told him. 'I'll have one.'

Meroe, a strict vegetarian, was delighted to find that there were more veggie dishes than meat. She selected tomato borek, village salad, pickled lettuce, felafel, fried chickpeas and baked haloumi.

'I am making a pig of myself,' she confessed.

'Hey, me too. But don't eat too much, this is just the entrée. There's moussaka and lemon chicken and you can have the broad bean and artichoke casserole, it's terrific.'

'I can't imagine why Greeks are so healthy,' she commented.

'They don't worry too much,' boomed Del. 'They eat and drink and sleep like dogs. You like Greek food?' he asked Meroe.

'It's wonderful,' she assured him, and he clapped her on the shoulder and went on to gather more dolmades, which he ate two to a bite. He then poured Daniel and me a big glass of ouzo and raised his glass in a toast, which meant that I had to skol a glass of ouzo, which meant that thereafter the proceedings were clothed with a gentle pink glow. I noticed that Jon and Kepler were managing to eat Greek food without trouble. Kepler was fascinated by the exotic fare, as I had once been with Chinese cuisine. The only thing that Kepler left on his plate was baked cheese. Nothing is going to make Chinese people like cheese.

Jason had started at the far end of the table and was working his way along it, in the manner of a vacuum cleaner.

The dinner was moving on to main courses and still the Professor had not come. Where was he? I had a conversation with Mrs Dawson about that providential gun.

'Well, dear, when it appeared that my son was going to do a very brave thing, I felt that I ought to be prepared,' she told me, eating pickled octopus with skill and grace, which I never could. 'So I joined a pistol club. It isn't hard at all,' she said. 'In fact I don't know what men make all that fuss about. Just a matter of a good eye and a steady wrist.'

'Did you move here because he was hiding here?'

'No, he was hiding here because I moved here,' she said.

'I know the graziers, of course, and they were happy for my son to get some use out of the apartment. I once danced with their ancestor,' she said. 'He stood on my foot. He was a clumsy man. I didn't, of course, realise the lengths to which those scoundrels would go. I would not willingly have put you all in danger. When I saw those poor girls threatened, I was appalled at what I had done in bringing Ben here.'

I watched Kylie and Goss put the moves on George—their taste in men was abysmal. They giggled, a little elevated by danger, but apparently unharmed.

'I think they'll forgive you,' I said.

'They shouldn't. Once I saw those twins, I knew that I had to do something about the—they were my fault. But how did you and Daniel get free?'

'I had a knife in my pocket. What I want to know is how Kepler and Jon got free. I know the knife hadn't reached them.'

'You can't tie Kepler up with ordinary rope,' said Jon.

'I told you, he teaches martial arts. It was just a matter of manoeuvring the attacker into a situation where he couldn't kill anyone else before we disarmed him.'

'What did you say to Jon in Chinese?' I asked Kepler.

'If this doesn't work, I'll see you in heaven,' he said.

'Only one thing we need to know, then,' I said. 'Where were those—'

The door opened. Professor Monk came in. Behind him, rather shyly, came Selima and Brian and both of the chocolate shop sisters. Vivienne had brought Kat with her.

'We have had some discussion,' announced Professor Monk.

'And Vivi and me have agreed to accept the Professor as our new uncle,' said Juliette.

'Since we are staying at Heavenly Pleasures,' said Vivienne.

There was a cheer. The sisters were gathered in and supplied with plates and delicacies. Selima recognised most of the food and guided Brian in his choice. They were sweet together, shy and devoted. I got a glass of wine for Juliette. Vivienne and Kat stuck to ouzo. George sidled up to Juliette.

'So, do I still have a job?' he asked, exerting every ounce of his charm. He positively reeked of it.

'Well,' she said. Del arrived next to her.

'You take him back, I keep him in line,' he said in his big, hoarse voice. 'He make trouble, I give him to his Yai Yai.'

The tiny black-clad old lady in the plushest armchair gave George a look which went straight through all pretensions and pierced his worm-eaten little soul as on a hook.

'Yeah, okay, Uncle. I'll be good,' he said.

'I see you are,' threatened Del. Vivienne approved of Del. She held out a hand. 'Deal,' she said, and they shook. Then they all had to drink a big glass of ouzo to seal the bargain. George decided that discretion might be a good idea, and went to bring Yai Yai a nice plate of lemon chicken and a new glass of wine.

'In about three hundred years he might even turn into a passable human being,' commented Daniel.

'Not all his fault,' said Del. 'His rotten father leave his mother, my sister, alone. He never finds out what it is to be a real man. Now he learns,' said Del, and drank some more ouzo.

'That was very nice of you, Dion,' said Mrs Dawson to Professor Monk, handing him a glass of the good wine.

'Not at all,' he disclaimed virtue with an elegant wave. 'They had been betrayed by one uncle. I was quite fooled by Max. I thought that they could do with another. And I am excellent uncle material.'

'They are lucky to have you,' said Mrs Dawson warmly. 'Every grown-up woman needs an indulgent uncle, who will take her out to lunch occasionally.'

We were all full of food. The wine was running low. Vivienne popped outside for a moment and brought in a couple of large thermos jugs, the sort that big caterers use.

'You will need cups,' she said. 'But you'll like this.'

'What is it?' asked Jason, emptying his wineglass and lining up for whatever was going. He had eaten at least three ordinary dinners and would undoubtedly take home the residue. For night starvation, from which he suffered, he told me, cruelly.

'Chocolate grog,' said Juliette, lining up cream and nutmeg on the denuded table.

Letty White came in at this point, to be loaded with leftovers and smothered with good cheer. It was generally felt that if it hadn't been for her devoted care, we might all be seriously dead, and we were very pleased to see her. With her came Mistress Dread, who had been detained at her dungeon, and three nerds, who dived on the food as if they hadn't breakfasted on tacos a mere four hours ago.

Now we were all here excepting Mrs Pemberthy, who was staying in bed. I raised my voice for silence. 'We've covered all the events of the last few days,' I said. 'And we are all friends here. Will you please, Ben, tell us where the disks are?'

'There are no disks,' he said, straight-faced. 'But if some of my guests would care to look at the table, they may find something interesting there.'

We all looked. Remains of sumptuous Greek feast, which was still being mopped up by appreciative latecomers, yes. Plates, cups and glasses, yes. Horrible sculpture, yes. No disks.

Then the three nerds, Daniel and Kepler began to laugh. They laughed quite a lot. The rest of us were as mystified as ever. I jabbed Daniel in the side.

'Explain!' I said.

'There,' he pointed. All I could see was an ugly sculpture made of flat lead and plastic slugs. Grey ones. Wait a moment. I had seen something like that before.

'Thumb drives,' giggled Rat, or possibly Taz. Gully was the one with the long stringy feral hair. 'The whole thing's made of thumb drives. Except for the fish. The fish is extra.'

'Which go in a laptop,' I said. 'What a very pretty idea. Very Edgar Allen Poe.'

'I was lucky that they didn't send anyone who knew about computers,' Ben said. 'But I didn't think they would. Everyone knows about computer disks. Not everyone knows about thumb drives.'

'Hidden in plain sight,' said Letty White. 'And the real ones are now somewhere very safe.'

'Until Tuesday,' said Ben.

The chocolate grog was a rich, velvety chocolate drink with—brandy, perhaps?—in it, topped with nutmeg and whipped cream. Perfect for a cold night and a celebration. And the end of a story, for goodnight and sweet dreams. For all of us.

Recipes

Chocolate is not as tricky as it sounds, as long as you remember that it has to be melted either over boiling water or in a microwave, where it rather eerily melts but keeps its shape, like a Pompeiian citizen, so has to be stirred. Couverture is too delicate for cooking. Cadbury make a very good baking cocoa, and I prefer Plaistowe's bittersweet chocolate for melting. It's reliable and it doesn't cost the earth.

Chocolate Orgasm Muffins

Be careful eating these. Straight out of the oven the melted chocolate can burn your tongue, like the hot jam in a doughnut. Refresh them when cold with 20 seconds in the microwave.

For the muffins:
> 2 cups self-raising flour
> 1/4 cup cocoa
> 1/2 cup brown sugar
> 125g melted butter
> 2 eggs
> 1 cup milk

For the filling:
> 200g bittersweet chocolate
> 1/2 cup thickened cream

Preheat the oven to 200°C and grease two 6-cup muffin trays. Make the filling by melting the chocolate and cream together, either 2 minutes in a microwave or just stir it in a saucepan on the stove until it melts and combines. Set it aside.

For the muffins, mix the flour, cocoa and brown sugar together in a large bowl.

Using a separate bowl, mix together the butter, eggs and milk. Pour the egg mixture into the flour and slap it about a bit.

Using a metal spoon, put a glob of muffin mix into the tins, filling them less than halfway. Then put a glob of filling into each tin, then top with the rest of the muffin mix. You now have muffins with a spoonful of chocolate sauce in the middle of each one. Do this quickly, or they will still taste nice but they won't rise.

Shove into the oven and bake for about 12 minutes (you should know how your oven works). They are cooked when they spring back when poked.

Chocolate Grog

Beware of this—it is utterly delicious and very alcoholic. It is Cocoa for Grown Ups. Thinking about it will put you over .05. But it warms the cockles and all other places. This is a serve for two.

> 500ml milk
> 75g bittersweet chocolate
>   (or you can use couverture for this)
> pinch each of allspice and ginger
> 1 tablespoon honey
> 75ml rum
> 200ml brandy
> 1 cinnamon stick
> nutmeg to sprinkle
> whipped cream to top

Put all the non-alcoholic ingredients together, heat and stir. When it is a little too hot to drink (but don't let it boil), add the alcohol and a cinnamon stick. Serve topped with nutmeg and whipped cream. You won't regret it. Until, perhaps, tomorrow.

French Onion Soup

    6 big onions
    2 tablespoons sugar
    olive oil
    chicken stock (you can also just use water)
    baguette
    gruyère cheese
    cognac

Slice the onions, sprinkle the sugar over them and fry them in a little olive oil until the sugar metls and they caramelise (about 15 minutes, depending on the onions). Keep stirring. These are stirring times. When they are golden brown but before they burn, pour in the chicken stock and cook the soup until everything is transparent and delicious. If, as happened to me the other day, the onions caramelised but stayed obstinately clear, use Parisian essence to colour the soup and don't tell anyone (it will be our secret).

Slice the baguette and lay rounds of it on an oven tray, and bake it in a slow oven until it is very dry but not brown. Then lay one piece of toast on the bottom of a bowl, top it with grated cheese, pour over soup and add, at the last minute, a teaspoon of cognac.

A superb winter dish and now there is no excuse for saying there is nothing to eat if there are onions in the house.

To receive a free catalog of Poisoned Pen Press titles, please contact us in one of the following ways:

Phone: 1-800-421-3976
Facsimile: 1-480-949-1707
Email: info@poisonedpenpress.com
Website: www.poisonedpenpress.com

Poisoned Pen Press
6962 E. First Ave. Ste. 103
Scottsdale, AZ 85251

CPSIA information can be obtained at www.ICGtesting.com
Printed in the USA
BVOW08s1530021215

429154BV00007B/222/P